PROJECT EX

Helen V Reese

This is a work of fiction. Names, characters, places and incidents either are the product of the author's imagination or are used fictitiously. Any resemblance to actual persons, living or dead, events, or locales is entirely coincidental.

Copyright © 2015 Helen V Reese
All rights reserved, including the right to reproduce this book or portions thereof in any form whatsoever.

ISBN: 0692470891
ISBN 13: 9780692470893

DEDICATION

To my beloved brother, Kopi Saltman. You brought joy and laughter to everyone whose life you touched. Your gentle wisdom still guides me every day. You're forever in my heart.

I sat there on the deck of my cabin on the SS Vandermeere, *staring at the ocean. The sea was calm now, but it had been a rough night, waves crashing against the ship with terrifying ferocity. I told myself it was the violent rocking of the ship—flinging me from one side of the bed to the other—that had kept me up all night. However, I knew it wasn't true and I would have had an endless night of tossing and turning even if the ocean had been calm. By 4:00 a.m., when the waves began to subside, my thoughts were still churning. Finally, at 5:30, I crawled out of bed, splashed cold water on my face and crept out to the balcony, tiptoeing past my best friend Carol, who thankfully was an Olympian sleeper.*

Tomorrow we'd dock in Costa Rica, and while Carol was whizzing through the rain forest on a zip line, I'd be on a plane, heading home to Philadelphia to try to pick up the pieces of my life—the life restaurant critic/investigative reporter and all-around scumbag Jared Abrams had worked so hard to destroy. I scrunched my eyes shut, and as my head lolled back against the soft cushion of the chaise longue, I tried to force all thoughts of Abrams from my mind. However, the ache in my back and the emptiness gnawing at my heart reminded me of another sleepless night—almost eleven months earlier, right after my 50th birthday—when I'd placed the fateful ad on Facebook that had changed everything. Turning fifty had kindled something in me—a yearning for change, for coming to terms with the past, for letting go and moving on. The realization that I'd lived for half a century—half a century!—had consumed me, propelling me to take action on fulfilling my dreams…now.

Maybe if I sort through all that's happened since last January just one more time, I thought, I'll be able to figure out what went wrong and how I can get my life back on track. The ad on Facebook—that was the catalyst. And then Project Ex took on a life of its own…

PART I—LYDIA ONLINE

CHAPTER ONE

Sick and tired of being an ex-boyfriend? If you're also one of my exes, I'd like to hear from you. I'm a therapist conducting research for a special project on dead-end dates and failed relationships. No strings attached, no hidden agendas, and no cost to you. Call Lydia Birnbaum, MSW at 610-555-9987, or email: projectex@hotmail.com.

It was two a.m. and I was still awake. I'd gone to bed around ten but knew I wouldn't get much sleep since I'd just returned home from yet another date from hell with a man I'd met on a singles website.

Truthfully, I was the one who was sick and tired. Sick and tired of the dating scene. Sick and tired of listening to men I barely knew tell endlessly boring stories about their endlessly boring lives. Sick and tired of sitting face-to-face with men who'd assured me they looked just like Boris Becker but who turned out to be dead ringers for Boris Karloff. And I was particularly sick and tired of my pattern of running to my own therapist—as wonderful and nurturing and gifted as Gwen was—every time I encountered another rejection. I'd just turned fifty and I was feeling sick and tired of just about everything when the idea to place the ad popped into my head.

I had to face it—my life was going nowhere. My job as case manager at Briarside Behavioral Health was rewarding but demanding and seemed to sap most of my energy. I had only a few clients left in the private practice I'd been struggling to build in the few odd hours I could devote to it over the last six years, and, as evidenced by tonight's disastrous date, my social life was nonexistent.

I'd met the latest CyberPsycho at a little Italian bistro about ten minutes from my home in Bryn Mawr—a gingerbread "Seven Sisters" town located on the Main Line, the exclusive and exclusionary suburbs that were home to many of the wealthiest and most influential people in the Philadelphia area—except for me, of course. And actually, he did look just as cute as the photo he'd posted in his profile on JDate. However, although I remembered that he'd described himself as separated, it took only five minutes for me to find out he was still living with his wife.

"Let me get this straight," I said. "You and your wife are still living together…in the same house."

"Well," he replied, "now that my girlfriend broke up with me, I'm back in the house with my wife."

"Now that your girlfriend broke up with you—what do you mean?" I began feeling a little dizzy, although I hadn't even taken a sip from the glass of Sauvignon Blanc I'd ordered only a few minutes earlier.

"We were madly in love, my girlfriend and me. She wasn't the first woman I've been with since my wife and I separated, but she was the best, and it was wonderful."

"So, what happened?" I asked, although what I should have said was, *Excuse me, I think I left the oven on and I need to get home immediately.*

"Well," he said, looking sadder than the most depressed of my few weekly clients, "things just didn't work out. She said I wasn't ready for commitment."

"I disagree," I said. "I think you're screaming out for commitment. I just wonder if there are any beds available at the psych hospital where I work."

He stared at me in disbelief. "What did you say?"

"Oh, never mind, never mind," I said. "I'm obviously wasting your time as much as you're wasting mine, because…because—I'm a lesbian."

He was frozen, dumbstruck. I downed the Sauvignon Blanc in two gulps. "Why the hell did you answer my ad if you're a lesbian?" he eventually sputtered. "What are you, a frigging lunatic?"

"One of us is a lunatic," I hollered back, grabbing my pocketbook and heading for the door, "but it isn't me."

To be honest, this isn't how things turned out, and no, I'm not gay. This is just one of the myriad fantasies I've invented about the single men I've met over the last twelve years. It helps my ego, temporarily at least, if I can visualize myself as the one who walks out the door with her chin held high, even though in reality things rarely turn out that way.

The reason I didn't say what I was thinking was simple: this guy was ten times cuter than anyone else I'd met in the last six months, and he had a certain vulnerability about him that was almost endearing. Besides, once you turn fifty, you find yourself trying even harder to make a silk purse out of a sow's ear—or a horse's ass.

So I sipped my drink, smiled empathically, and thought, *Well, maybe it's not crazy to put your profile on JDate even though you broke up with your girlfriend five minutes ago and are now back in the house with your wife. Maybe this guy is just confused and needs a little time, or a little therapy.*

Maybe Lydia the therapist could–should take him on?

And I did, right there at the restaurant, as we sipped wine and I stuffed my face with spaghetti *alla putanesca*. "You're not ready for another relationship right now," I said.

"What do you mean?"

"You seem…well…confused." Never mind that I was confused about why I was sitting there with him on what was allegedly a date when I knew very well I was wasting my time.

That's the problem when you're a therapist—you feel you ought to help people, no matter how pathetic their story. However, it doesn't help your social life—or your sex life, for that matter—when the reason you're staring into someone's eyes is to make sure they're not glazed over. Or if you discover you're hanging on to his every word because you're trying to figure out which diagnostic category he fits into in the DSM—you know, the therapist's bible, the diagnostic, not the liturgical one. I'd finally come to the realization that most of the men I'd dated since my divorce were:

a. searching for the "perfect" relationship with
b. the "perfect" woman who also happened to have
c. the "perfect" body (of course) but were
d. emotionally unavailable and/or commitment phobic, not to mention
e. totally clueless about how to relate to other human beings, or to sum it up in one nonclinical term…
f. just plain nuts.

Lying in my bed hours later, I felt as if everything was falling into place. I'd been thinking about starting a research project for some time but hadn't selected a topic yet. What better topic for my project than the men I'd dated over the last twelve long, lonely years? If I could meet with them, maybe I could gain some insight, understand why so many had rejected me, why in turn I'd rejected some of them. And what better way to track down exes than by placing an ad on Facebook? I used to think Facebook was only for the under-fifty crowd but, like Facebook itself, I knew better now. I'd signed up six months ago, and since then I'd posted updates almost every day. I had a whole network of friends and had even reconnected with some long-lost buddies from high school and college. I'd never placed an ad on the site before, but I figured it was worth a try, especially since I could target a specific population: single men in the Philadelphia area between the ages of forty and sixty, i.e. men I had dated. I was hoping once my name and my ad were posted, they would catch the eye and pique the interest of some of my exes, who might at least remember the name Lydia if nothing else.

The idea for the research project had also been fueled by my commitment to extricate myself from the financial morass I'd been in since my divorce. I'd finally faced the fact that my paychecks were barely covering the mortgage and my always-dwindling private practice would never make up the difference. I'd decided that teaching a few undergraduate courses at one of the local colleges could be a source of much-needed additional income. I was hoping Project Ex would provide me with material for an article—or maybe a series of articles, or eventually even a book—about how to find and maintain intimate and loving relationships, and how to identify the ones that were destined to end in frustration and heartbreak. Getting published in a peer-reviewed professional journal like *Annals of Psychological Theory* might help me land a part-time teaching job and could even lead to more writing projects in the future.

I was so glad I'd crawled out of bed to write the ad. It was a stroke of genius, really, and the perfect way to launch Project Ex. As I read it over one more time, I began a running tally of my exes in my head. There was that loser Todd who never had any money in his wallet when it came time to pay for dinner—most of the time he didn't even have a wallet, it was usually in that mysterious "other pair of pants"; that son of a bitch Leon who told me he was a famous local entrepreneur but turned out to be a shoe salesman at Macy's; and two-timing Sid who'd never bothered to mention—until I'd gone to bed with him, of course—he was already engaged to someone who conveniently happened to live out of town. Just as I was mentally aiming the red patent leather stiletto I wished I were wearing at his head, he'd added, "We can keep seeing each other after I get married—discreetly, of course." I'd dated plenty of men—more than I wanted to think about at the moment—and if I could find at least a few who would agree to be interviewed, I should have more than enough material for a decent article.

I took a deep breath, then entered my credit card information and pushed the "send" button. The ad would be posted the very next day—January 15—and would run through Valentine's Day—an added bonus. My chest felt tight and my heart started to flutter. *I need to calm down*, I thought as I got up and headed for the kitchen. *Maybe a little chamomile tea will help me sleep, along with that strawberry cruller I was saving for breakfast tomorrow morning.*

CHAPTER TWO

The next day was Saturday, but I couldn't sleep in because I was expecting Cassie McMillan, my first and only client of the day, at 9:00 a.m. I dragged myself out of bed at 8:15, showered, and was in my home office by 8:45, a cup of strong coffee on my desk. When my business line rang, I picked it up immediately, expecting to hear Cassie's voice on the other end. I figured she was calling to cancel at the last minute again.

"Hello," I said, feeling slightly pissed off. I was getting tired of her calling ten minutes before her appointment to tell me her car wouldn't start, her babysitter was late, her hair wasn't dry, her cat had a hairball. This time, she'd have to pay whether she showed up or not.

"Hello, Lydia," a male voice said. "Do you know who this is? It's Barry—Barry Marmelstein—*Dr.* Barry Marmelstein. Remember me? It's been a long time…"

"Barry," I said, "Of course I remember you."

"I saw your ad," he said, "and you know I never could resist anything for free."

Hell, I thought, *why did that cheap bastard have to be the first one to respond to my ad?* However, I had the presence of mind to ask, "How's orthodontics these days?"

"Oh, it's fine, but I'm not having any luck with women at the moment and I can't figure out why."

I can, I thought, as I remembered all those early-bird specials we shared together at the diner and those coupons from the *Entertainment Book* he brought along in a plastic bag on every date. However, what I said was, "Well, then, you're a perfect candidate for my research project."

He seemed happy enough with that reply and scheduled an appointment for the following Saturday at 9:00 a.m.

I spent a lot of time over the next few days thinking about my short-lived relationship with Barry. Although it had been brief—I dated him for six weeks, maybe seven—I knew it had lasted much too long, at least from my point of view. I wanted to try to figure out why I'd continued going out with him when I'd known from the beginning that the sexual attraction just wasn't there for me. I had no idea how I managed to make it through our boring dates when most of the time how I felt, what I wanted, or what I had to say didn't seem to matter. And it wasn't just me. Many of my friends had had similar experiences. They'd hung in there for weeks—sometimes months and even years—with men they tolerated but didn't really like and knew they could never, ever love.

I did a lot of soul-searching and at last I came up with an honest but painful answer: I'd met Barry only a couple of years after my divorce, when I was raw and vulnerable and believed my chances of finding someone decent and desirable were slim to none. And, as bad as Barry was, he'd still provided some diversion from the never-ending responsibility of raising two resentful and rebellious teenagers mostly on my own. I wasn't happy with the answer, but I jotted down some notes about my revelation, figuring it might be important for my research.

The following Saturday, Barry showed up at my door right on time, looking exactly the way I remembered him. His receding, salt and pepper hair was parted to the left, and he peered out at me from behind black-rimmed glasses the likes of which I hadn't seen since the 1980s, when they were already considered retro-50s. The glasses seemed comforting somehow; my knowing he'd probably bought them on sale at Sears Optical confirmed he hadn't changed over the last ten years. He was still cheap old Barry, always looking for a bargain. As I remembered all the diners we'd been to together, I felt my annoyance growing. *Was I just annoyed with him*, I wondered, *or was I upset with myself too because I'd never mustered up the nerve to confront him about his shortcomings?*

"Hello, Barry," I said, as professionally as possible. Barry stood there, looked me over, and then stepped into the foyer.

"You've lost some weight, Lydia," he said. "It suits you. Your teeth look great too, although I could make them even whiter."

"Hmm," I said, not sure whether I'd just received a compliment or not. "Perhaps we can talk about that at the end of the interview. Who knows, maybe you'll give me a discount in exchange for whatever advice I can give you," I added, watching his face turn whiter than my teeth would ever be.

"There's no gimmick or anything, is there? I mean, it's not going to cost me anything to be part of this research project?"

"Of course not. Just like I said in the ad, I'm doing some research on the singles scene—trying to figure out why so many older, divorced singles can't seem to find anyone to date, let alone fall in love with. Actually, you're helping me. There's no charge."

"Well, then, what are we waiting for? Let's get started." He smiled and attempted to squeeze my arm, but I turned quickly and started down the hall. When we reached my office, I moved to the leather chair where I usually sat during sessions, motioning for him to sit on the couch.

"Why don't we get the paperwork out of the way first," I said and handed him a release form.

"Is this really necessary?" Barry was as paranoid as he was cheap.

I smiled as sweetly as I could. "Well, I hope to write an article after I've completed all the interviews, and I may want to include something that comes up during our meeting. But if you don't want to sign it…"

"No, I'll sign it—as long as you don't misquote me or anything."

I pointed to the tape recorder on my desk. "That's included in the release too. I plan to record these interviews, in case I need to refer to them later. I won't use your real name, regardless."

He seemed satisfied with my explanation, so he read through the release and then signed it. "Now," I said, "tell me why you answered my ad."

He flashed the perfect white teeth that were his best advertisement. "I was curious and wanted to check you out… You know, after all these years." He hesitated and then added, "But mostly I'm here because I haven't had a relationship for three years—since my second marriage fell apart."

Second marriage? I couldn't believe it. Two women had actually been foolish enough—or desperate enough—to marry him?

"I just can't seem to find the right person."

"What do you mean?"

"I never seem to get past the second or third date anymore. I meet someone, go out with her once or twice, and then…it's over. I call and she doesn't answer or she says she's busy or she's back with her old boyfriend. I don't get it. I mean, I've always had a way with women." He winked. "I bet you remember that."

I winced inwardly as I remembered our few sexual encounters. Truly, it hadn't been his cheapness alone that had prompted me to end the relationship. Making out with Barry had been about as much fun as having your braces tightened without any of the benefits, like ending up with a great smile on your face.

"I guess I'm here because I'm looking for insight—your insight. I thought you might be able to help me figure out how to find the kind of woman I'm looking for—someone who's going to hang in there for the long term, or at least longer than, you know, the first date."

"Do you have any ideas about how to change things?"

"Well, I was thinking about joining a yoga class—I had a friend who did. He was the only guy in the class and he loved it. But I'm not sure yoga will work for me."

"Why not? It's a great way to relax and you could meet a lot of women."

"Yeah, but it's so expensive." Drops of sweat broke out on his forehead. "My friend told me it cost him a hundred dollars just to join the damn place—some 'initiation fee' garbage—and then he had to pay for every class."

I blinked as an image of Barry in the lotus position flashed through my mind. *Maybe it's not the best option for him,* I thought.

"How about a dog?" I asked. "Walking a dog is a neat way to meet women."

"A dog?" He scratched his head. "I don't really have the time for a dog. I'm not good with, you know, responsibility. Plus, they're so expensive. Do you know how much a vet costs?"

"Actually, Barry, I think we're getting a little off track. What I want to talk about are those dead-end dates you mentioned. Do you have any insight about why those women didn't want to see you again?"

He glared at me. "It's not about me. It's the women I've been meeting lately. They're not like the women I used to go out with. They're different."

"Different? How?"

"Well, for one thing, they have expectations."

"Expectations?"

"You keep repeating what I say. It's unnerving."

I almost repeated "unnerving" but caught myself. "I'm just trying to find out whether you have any behaviors that might get in the way of your getting what you want with women."

"You don't understand. It's not me. It's them. I'm still the same guy I used to be. We dated for a while. You must remember something about me…"

Before I could stop myself, I blurted out, "What I remember is that you've always been pretty wrapped up in yourself. That doesn't do a lot for your love life, if you know what I mean."

"Me—wrapped up in myself? How could you say that?"

"Well, every time we went out to dinner, you always picked the place. And it was usually a restaurant that was featured in the *Entertainment Book*. Or, you'd make sure to pick me up at five o'clock so we could get the early-bird specials. We'd run ourselves ragged to get to a restaurant before six, and then I'd be feeling so rushed—not to mention annoyed—I'd lose my appetite." I felt a surge of happiness. At last I was getting out the words I should have uttered years ago.

Barry swept his hand over the few hairs on top of his head. "I never knew you felt that way. Why didn't you tell me? I noticed you never ate much, but I thought you were always on a diet or something."

It took me a few moments to process that he really didn't have a clue about how his cheapness had ruined our relationship. I figured it probably hadn't done much for his two marriages—or his recent dates—either. "You know, I've found that people who are obsessed with saving money usually have something else going on. I mean, that kind of cheapness comes from some place, and often it's a place of great pain."

Now it seemed both of us were astonished. Quite honestly, I couldn't believe I could feel any empathy for this self-centered man who had schlepped me to every two-for-one place in town, and he seemed floored by my honesty.

"Barry, are you okay?"

"I've been better, I'll tell you that. The truth is, after I called and scheduled this appointment with you, I started doing a lot of thinking, especially about Sarah, my second wife. So I called her and told her I needed to see her."

"What did you want to talk to her about?"

"Well, I thought maybe she could give me some answers—you know, about why I'm not getting anywhere with women these days."

"And?"

"I don't think she really wanted to talk to me. I mean, the relationship ended pretty badly. You'd think that since we were married for only three years and we didn't have any kids together, we could have resolved things without a lot of animosity. But that's not how it happened at all." He stared off into space.

I was lost in thought for a moment too, as memories of the disastrous end of my own marriage came flooding back. It was mid-December and I was curled up on the threadbare couch in the tiny den of the home where my husband, David, and I had lived for fifteen years, bundled in my fleece bathrobe, watching *I Dream of Jeannie* reruns on TV, and feeling terribly alone. I heard his key in the lock but for some reason I didn't get up to greet him as I usually did. When he came into the den, he didn't bend over to kiss me but just sat down beside me on the couch. "I have something to tell you," he said.

"Why did your marriage end?" I asked, pulling myself back to the present. Barry shot me a look that made it clear he didn't want to talk about any of this.

"Why did it end? She said there was no excitement anymore. She said I never listened to her and I had no idea who she was. That she was done raising children—she had two grown kids from her first marriage—and she wanted to have fun. She said I was boring and predictable and I didn't really care about her." He glared at me. "And she said I was cheap."

"Why are you glaring at me like that?" I asked, meeting his gaze.

"Well, because you just called me cheap too. Sarah talked about the early-bird specials too—what's wrong with them, anyway? And the roses I bought her that died the next day—how was I supposed to know you shouldn't buy roses from Daisy Depot—and the jewelry she wanted but never got. I'd heard all of it before, but..."

"But?"

"When I was talking to her, I suddenly realized what I'd lost and I wanted to kick myself."

"Why?"

"Well, I loved her, you know? So, why didn't I give her what she wanted? What's wrong with me?"

We sat together quietly for a few moments as Barry struggled to pull himself back together. My mind drifted again to David and all the lies he'd told me. Even when he said he was leaving, he didn't have the nerve to acknowledge he'd been running around for months with a young associate in his law firm. When I found out about her—the unforgettable Tawny—I went berserk, rifling through his briefcase while he was in the shower, following him in my car when he went to "meet clients" at night. It was only later, after David moved out—tossing every card, every memento I'd ever given him into the trash—that I was able to turn my fury into acceptance, mostly because I wanted my children to come through everything as unscathed as possible but also because I needed his financial support.

"And I need to know what you meant when you said cheapness is about more than money," Barry said, his voice catapulting me back to the present. "What did you mean just now when you said sometimes it comes from a place of great pain?"

"I think you know, Barry. Tell me where you think it comes from." But what I was thinking about was my own pain—and the humiliation of losing a husband I loved to a woman named Tawny.

"Oh, you're trying to psychoanalyze me. Don't give me that bullshit—just tell me what you meant," he said, his voice rising. He got up and began to pace back and forth in the small room.

"Barry, please sit down," I said.

He glared at me, but he sat down.

"Let me ask you something—why did you get so agitated when I asked you where you thought your cheapness comes from?"

"It's always about your parents and how they treated you, or some deep, dark secret you're harboring. Well, none of that is true. My parents were decent people and I don't have any secrets."

"Then I guess you're just cheap. Is that it?" The words came out before I could stop them.

"Yes, I guess that's it. And what's so terrible about that, anyway?"

"Well, you were just telling me that maybe it was at least partially responsible for the end of a relationship with a woman you loved very deeply, but other than that, nothing."

Thankfully, at that moment, I glanced at my watch and decided it was time to bring our meeting to an end.

"Listen," I said, "We've covered a lot today and I know some things we talked about brought up painful issues for you." *And for me*, I thought. "Why don't we break here and you can think over what we discussed when you get home. Feel free to call me if you'd like to talk again. I really appreciate your willingness to participate in my project. This interview gave me a lot to think about. I can see now that when we were dating, I wasn't totally honest about how I felt. I didn't realize I was still harboring so much resentment."

Face flushed, he jumped to his feet. "This is bullshit. I came here to get some advice. I thought if I helped you, you'd help me too. But that's not how things turned out, and I've changed my mind. I don't want to be part of your stupid research project. Give me back that release I signed. If you dare to print anything I told you today, I swear I'll sue."

I pointed to the release still sitting on my desk. He grabbed it and tore it into shreds. Then he flung his coat over his arm, turned, and strode out of the office; an instant later, I heard the door slam behind him. I sat there for the next half hour, trying to unwind. *I need to do some thinking before I proceed with this research project*, I thought. *If I end up pissing off all my ex-boyfriends, I won't have enough data for a bumper sticker, let alone an article.*

CHAPTER THREE

Barry White on Soul FM woke me up the following morning, swearing he was never, never gonna give me up. I took it as an omen, maybe related to my encounter with Barry yesterday, maybe—hopefully—not. I quickly showered and kept myself busy with errands all day so I wouldn't have time to check my emails or voice mail messages. I knew I needed to do some thinking about Project Ex before I scheduled any more interviews. I felt I'd crossed a line with Barry. I'd allowed him to trigger too much in me, and I felt uneasy and ashamed. I hadn't been prepared for the flood of memories and sad feelings our session had brought up in me—feelings about David, the breakup of our marriage, and my inability to find a meaningful relationship over the past twelve years. I tried to perk up by reminding myself that my therapist Gwen had helped me come to terms with the problems in my marriage and to understand that just because things hadn't worked out with David, it didn't mean I was incapable of finding happiness with someone else. However, it was tough to push those old feelings down once they resurfaced.

When I returned to work on Monday, I didn't have to worry about obsessing over Project Ex. Things there were as hectic and unpredictable as usual, and by the time I returned home at the end of the day, I was exhausted. On a good day, it took me over half an hour to get to work, but most days, the drive into Philly on the Schuylkill Expressway, the outdated and much-maligned main artery, was not only time-consuming but anxiety-producing, frustrating, and downright suicide-inspiring at times. I loved working in Old City, the historic heart of Philadelphia, but hated the commute and had been yearning for years to move into the city. Something about the Main Line always felt unreal and affected to me, even though it had become more diverse over the years, with more Jews and now blacks and Asian Americans moving there to offset what was once a most unwelcoming Wasp-ness. I felt like I belonged in Center City Philadelphia, especially now that my children were no longer at home. However, the expense of a move, along with the even more outrageous cost of real estate in the city and the additional cost of parking—so outrageous that one developer even opened his own "parkominium," a cars-only condo!—had so far prevented me from doing anything more than dream about taking the plunge and putting my modest ranch house on the market.

It was seven o'clock and I had just arrived home, a takeout salad from a nondescript local restaurant in a brown paper bag under my arm. Before I could even think about devouring it though, I went to my computer and began checking my emails. One subject heading immediately caught my eye: *You shouldn't have dumped me back in 2000.*

I began to read: *Remember me? We went out together for a couple of months back in 2000, but things didn't end very well, thanks to you. I'd be happy to come and talk to you, although you may not like what I have to say. Larry Kimmelman.*

Larry Kimmelman. I repeated the name several times. I had no idea who he was, although it certainly sounded familiar. His attitude bothered me. I wrote back quickly, recommending that he give me a call so we could schedule an appointment. I made no mention of his reference to the fact I'd done him some grave injustice. Obviously he'd let me know all about it when he came to see me.

Larry called the next day and asked if he could see me the following Monday evening after work. He was cool and said nothing more about how I'd done him wrong, nor did I ask.

It was difficult to concentrate on my clients at the clinic for the rest of the week. All I could think about was the upcoming session with the mysterious Larry Kimmelman and any other emails from my exes that could be waiting for me at home.

I woke up early on Saturday morning and once again headed straight to my computer. Checking through my new emails, I was surprised to find one from Josh Samuels. No chance I could forget him. He was a real hunk and I'd flipped over him the minute I laid eyes on him. We'd had a few dates and everything seemed to be going well until he disappeared—and remained disappeared until 11:45 p.m. last night, when he resurfaced as a phone number, a Gmail address, and an abrupt "call me when you can."

I closed my eyes, trying to remember the last time we were together. I knew it had been at least several years ago. We had drinks at a funky martini bar on Market Street then walked around, holding hands. We made out for a while on a bench on Penn's Landing, the harbor area where you can watch the boats sail by, and it seemed as if he couldn't tear himself away when the night was over. He kissed me passionately when we said good night, and then…I never heard from him again.

He lived in New Jersey, and I had kind of convinced myself that something terrible had happened to him when he was on his way home that night. There seemed to be no other reasonable explanation for why he never called again when the date had gone so well and he'd seemed so into me. I took some comfort in my perverse fantasy that his car had plunged over the railing of the Ben Franklin

Bridge. Of course, I knew it was only a fantasy, and it wasn't as if I was wishing that anything disastrous would happen to him. But when you've been disappointed and disillusioned by relationships as often as I have, you pray that the reason you've been rejected has nothing to do with you and everything to do with circumstances beyond your control, like a car wreck or an earthquake. I figured that someday, when the police were dredging the river looking for something else, there he'd be—Josh Samuels, my former almost-boyfriend, trapped in his car at the bottom of the Delaware, his hands still on the steering wheel. No matter that, as far as I knew, no article had ever appeared in the newspaper about a terrible tragedy on the bridge or a missing hunk named Josh from New Jersey.

I glanced out the window. It was a beautiful, sunny day. It seemed unlikely Josh would be sitting around on a day like this, so I decided it was a good time to give him a call and leave a message. When he picked up on the second ring, I was surprised. "Hi, Josh. This is Lydia Birnbaum," I said. "I got your email and I'm calling to set up a time for us to meet." *You bastard*, I thought. *How could you have the nerve to still be alive?*

"So, what's this project of yours all about? I was just curious, you know…"

"Just what I said in my ad, Josh. I'm doing some research on relationships—why they work and why sometimes they don't—and I thought there was no better place to start than with my own experiences. Are you still interested?"

"Well, what do I have to do?"

"All you have to do is make an appointment to come and talk to me. Then we'll take it from there."

"But what if I have nothing to say?"

Well, then we'll just sit and look at each other, I thought. Not a bad thought, really, since Josh was such a looker. "If you have nothing to say, then perhaps you shouldn't come."

There was a long pause. *Oh no*, I thought, *I turned off another guy—even before I had the chance to turn him off in person.*

"No, I'll make an appointment," he said at last. "Why not?"

Once that interchange was over, Josh seemed anxious to come as soon as possible—*what odd creatures men are*, I thought—so we scheduled an appointment for Tuesday evening at seven. Larry Kimmelman on Monday and Josh on Tuesday—next week was really shaping up.

I was about to return to my grilled chicken salad when the phone rang. I picked it up quickly, noticing the call was on my business line.

"Lydia Birnbaum here," I said, wondering if another ex-boyfriend was on the other end.

"Lydia, are you all right?" The familiar voice of my mother came through—the crispest, clearest, most authoritative seventy-five-year-old voice I've ever heard.

"Of course, Mother. I'm fine. How are you and why are you calling on my business line?"

"You didn't answer your other line. I've been trying to reach you all morning, but you didn't call back, so I decided to try your other number. I was worried," she said. My mother who professed to worry about everything but who had barely a wrinkle on her face, while I felt that mine looked like a picture I'd recently seen of the Grand Canyon.

"When couldn't you reach me?" I asked, feeling my face redden just like it did when I was fifteen and she caught me necking in the living room with Michael Himmelfarb.

"Why, this morning. I know your routine, so I called early, but no one answered. Where were you at seven?"

"In the shower. Where else would I be?" I asked. I wondered why Lydia the therapist couldn't handle Miriam her mother the way she had just handled Josh the research subject and ex-boyfriend.

"But I left a message and you didn't return my call. I specifically asked you to call me as soon as possible."

"I guess I forgot to check my messages."

"Are you dating that musician again?"

"Mother, I broke up with Robert six months ago, as you know. And what does the fact I haven't checked my messages yet today have to do with Robert, anyway?" I felt the familiar pain seep through me at the mention of his name. I really cared about him. He was exciting and sexy and even claimed I was the inspiration for two of his songs. But I could never rely on him. It seemed whenever I needed him, he let me down.

"Oh, I know he stayed over and you tried to hide it from me. You used to turn off the ringer on the phone so I couldn't reach you."

Yes, I longed to say, feeling lonelier than I had in a long time. *When Robert and I were in the middle of making mad, passionate love together, nothing would have excited me more than to pick up the phone and hear your voice on the other end.*

What I actually told her was, "This has absolutely nothing to do with Robert. I've been busy all morning, and I haven't had a chance to check my messages yet. Is anything wrong?" I knew my mother was a drama queen, but lately I'd also been acutely aware that she was getting older. Although she knew my pressure points and how to play them, the stakes of this seemingly light-hearted but painful game we played were getting higher. One of my deepest fears was I'd become so inured to her manipulations that someday I'd ignore her call for help when she really, truly needed me. *There's a psychological term for this dance we do,* I thought, *but I don't want to think about that right now.*

"I'm getting ready to go to Myrna's house. Her daughter is taking us into town today for lunch. I just thought maybe you could drop me off at Myrna's, but if you're seeing a client today…"

My mother knew the chances of my seeing a client on Saturday afternoon were slim to none. I usually saw my few private clients before ten a.m. There was very little that happened in my life that escaped her expert scrutiny.

"I'll take you to Myrna's house," I said, thankful that none of my clients was around to hear their therapist engaged in this decidedly dysfunctional interchange with her mother.

"I know you're busy."

"Mother, can we stop this right now? You called because you want a ride to Myrna's house. I'll take you. There's no need to discuss it any further." I looked with longing at the answering machine and wished I had let it fulfill its God-given purpose and pick up this call.

"I have to be there at eleven."

"That's fine," I told her. But the problem was, I didn't want to take her, especially since I knew the bus practically stopped at her doorstep and would deliver her exactly where she wanted to go. But her message had come through loud and clear: *Myrna's daughter has time to take us to lunch. The least my daughter can do is deliver me to Myrna's house so I can enjoy a little pleasure, even if it's not with my own flesh and blood.*

"I was hoping maybe you'd join us for lunch," my mother said when I picked her up later, glancing at her watch as she got into my car at 10:45 and eyeing with disgust the shabby sweats I was wearing. I had changed specifically so I wouldn't have to join Myrna, who mentioned every five minutes that her daughter, Candice, could do no wrong; Candice, who agreed wholeheartedly with her mother's assessment of her; and my mother, who mentioned every five minutes that her own daughter had so little time for her—for a lunch guaranteed to be followed by an entire bottle of Pepto-Bismol.

Somehow they did persuade me to join them for lunch in spite of my apparel, and when I returned home several hours later, I consumed not a bottle of Pepto-Bismol, but a bag of peanut M&Ms, followed by an entire pack of Tums.

I couldn't shake my mood, and after dinner, I was still out of sorts. Feeling restless and unmotivated, I plopped down in front of the TV, a bag of microwave popcorn by my side. Popping the kernels into my mouth, I began to review the afternoon with my mother. It struck me she'd seemed unusually quiet. She generally grilled me mercilessly on just about every aspect of my life. If I didn't tell her what was going on, she'd call one or both of my kids and worm as much information as she could out of them. That's how she'd found out about Project Ex. I wasn't exactly trying to keep it a secret, but I didn't see why I had to tell her all the details, beginning with the fact that it existed. However, one day my daughter Stephanie dropped by to see her and "just happened to mention" I'd posted an ad on Facebook to locate my former boyfriends. My mother called me up as soon as Steph was out the door, and boy, did I get an earful, ending with: "Digging up your old boyfriends is a pretty desperate way to find dates, if you ask me."

I sat there, mindlessly stuffing popcorn into my mouth, ruminating about our day together. She was usually fixated on Project Ex, but today she'd barely mentioned it. Of course, she'd never bring up what she considered my crackpot project in front of Myrna and her family, but we'd had plenty of time alone together. Just then, the phone rang; I chucked another popcorn kernel into my mouth and pressed the "talk" button.

"I just wanted to call and thank you for spending so much time with me today," my mother said.

I began to choke as the popcorn kernel lodged in my throat.

"Lydia? Are you all right?"

I coughed and then grabbed the glass of water on the coffee table. "I'm fine," I said, after taking a long swallow. "I was just snacking on some celery sticks and one of them went down the wrong way." *If I tell her I'm eating popcorn,* I thought, *she'll start harping on me as usual about my eating habits and then she'll say, "Don't call me to complain when you feel bloated and your pants are too tight."*

"Celery sticks, huh? I've been munching on Reese's Peanut Butter Cups myself. At least you're eating sensibly. I've put on some weight these last few months," I was surprised to hear her say.

"I doubt that. You haven't gained an ounce in the last thirty years."

She laughed but the laughter was strained. "By the way, how are the children? Anything new since I talked to them last week?"

I suddenly realized she'd barely mentioned the children all day. Both grown and relatively independent, they were the apple of her eye, and she usually bombarded me with questions about them. Nate, twenty-four, graduated from college a couple of years ago and then moved to Vermont so he could be near his girlfriend, Jodie, and pursue his passion for snowboarding, skiing, and mountain biking. Unfortunately, he didn't seem to have much passion for finding a full-time job, but so far he'd been getting by on temp work. Stephanie—who has my dark, curly hair and the kind of knockout figure I'd always dreamed of—had just turned twenty-seven. She had a terrific job as a graphic artist, a boyfriend, and an apartment in Hoboken.

Both of them adored their grandmother. On some level, it bothered me that my children had such an easy, open relationship with my mother, since there'd been a strain between the two of us for as long as I could remember. There was a formality between us, as evidenced by the fact that I almost always called her "Mother," rarely "Mom." If there was anything that defined our relationship, it was the difference between those two words. I felt like I had to work hard to be the kind of daughter she wanted me to be. But Nate and Stephanie were her grandchildren and she accepted them just as they were.

"The kids are fine. Nate spends all his free time up in the mountains on his new bike, and Steph barely has time to talk to me anymore, now that she and Les are an item. Everything's the way it should be, I guess."

She sighed. "Their lives are just beginning. They have so much ahead of them. But for me, well, how much do I have to look forward to?"

"Is something wrong?"

"No, honey. Everything's fine. I'm feeling a little sorry for myself, that's all. I spend so much time alone. I just have too much time to think."

My mother was the busiest senior citizen around. She met her closest friends—Sylvia Sondheimer and Ethel Blum—for lunch at least twice a week, played mah-jongg at the senior center every Tuesday and bingo at the Jewish Community Center every Thursday. She was also president of the Golden Years Club—a group she'd founded a few years after my father passed away—which hosted biweekly Friday night services and dinners at the clubhouse in her condominium.

"But you have so many friends. You're with people all day long."

"Exactly. I'm surrounded by people all day and by myself all night. I've been alone for a long time, Lydia—a long, long time. That's why I was wondering."

"Wondering about what?"

"About that research project you started. I didn't like the sound of it at first, but after I thought about it for a while, I decided it's not such a bad idea. Not bad at all."

"Thank you, Mother," I said, knowing she was oblivious to all forms of sarcasm.

"I just hope you're keeping me in mind."

"Keeping you in mind?"

"For heaven's sake, Lydia, I need a man around here. Maybe one of those men you're interviewing has a father who's a widower—someone who's just as lonely as I am and looking for companionship."

"Are you asking me to fix you up?"

"Yes, I guess I am. You can't fool me. You're hoping one of these men will work out for you, so why shouldn't there be someone for me too?"

"Mother, I can understand that you're feeling lonely. If you feel like you're ready to meet someone after all these years, that's great. But you don't understand what my research project is about. Most of my ex-boyfriends weren't Mr. Right to begin with and won't be now either. I'm interviewing them as research for an article, not to convince them to date me again. I doubt there's a decent guy in the whole rotten bunch, let alone a decent man for you."

"All right. If you feel that way, I guess I have no choice but to consider Irving."

"Irving? Who's Irving?"

"Irving Melnick. He joined the Golden Years Club a couple of months ago. He's been asking me out, but I've been resisting."

"Why?" I was relieved that her feistiness had returned but worried that Irving might be the senior-citizen version of Ted Bundy.

She lowered her voice. "I think he's just looking for sex."

This is great, I thought as I contemplated hitting my head against the wall. *I'm sleeping alone and my mother's going to be some eighty-year-old's sex toy?*

"He's only about 5'4" but he's got quite a physique for a man his age, I'll tell you that."

"I think you should talk about this with Sylvia and Ethel. It's a bit much for me." Even thinking about the possibility of my mother having sex with anyone was making my stomach lurch.

"Oh, I see. You'd rather give free advice to your rotten former boyfriends than to your mother."

"We both know you don't need my advice. You already know exactly what you're going to do."

I could hear her chuckling as we said our goodbyes.

Unlike her divorced and dateless daughter, she won't have to worry about those long, lonely nights for much longer, I thought as I got up to check out the dinner possibilities in the freezer.

CHAPTER FOUR

On Monday when I arrived at work, Dr. Crenshaw, who was the head of our treatment team, told me with a twinkle in his eye that there was a full moon, "And you know what that means." I laughed and shrugged it off, but when I saw Betty Anne Buford, the homeless schizophrenic who had been in and out of the hospital for years, I became a believer in the power of the full moon. Dressed in a purple tutu, yellow tights, and black work boots, and weighing in at well over 300 pounds, she definitely was not a sight for sore eyes. I prayed she was wearing underwear this time, remembering with a grimace what the nurses had discovered last time she was brought in on a commitment.

As I approached her, Betty Anne was staring suspiciously at the mirror on the ceiling. "Hi, Betty Anne," I said. "I'm Lydia. We met last time you were at Briarside, remember?"

She waved me off, never taking her gaze from the mirror, and began whispering her usual nonsense as if she were disclosing Cold War top secrets. "The men are the women and the women are the men."

"That's a security mirror. It's here to protect you." *And us*, I thought.

She gave me another suspicious look and then continued to stare at the mirror and whisper simultaneously, "I'm having a baby when the cows come home." She looked carefully from side to side and proceeded down the hall, muttering to herself.

I looked at Nancy, my favorite nurse on the unit. "Did you hear that?"

"Yeah, sounds like she hasn't taken any meds since she was here last month," she said.

I was busy all day as usual, but I couldn't get Betty Anne off my mind. A few minutes before five, I stopped by the nurses' station to review her chart. The only "permanent" address listed was a shelter where she crashed every now and then when she needed food. I read Dr. Crenshaw's psychiatric evaluation carefully. He had noted that, as usual, her speech was disorganized—jumbled and difficult to follow. However, in the midst of her delusional ramblings, there did seem to be a common theme: she believed she was pregnant. I seemed to remember that Betty Anne had talked about being pregnant the last time she was in the hospital too. Leafing back through her chart, I found last month's notes. Sure enough, she'd also been preoccupied then with "having a baby when the cows come home." *I wonder how old she is now*, I thought as I checked her date of birth and discovered she'd just turned forty-two a couple of weeks ago. She looked ten years older—was it possible we'd all dismissed the idea she could be pregnant, thinking she was simply too old to have a baby?

It's just some delusional system she's created, I told myself. It was so hard trying to gather a history from paranoid schizophrenics or other psychotic patients. There was often some piece of reality woven into their elaborate and colorful stories, but you could never be sure. I decided to remind Dr. Crenshaw in rounds the next morning that pregnancy had been a central theme in Betty

Anne's ramblings since her last admission. Satisfied with my investigation, I closed the chart and put it back in its place. Glancing at my watch, I dashed to my office, finished up my paperwork, locked all the files into my ancient filing cabinet, grabbed my purse, and then headed out the door.

I rushed home from work and grabbed a Lean Cuisine from the freezer. It was almost six o'clock and Larry Kimmelman was coming in an hour. As the microwave nuked my dinner, I racked my brain, trying to remember who he was. When the buzzer rang, I pulled my gourmet dinner out of the microwave and sat at the kitchen table, where I gobbled every bite of my turkey tetrazzini in less than five minutes. *You'll be hungry later,* I told myself, glancing longingly at the drawer where I kept my stash of Hershey's Special Dark with Almonds.

By 6:45, I had cleaned up the kitchen—not hard to do after a frozen meal; listened to the messages on my answering machine, which also wasn't hard to do since there was only one and that was from my mother; and managed to spend ten minutes doing some deep breathing to calm myself down before the session. Don't ask me why this guy had me rattled, but he did.

At 7:00, I was in my office, waiting for the doorbell to ring. By 7:10, I had looked at my watch at least ten times and checked the answering machine four times to make sure I hadn't missed his call. By 7:15, I was convinced that Larry Kimmelman was a passive-aggressive son of a bitch who was paying me back for whatever injustice I had allegedly committed.

At 7:20, I decided to call and find out whether he was still at home. If he was playing some sort of game with me, I wasn't going to be taken in, that's for sure. I was the one conducting the interview, and he damn well better play by my rules.

I had just found his phone number in my appointment book and was about to call him when the doorbell rang. I checked my watch—7:22. I attempted to hide my annoyance as I opened the door. I mean, maybe the poor guy had been mugged or was in a terrible accident.

On my doorstep stood a short, pudgy man in a toupee. Actually, it wasn't a bad toupee and some people might not have noticed it right away. But as soon as I saw him, my eyes went straight to that stupid toupee and I remembered everything. In spite of myself, I felt my face begin to redden as the memory of our last nightmarish night together came flooding back.

He stood there, staring at me. "Hello, Larry," I said, extending my hand. "Why don't you come in? It's kind of cold out there."

He shook my hand and walked into the foyer, looking around as if he thought this was a drug bust and several FBI agents were going to pop out of my umbrella stand.

"Let's go into my office so we can sit down and talk," I said, leading the way.

Again he just stood there for a moment, as if he were considering turning around and dashing out the door. But he followed me into the office and sat down on the couch, his hands folded in his lap, his eyes riveted on mine.

Just when I was beginning to wonder whether I'd be the only one to open my mouth, he spoke. "Lydia Birnbaum, I've certainly thought about you over the last five years." There was a definite innuendo in his tone, and I wasn't sure I liked it.

Now it was my turn to stare at him. Was this guy going to spend our time together lambasting me for something I'd done five years ago? *Maybe if I apologize, he'll leave and then we can both forget about his taking part in my research project*, I thought.

"Hey, Larry," I said, "I've had the distinct impression—first from your email message, then our phone call, and now from your comment a few moments ago—that you're angry with me."

"Gee, you must be a perceptive therapist," he said, a smirk crossing his round face.

"Well, we're not going to get anywhere until you tell me why you're so angry. There's no way we'll be able to exchange information if you feel I've wronged you in some way."

"Wronged me in some way—you're really something. You know very well what you did to me… And still, all these years later, I don't understand why." His voice shook with emotion.

"Larry, I'm going to be honest with you. When I got your email, I racked my brain but I couldn't recall who you were. Even speaking with you on the phone, I drew a total blank. But when I saw you on the doorstep, I recognized you immediately. And of course I remember how our relationship ended. How could I forget?"

"Relationship? I'd hardly call half a dozen dates a relationship."

I'm trying to apologize here, schmuck. Why don't you let me get on with it? "You're right. We only dated for a little while and things didn't go very well."

"What do you mean, 'things didn't go very well'? I thought you liked me. I mean, you liked me enough to go to bed with me, didn't you?"

"Larry," I said as gently as possible, "I'm talking about the last night we were together. I'm sure you remember what happened…"

"I certainly do," he said, smoothing his hand nervously over his toupee. "I certainly do. That's why I'm here. You owe this to me, Lydia. You messed up my head all those years ago, and I've never gotten over it."

Oh my God, I thought, *this guy is really going to lay a trip on me.*

"I remember we were at your place and you put on some soft music, lit a couple of candles, and before we knew it, we were in bed together." Actually, I remembered a lot more and I'm sure he did too, but I didn't want to embarrass the poor guy by going into all the details. What I remembered was things got hot and heavy fast and I began to run my fingers through his hair—or at least I thought it was his hair. He'd never told me he wore a toupee, and I guess I was super naïve at that point in my life, because, although his hairstyle always looked kind of strange, it had never occurred to me that the hair on his head might not be his own. I felt something move and suddenly his hair was flying through the air. I thought I scalped him and I started screaming, but he didn't move. When the damn thing landed on one of the candles and he finally jumped up and ran for the fire extinguisher, that was it for me. The fire was out for good—in more ways than one.

I recalled the burning hairpiece and suppressed a giggle. "We nearly burned your house down that night."

He gave me a hurt look. "Are you laughing at me?"

"I'm not laughing at you, Larry. But looking back now, can't you see just a little humor in what happened?"

His lips began to turn up at the corners. "I guess," he said, grinning now. "It was what you call a true hair-raising experience."

"I forgot what a great sense of humor you have."

"For a guy with no hair, you mean."

"With or without hair, you're a great guy."

"Then why didn't you give me another chance?" he asked, his voice taking on a petulant tone. "If I'm so terrific and if the toupee wasn't the real issue, then why didn't things work out for us? You have no idea how I've agonized about this. I mean, the whole thing was humiliating and everything, but why couldn't you get past it? You obviously didn't care enough about me. Or maybe you never cared about me at all."

I paused and thought for a few minutes. The truth was, no one was more surprised than I was that I ended up in bed with Larry that night. We hadn't been dating for long, but I already knew that the sexual attraction was a lot stronger for him. And it was a shame too, because he really was a sweet guy. Kind. Attentive. Nice. But although I was always glad to see him, I didn't yearn to see him. It was the lack of yearning that made all the difference. But there was no point in saying that now.

Larry was staring at me, waiting for me to go on.

"I guess the romance was gone for me after that night and I just couldn't get it back," I said. "If the toupee fiasco hadn't happened, who knows how things might have turned out. Maybe after a while I would have pissed you off in some way, and you would have broken up with me. Or either of us could have met someone else. But, since we're both good people, I'd like to believe that eventually we might have ended up as friends and you wouldn't have had to carry around all that hurt and anger for the past five years." That was honest, wasn't it? Or at least, it was honest enough. No point in telling him now that I'd had to work at the chemistry to begin with and watching his toupee fly through the air hadn't helped the situation.

Larry's face turned pale. Had I scarred the poor man for life?

"It never occurred to me there was the possibility I might have broken up with you. Are you just saying that to be nice, or do you really think that's what could have happened?"

"I think there was a 50-50 chance you might have broken up with me. You never know how relationships will end up."

When Larry's face lit up, I knew my response had resonated with him.

"Can you tell me what you're feeling right now?" I asked.

"Well, I guess I'm feeling relieved…and enlightened too. I really liked you, Lydia, and I knew that gave you the upper hand. I guess that's why I never told you about the toupee. I was afraid it'd be a turnoff."

"I liked you too, Larry. You're a really nice guy. As for the toupee—well, I guess if you'd been able to tell me about it beforehand, you wouldn't have felt like you had to wear it to bed. But I can understand how vulnerable you must have felt. I just wish we could have talked about what happened that crazy night, maybe not right at that moment but later—although I'm not recommending five years later. One thing I want you to know—I never meant to hurt you." I knew I had a tendency to run away from relationships when things weren't going well. I simply couldn't face endless hours of discussion about how to fix whatever had gone wrong. Maybe it was because I was a therapist and spent so much time listening to my clients sorting through their problems. Or maybe it was just some shortcoming in me, a lack of patience, or a fear that if I looked back, I wouldn't have the courage to move on.

"Talking to you today helped a lot. I'm really glad I answered your ad. I think I'm finally ready to make an important decision I've been considering for a long time."

"What's that?"

"I think I'll go *au naturel*, as the French say," he said, pointing to his toupee. *I hope the French don't say it the way you just pronounced it*, I thought. "I've read that some women really go for the bald look these days." Glancing down shyly at his bulging midsection, he added. "Hey, maybe I'll lose a few pounds too—couldn't hurt, right?"

I felt pretty good after Larry left, as if both of us had reached some kind of epiphany. I carefully put my notes in the top drawer of my desk and then paced around the house for a while, ideas for my article circulating in my brain. Then I decided to call my best friend, Carol, to see if she had plans for the weekend. Maybe we could get together for dinner or a movie. When she didn't pick up, I suddenly remembered she was in California on a business trip so I left her a message. "Hi, Carol. Give me a call when you get home. I really miss you."

When I hung up, I realized I hadn't checked my voice mail or email since yesterday. I was surprised to discover I had five new voice mail messages and several emails. Adam Rosen. Mark Kornblau. Sheldon Edelman. *This is getting exciting*, I thought as I sat down at my desk. *It's raining exes!*

CHAPTER FIVE

The next morning I woke up an hour later than usual. No surprise, since I'd stayed up responding to emails until 2:00 a.m. I got myself together in record time and rushed out the door but was still fifteen minutes late for rounds, which meant I'd missed Dr. Crenshaw's report on Betty Anne's progress. I approached him sheepishly when rounds were over and asked if we could talk for a few minutes. He had a stack of charts under his arm and I heard his beeper go off. He checked the number as he asked what I had on my mind.

"I'm sorry I was late today, Dr. Crenshaw. I don't know what happened—my alarm never went off."

"Don't worry about it," he said, looking at his watch. "I have to get to the locked unit. Something's going on…"

"I wanted to talk to you about Betty Anne Buford," I said. "Did you read my notes?"

"I did, and I think you're right. We shouldn't assume the pregnancy is a delusion. I talked with her yesterday after you left and asked if she'd agree to a pregnancy test."

"What did she say? Did she agree?"

"She told me not to worry since the baby's not due until the cows come home. The cows, it seems, aren't home yet, but I ordered the blood test anyway. Since she's here on a commitment, I felt justified in going ahead with it whether she agrees or not."

"Good," I said. "If she is pregnant, what will we do?"

"Well, it's going to make it difficult to medicate her. And if we have to keep her here a long time—which seems likely, even if she agrees to sign herself in, since we can't exactly discharge a homeless, pregnant schizophrenic to the street—I don't know what we'll do. We've never delivered any babies on the locked unit, and we certainly aren't going to start now."

"Dr. Crenshaw, don't even go there. I'm hoping, if she is pregnant, I'll be able to find a place for her to go."

"Lydia," he said, a sad expression on his kind but weary face, "I know how hard you try to take care of everyone. But this is going to be tough—really tough. We've never been faced with this kind of challenge before." He glanced at his watch again. "I have to go. We'll talk more about this tomorrow. We should have the test results by then."

"Thanks, Dr. Crenshaw. I appreciate your taking my notes so seriously and ordering the blood test and everything. Not that it'll do poor Betty Anne any good…"

"Well, it will be a blessing that she hasn't been taking her meds if it turns out she really is pregnant."

"I know," I said. Just then, my beeper went off. I glanced at the number. "It's the locked unit. Something's definitely up."

"Let's go." Dr. Crenshaw started off at his usual high-speed clip.

We heard the commotion as soon as we got to the unit. It was Betty Anne.

"I'm leaving now!" she yelled, glaring at the circle of technicians and nurses who surrounded her. "The cows are coming, the baby's coming, and I'm leaving now!" She tried to push through the crowd, using the bulk of her weight to get through.

As Dr. Crenshaw stepped forward, he nodded to the techs closest to Betty Anne, who had grabbed her arms. They let her go and she stomped over to him, pointing her plump finger right in his face. "Listen, Doc," she said. "I'm done here. I need to get out now. The men are the women and the women are the men and the cows are coming home right now."

"Let's go into my office and talk," Dr. Crenshaw said. "I'm sure the cows can wait for a little while."

"Do you have any Tootsie Rolls?" she asked.

I stepped forward, smiling, and said, "I don't think he has any Tootsie Rolls, but he has a big jar of M&Ms on his desk."

"M&Ms are good but Tootsie Rolls are even better," she said as she followed Dr. Crenshaw to his office.

I looked at Nancy the nurse and grinned. "Thank God for Dr. C.," I said.

"There's not a schizophrenic around who can resist him," she replied.

The rest of the day was relatively calm compared to the incident with Betty Anne, but I felt discombobulated because I'd missed rounds and had a lot of catching up to do. By the time I finished my paperwork, it was 5:30 and I rushed home to gobble another frozen meal—Kashi low-fat Dijon chicken with mashed potatoes and string beans, 320 calories and not very satisfying—before my appointment with Josh Samuels. I was just putting my fork in the dishwasher when the doorbell rang. Glancing at my watch, I noted with pleasure that Josh was right on time and headed to the front door.

As soon as I opened the door and looked up into Josh's soft brown eyes—I forgot how tall he was, at least 6'2"—my heart started to flutter. He was just as gorgeous as I remembered. His dark hair was cut short and spiky, which only accentuated the fact that every single feature was perfect. If he wasn't quite Clooneyesque, he was at least Brolinesque—James or Josh, either one would do.

I realized how vulnerable I felt. I'd had the upper hand with Barry Marmelstein and Larry Kimmelman because I'd rejected them. But Josh had dumped me. Suddenly I wasn't so sure I wanted to find out why he'd disappeared three years ago. As we walked toward my office, my mind was racing. Instead of feeling furious with this guy—*the way I ought to feel*, I told myself—I was trying to resist my impulse to invite him upstairs for a little quickie.

Josh seemed pretty ill at ease too; as he sat down, his eyes darted around the room. *Is he looking for an escape route*, I wondered? Frankly, I was having trouble getting my mind off his butt, which I had already noticed was just as cute and tight as it had been three years ago. *These interviews I'm conducting definitely aren't therapy*, I thought. *If this is a research project and not a therapy session, I wouldn't be violating the Social Work Code of Ethics if I tried to seduce him, would I?*

He was staring at me, waiting for me to begin. Every now and then, I'm really, really thankful other people can't read our minds. This was one of those times.

"So, Josh," I said, "what have you been up to over the last few years?"

"Well," he began, "things have been kind of rough."

"What do you mean?" I asked, trying to hide my shock and annoyance. Did he really think I'd accept some lame excuse for why he'd never called me again?

"Having two nervous breakdowns in three years was no picnic, I'll tell you that."

"Why? What happened?"

"Nothing. I mean, it wasn't nothing—more like everything, really. It's just—it's me."

"You? I never knew."

"No one knew…until my life fell apart. I look normal, don't I?"

"Yes, you certainly do. You look about as normal as anyone could be." *Some therapist you are*, I said to myself. *You never even considered that the guy might be having serious problems. Not to mention that you should be focusing on your research project instead of how cute he is and how angry you are because he dumped you.*

"Is that a good thing or a bad thing?"

"I'm sorry," I said, realizing I'd let my feelings about him spill over. "It's just that, even though we only dated for a couple of months, I thought you were so…together."

"You and everyone else. Women in particular. They always think I'm the same on the inside as I look on the outside."

"How are you on the inside?" I asked as it sank in that, in spite of his rugged good looks, this guy was pretty fragile.

"Well, I'm…insecure, anxious, always questioning my decisions. The truth is, I'm a disappointment to myself and just about everybody I know."

"Sounds like you spend a lot of time beating yourself up."

"Oh, yeah, I'm an expert at that."

"So, how long ago were you hospitalized?"

"It was just about three years ago—not long after our last date. I'm sorry I never called, but I was still in pretty bad shape when I got out of the hospital. I was on Prozac for two years for depression, and now I'm taking Klonopin for anxiety. I kind of hibernated for a long time. Somehow I got myself to work every day, but then I'd go home and crawl into bed. It was terrible."

"You don't have to apologize. Now that I think about it, I should have called you to find out if you were okay. I should have known you weren't one of those guys who would just disappear without an explanation. So, I really owe you the apology." My throat felt scratchy and I took a sip from the glass of water on my desk.

"No, I should have called you. But I couldn't because all I could think about was how I'd let you down—along with everybody else—and how much I'd probably hurt you. It never even crossed my mind that you should have checked up on me."

"So, how did you get your life back on track?" I asked.

"It took a while, but things started getting better. I felt like my life was going in the right direction. I got a promotion and then I met someone new. Her name was Cindy, and I fell in love with her the minute I saw her. I know it sounds corny and stupid, but it's true."

"Did she feel the same way?"

He looked at me, his dark eyes moist. "She was crazy—really crazy—she had these unbelievable mood swings and she refused to take her meds. I knew she was no good for me, but I couldn't stay away from her. The ending was terrible and I felt myself slipping back into a black hole. But this time, I reached out for help right away. It was still pretty bad, but at least I pulled myself out of it a lot faster. It hurt, though—a whole lot more than I wanted it to. Then I saw your ad on Facebook and I decided to come in and talk to you. I don't have a clue how to find a healthy relationship."

"Well, that's why I started this project, Josh. Even though I've counseled lots of people on relationships, I'm pretty clueless about applying what I know to myself. I'm doing this research with the people I've dated to try to figure out how we can turn things around and save ourselves a lot of pain."

"Pain? I'm used to it. It seems that no matter what I do, I cause pain to myself or to the people I care about. I don't know if I'll ever be able to figure out this relationship stuff. If anyone does, I mean. I don't know. Someone has to, right?"

I sat there, looking at him, this gorgeous hunk of manliness, and suddenly it hit me like a ton of bricks: Josh disappeared three and a half years ago because he was troubled and on the verge of a breakdown, not because he didn't like me or because I wasn't pretty enough or sexy enough or exciting enough for him. In other words, *It wasn't about me.* My fantasy about him plunging off the bridge had been my way of trying to convince myself it wasn't my fault that he never called again. It was a lot easier to accept that some terrible catastrophe had befallen him than it was to acknowledge my underlying fear that it was some basic flaw in me that had driven him away. Now I realized it was neither. I realized something else too: the attraction I'd felt when Josh crossed the threshold today had melted away as soon as he began to talk about his issues. I was sick and tired of rescuing the men I dated. I didn't want to work so hard anymore or to feel like the men I dated needed to be rescued.

Just as we were wrapping up, Josh told me his therapist had recently moved away and asked if I'd consider taking him on as a client. I told him I was flattered by his request but couldn't honor it for ethical reasons since, after all, he was still one of my exes. He didn't look happy when I gave him the name and phone number of one of my colleagues, but he seemed to understand.

After he left, I went into the kitchen for a snack, taking my appointment book with me. Leafing through my appointments for the next week, I was surprised to see what a full schedule I had. Jeff Portman was coming to see me the day after tomorrow. He was the guy who'd dumped me after our last disastrous date at the Jersey shore on New Year's Eve. He'd run out of gas on the Atlantic City Expressway on the way home and had left me alone in the car by the side of the road while he set off on foot to find a gas station, the sixty dollars I'd won on the slot machines tucked in his pocket. Somehow he seemed to have left his credit card at home, and he told me he'd lost his last dime at the craps table. Maybe that's why he "forgot" to fill the tank before we got on the road. And I was seeing Craig Meyers next Saturday. Craig Meyers…the name sounded familiar, but I couldn't place him. *Probably just as well*, I thought, munching on a cookie.

I was starting to feel concerned and more than a little anxious that I was turning to food again for solace, a pattern that had begun shortly after David left. During that terrible time, food had become my comfort, my escape, my outlet. I'd suddenly developed this insatiable hunger and couldn't stop eating. It seemed as if no matter how much I ate, I wanted—no, needed—more. I told myself it was sensible to need more calories at such a stressful time. After all, I was on my own—juggling my full-time job and raising two adolescents—and I had to be burning at least twice as many calories as I did before.

Of course, that was bullshit but I talked myself into believing it. Naturally, I knew about compulsive eating, but it was a term I used in relation to my clients, not myself. I was the therapist—the one who needed the calories in order to absorb my clients' pain. I was definitely not the one in pain—the one who was stuffing her feelings or seeking comfort in food.

I began craving things I'd never cared about before, except when my PMS was raging—chocolate, potato chips, pretzels, chocolate, and more chocolate. I learned that if I stuffed a bag of M&Ms into my mouth, I felt sick when it was empty but, for a little while at least, I didn't feel so frightened or so alone.

Although my clothes were getting tighter, I refused to acknowledge my compulsive overeating was making me gain weight. I told myself I was retaining fluid, didn't have time to exercise as much anymore, and needed to rev up my metabolism. It took me months to realize the "hunger" I'd been feeling had nothing to do with food. I was hungry for attachment, for intimacy, for love. I was yearning for a truly loving relationship and terrified I'd never find it.

I told myself I didn't have the worst divorce in the world. As a matter of fact, my friends said I had the nicest divorce they'd ever heard of, but that's no surprise. Why wouldn't a person who goes out of her way to make sure other people are happy have a "nice" divorce? I was so busy making sure my husband didn't feel guilty and my children weren't going to be scarred for life that I wasn't concentrating at all on my rage—which I shoved down, along with a whole bunch of other feelings.

I was in total denial in the months leading to the end of our marriage. Believe me when I tell you that the New Underwear Myth is based in reality. I should have known something was out of whack when David suddenly decided those old, torn, ratty briefs he'd loved for so many years had to go. He never had any compunctions about parading around the house after work in his dress socks with the drooping briefs and stained undershirts he claimed gave him some sense of security or something. Although I always felt slightly nauseated when I saw him in this getup, as a loving wife and ever-the-therapist, I gave up on nagging him and decided that all couples must reach that point of comfort when such things don't matter anymore. However, I did wonder if all wives felt quite as nauseated as I did, or felt their libido take a dive, as mine did.

Sure enough, as soon as he found another woman, he made a beeline for the men's section at some fancy department store and bought a complete line of new briefs, including bikinis, silks, even a pair of thongs. When I looked at him like he'd lost whatever vestige of sanity I thought he still had, he told me, "I'm entitled to a midlife crisis. You spend money on makeup and jewelry… Well, this is my way of making myself feel good."

When you say that to a therapist, what response do you think you'll get? Of course…I felt guilty. My husband was in the midst of a midlife crisis and I didn't even know it. Maybe I'd caused the damn thing by nagging him about his underwear in the first place. If I'd kept my mouth shut, I wouldn't have had to look at him in those ridiculous silk bikinis he always seemed to put on the day he was leaving for a "business trip."

It wasn't until much later that I put everything together and realized he only wore all the new stuff when he was going "out of town." At the time, I was too busy feeling guilty to pay much attention to details. Of course, I should have realized what was going on, not just with our marriage but with me, too.

Now, thinking back on that painful time, I said to myself, *you're turning to food for comfort again and that means you're eating for reasons that have nothing to do with hunger. You'd better figure out what's eating you or you'll be a candidate for* The Biggest Loser *before you know it*.

CHAPTER SIX

Another few weeks went by and suddenly it was the middle of March. I woke up early one brisk, clear morning and decided to go into Philly for a bike ride on Martin Luther King Jr. Drive, or West River Drive, as it was formerly and still most commonly known. I'm not what you might call the athletic type, but I do own a bike—nothing fancy, just three speeds. Since it takes only about half an hour by car to get there from my house, I figured I could ride for an hour or two and still be home well before noon. After an invigorating bike ride, I planned to spend most of the afternoon working on an outline for Project Ex.

West River Drive, along with its mirror image, East River Drive—which is also known as Kelly Drive, after Jack Kelly, Jr., brother of the gorgeous actress Grace Kelly—provide a spectacularly scenic view of Philadelphia. *How perfectly Philadelphia in all its inconsistency*, I thought. *We name one avenue after Martin Luther King, Jr. and another after a wealthy man whose sister became a movie star and a princess.* It's a fun place to go for a ride, although, unless it's bitter cold or oppressively humid out, it's usually jammed on weekends with bikers, joggers, skateboarders, gawkers, and Canada geese.

I grabbed a quick breakfast and hooked up my bike rack, cursing as I did every time I went through the arduous process of attaching it to the car and then lifting and securing my bike onto it. There was no traffic and I made it to West River Drive in record time. Before I knew it, I was pedaling furiously, rejoicing in the warmth of the sun on my face, the wind rushing through my hair. *I should do this more often*, I thought, even though I knew I wouldn't.

I couldn't even remember the last time I'd taken my bike out for a ride. The truth was, I'd been pretty absorbed with Project Ex. My schedule was getting busier and busier and this was the first time in ages I'd been able to carve out any time for myself. Every day, I raced home from work to check my voice mail and email messages. There was usually at least one new message, sometimes more. Strangers contacted me too, just to let me know they'd seen my ad and were interested in contributing to my research. A few crackpots had responded also—guys with filthy minds who wanted me to fulfill their sexual fantasies. I wanted to let them know that not only didn't I own a maid's uniform, a policewoman's uniform and handcuffs, or a Catwoman costume, I wasn't fulfilling anyone's sexual fantasies lately, not even my own, but I just deleted their emails as quickly as possible.

After I'd reviewed my messages, I'd head into the kitchen to make myself a sandwich or a bowl of soup; then I'd retreat to my office, where I'd spend the rest of the evening at the computer or on the phone, setting up appointments for interviews. I kept a large spiral notebook in the top drawer of my desk so I could keep track of everyone who'd contacted me. I enjoyed leafing through it every day, checking off the names of the men who'd responded, making notes next to the ones I'd already interviewed. So far, I'd received responses from forty-eight exes, twenty-six curious

Facebook browsers, seven nut cases, and eighteen men who'd been referred by one of my exes, as in "I don't need to talk to Lydia about my past relationships but maybe you do." I'd already met twenty-eight exes face-to-face and had nine more interviews lined up over the next few weekends. When I'd posted the ad on Facebook, I'd been focused on finding interview subjects and so I'd defined the term "ex-boyfriend" rather loosely, i.e., anybody I'd dated, even for a brief time. However, something unexpected had happened: some of the men I'd already interviewed had found that talking to me about relationships was so helpful, they'd started sending their friends my way, not just as subjects for my research project but for therapy too.

I took a deep breath and slowed down a little. I looked over at the crowd of people on the sidewalk, some walking, some jogging, some rollerblading, and saw a toddler bend over to pet a fluffy-looking puppy that seemed to belong to an older, gray-haired man. His mother scooped the boy up quickly and carried him off, kicking and screaming. An adorable guy with a kerchief on his head and ominous-looking tattoos on his muscular arms and legs whizzed along on rollerblades. As I turned my head to check him out—not my type and about twenty years too young, but a looker nonetheless—another biker swooshed by, a little too close, and I picked up speed. I smiled as I whizzed by the Art Museum, remembering the happy times I'd spent there with my kids. Although I loved to linger over the artwork, Nate and Steph always wanted to head straight to their favorite rooms. Nate liked to spend his time in the room with the huge display of medieval armor and weapons, while Steph was drawn to the quiet of the meditation room, where she could sit inside a medieval cloister and listen to the gentle sounds of water trickling in a stone fountain. I brushed away a tear as I turned onto East River Drive. Thinking about the "good old days" brought up mixed feelings for me. While I yearned for the time when the kids were still at home, it had been hard—really hard—raising them on my own. And in some ways it was a relief to know they'd been launched—successfully, I hoped—at last.

By 11:30, I was feeling tired and hungry so I pedaled back to my car, hooked up my bike, and headed home. I realized how relaxed and clear-headed I felt. *Now I'm ready to tackle that outline for my article*, I thought. Although I'd achieved lots of things in my life, I could be a real expert at sabotaging myself when I was close to getting something I really wanted. I'd spent plenty of time talking to my therapist Gwen about that. Writing the article about Project Ex was the perfect example. I'd been gung ho about conducting the interviews, but now I was dragging my feet, putting my energy into projects that needed to be done around the house—*or taking a long bike ride*, I thought with a twinge of guilt.

I pulled into my driveway, parked the car, and went inside. Although I was still determined to get to work on the outline, I decided I deserved a little rest after all that exertion, so I plopped myself into my favorite chair in the living room. I leafed through the newspaper on the coffee table until I found the lifestyle section with its focus on arts, entertainment, and best of all, food. I loved reading restaurant reviews, and I usually read every one, even those written by Jared Abrams, whose name probably struck fear in the heart of every restaurant owner in the Philadelphia area. Although he definitely had a way with words, his reviews were often scathing and sometimes downright mean. I never trusted his ratings because he rarely had anything positive to say. Few chefs seemed able to prepare a dish that met his incredibly high standards, and few restaurants seemed to provide the ambience or service to warrant his praise. I wondered how he felt when he slipped into restaurants undetected, with his notepad or tape recorder tucked into his pocket, hungry for the opportunity to vilify the reputation of yet another of Philly's finest restaurants. Jared's columns deliberately ran without a photo, typical of most restaurant critics, even when he wrote about the occasional non-food subject. I'd heard a rumor that he was going to make a move to investigative reporting soon and said a silent prayer for anyone who might be on his "hit list."

Just thinking about reading about food was making my stomach rumble, so I put down the newspaper and headed to the kitchen to make a turkey sandwich. I pulled the ingredients out of the fridge and piled fresh turkey breast, romaine lettuce, and thick slices of tomato on whole-grain bread—complex carbs and, therefore, guilt-free. I added some crunchy tortilla chips with flaxseed on the side, poured myself a tall glass of ice-cold lemonade, and then carried everything on a tray into the living room. I'd just slid the tray onto the coffee table and had snuggled again into the cozy chair, prepared to take the first bite out of my yummy sandwich, when the phone rang.

"Hello," I said, holding the phone with my left hand and reaching for the sandwich with my right.

"I'm back." It was my friend, Carol. We've been best friends since kindergarten. I know it sounds corny, but it's true. Her last name was Greene then and mine was Glass—we'd both taken our husbands' names after we got married—and since our teacher liked to seat each class in alphabetical order, Carol and I ended up sitting right next to each other. The rest, as they say, is history.

"Boy, have I missed you," I said. Usually, we got together every couple weeks and talked on the phone almost every night. But she'd been in Los Angeles for almost a month and I'd been wrapped up with Project Ex, so we'd barely had time to talk or email each other.

"I'm dying to see you and I must hear what's been happening with Project Ex. How about if we meet around 1:30 for lunch at Christina's Place? I just got in this morning and I haven't even unpacked yet, but who cares?"

"Sounds like a plan," I said. "I was just about to eat lunch, but I'll wait." Christina's Place was my favorite neighborhood restaurant and Carol knew it. I loved their signature salad, a mound of organic greens, topped with slivered almonds, colorful pepper strips, and fruit—mango, strawberries, blueberries, pears—whatever was in season. I'd already taken a bite out of my sandwich, but I put the rest back on the plate and went into the kitchen to put it in the refrigerator.

Since Carol lives in Center City and Christina's is practically around the corner from my house, I assumed I'd be the first to arrive. Anyway, I knew that even if Carol lived next door to the restaurant, she'd arrive at least ten minutes late. I was used to that after all these years.

As I walked in, I waved at Christina, the owner, who was talking on the phone. She gave me a smile and pointed to a booth near the back. I'd been coming to Christina's since my kids were in high school, and she felt like an old friend by now.

I sat down, took off my jacket, and shoved it over near the window. A few minutes later, Carol opened the door and glided into the restaurant. She was built like a ballerina—tiny-boned, slim-hipped, and narrow. She walked like a dancer too, her back straight, shoulders in perfect alignment. With her olive skin and translucent green eyes, she was a total knockout. She had a closet full of the most fashionable clothes—usually purchased on sale at "Bloomies" or "Nordies," her two favorite stores. Today she was wearing a dark green cape that flowed as she moved. I half expected her to do a grand jeté, but instead she waved and headed in my direction.

"It's great to see you," I said, jumping up to give her a hug before she sat down. "I've really missed you. Next time you go away on a long business trip, you'll just have to take me along."

"No problem," she said, "as long as you can pull yourself away from Project Ex."

"Actually, I don't think I could at the moment. You wouldn't believe how busy I am."

"I can't wait to hear everything. Let's order and then you can fill me in." Carol opened the menu and gave it a cursory glance. She motioned to the waitress, Claire, a 40ish-looking—but probably 50ish—brassy blonde who'd been working at Christina's for as long as I could remember.

After we'd both ordered our salads, I said, "I want to hear all about California too. Knowing you, there are plenty of stories."

"Well, I did almost bump into Johnny Depp."

"Johnny Depp? You know how much I love him."

"He's even cuter in person, I have to say. Even through my binoculars, he looked pretty damn adorable."

"Binoculars? You didn't. Carol, were you stalking the poor guy?"

"Of course not," she said, her voice vibrating with indignation. "Let's just say I heard he was going to be in a certain place at a certain time, and I made sure I was there."

"With your binoculars tucked into your purse."

"But of course," she said, giggling.

"I gather you had some free time," I said. I knew very well that Carol was obsessed with pop culture. She read magazines like *People, Us,* and *Entertainment Weekly* from cover to cover and was hooked on shows like *The Dish* and *The Soup*. She loved following the intimate details of celebrities' lives but vehemently denied she was the gossiping type.

"I was working day and night, Lydia. I had very little free time."

"But when you did, you made a beeline for Rodeo Drive."

She grinned. "Well, sure—why not? Enough about me. I must hear what's going on with Project Ex."

"Well, you're not going to believe it, but almost one hundred men have answered my ad."

Carol arched her eyebrows. "Wow! That's a lot of exes. But I'm not surprised. You've been on a dating rampage ever since David walked out the door."

She was right. Within a few months after David and I separated, I became obsessed with finding ways to meet men. I spent a lot of time writing and answering personal ads and dragged Carol to plenty of bars and singles events too. Thankfully, my mother had helped out a lot with the kids, so Nate and Steph were well cared for when I wasn't home. I didn't bring a lot of men home either, and if I was lucky enough to be in a relationship and I had someone to sleep with, I usually stayed at his house or brought him for overnight visits to my house when the kids were with David. I felt good about that but not so great about all those nights I wasted looking for someone I still couldn't seem to find.

"Hey, wait a minute. You don't understand—they're not all my exes. Some guys were just curious when they saw the ad and wanted to find out more. And some of the exes I've already interviewed have sent their friends and even a couple of relatives my way. Project Ex is starting to have a life of its own."

"I bet if you average it out, you've probably met at least one or two men a month for the last twelve years."

"Well, probably, but I hardly remember most of them. It seems as if there were so few who really mattered, except for Robert, of course. Even though we only made it through six months together, we had something special while it lasted. But it's true, if you do the math…"

"That's a lot of men," Carol said, "whether they're memorable or not. You know, this project of yours has definite possibilities. I bet my friend Beth who works at *Philly Now* would be interested in hearing about it. It just so happens that she writes the 'What's Hot and Happening' column every month."

"And you think my project is hot and happening?"

"I think it's sizzling, and I'm going to send Beth an email as soon as I get home and tell her all about it."

"Go ahead," I said. "She'll probably laugh herself silly over it, but what the hell."

"You know how things happen in Philly," Carol said. "Once word gets out about Project Ex, you could become an overnight sensation."

"And a has-been the morning after."

"Stop being such a pessimist. I'm telling you, I think you're on to something here," Carol said, smiling at Claire as she brought over our lunches. "Hurry up and eat. I can't wait to get home so I can get that email off to Beth."

CHAPTER SEVEN

Sure enough, Carol's friend, Beth Murphy, called the very next day. She asked me a lot of questions then told me she planned to feature Project Ex in her next column and requested that I email my photo to her as soon as possible. Two weeks later, when the April issue of *Philly Now* hit the newsstands, there was my photo, along with a smartly written piece about my "hot and happening" project.

The day after the column appeared, a reporter from the *Philadelphia Globe* called and asked to interview me. I was surprised and flattered and agreed to meet her at a local restaurant. It turned out she was fifty-four, recently divorced, and a Project Ex aficionado. What seemed to impress her the most was that I harbored so little animosity toward my former boyfriends. She asked me lots of questions which I answered as honestly as I could. She didn't press me when I was evasive about how long it would take me to complete the interviews and get the article written. If she'd known the truth—that I'd written only three sentences of the first paragraph and so far I'd revised those three sentences eight times—she might not have been as impressed with me and what she later described in her article as an "innovative and ground-breaking project."

It wasn't long before I started hearing from other reporters and from producers at local radio and TV stations. Before I knew it, I was being interviewed on the radio and making guest appearances on TV talk shows. Most of the people who interviewed me were so taken by Project Ex—that I'd had the initiative to contact my former boyfriends and was willing to hear their feedback—they too paid little attention to the article I was supposed to be writing. Over and over, I was introduced as "Philly's relationship expert." It was unreal—no, surreal—hearing myself described as "the single guy's guru" when I'd had so many relationship failures of my own.

By the end of May I was exhausted, so I allowed myself a Saturday morning off—no therapy sessions, no Project Ex interviews, nothing but downtime. I had just plopped myself onto the chaise longue on my tiny patio and was luxuriating in the warm sunlight when my cell phone rang. As soon as I answered, a male voice asked, "Is this Lydia Birnbaum?"

"Yes, this is Lydia. What can I do for you?"

"My name is Sam Sloane. My friend, Troy Johnson, suggested I contact you. I'd like to make an appointment to come in and talk to you. A regular appointment, I mean."

"You're looking for a psychotherapist?" I asked. I remembered his friend Troy very well. He was a nice guy who'd been in some rotten relationships and had needed help boosting his self-esteem.

"Yes, I think I am."

He sounded uncertain, but I figured we could talk about that during our session. Sam wanted to schedule something as soon as possible and seemed delighted when I told him I'd just had a cancellation and could see him at 7:30 the following evening.

"I'll be there," he said.

I tried to return to my prior semivegetative state, but it was no use. My conversation with Sam Sloane had interrupted my reverie and I just couldn't get myself to unwind again.

The next day, Sam showed up right on time; as he walked in, he shook my hand and thanked me for agreeing to see him right away. He was a strikingly handsome African American man, probably in his mid-fifties, with a compact, muscular build and piercing dark eyes. His khakis and lavender Ralph Lauren polo looked freshly pressed—everything about him was crisp and precise.

He sat down on the couch in my office and began fidgeting immediately.

"You seem on edge," I said.

"Look," he said, "I want to be honest with you."

"I hope so. Therapy won't work unless you're completely honest with me and with yourself."

"Well, that's the thing. I'm not really here for therapy."

"You just need some advice about a specific issue, and you feel it can be resolved pretty quickly. Is that what you're trying to say?" How many times had I heard that before?

"No, what I'm trying to say is that I'm not here for therapy. I'm here to make you an offer—one you can't refuse, I hope," he added, smiling.

"An offer?" I asked, feeling the hairs rise on the back of my neck.

"Don't worry—this is totally legit. My friend Troy told me about you and your unusual project, and I've done some research of my own. Sounds like you've become quite the authority on relationship issues, which means you're exactly the person I need."

"Wait a minute, I'm confused. You just said you're not looking for a psychotherapist."

"I'm not but my listeners are."

"Your listeners?"

"I'm a radio producer. Talk radio—WKLR."

"Talk radio? What does that have to do with me?"

"Do you listen to KLR at all? We have lots of programs focused on all kinds of issues. At least you've probably heard about our most famous host, Henry Sanchez. He's always in the news because of some controversy he stirred up…"

I just stared at him and then I shook my head. "Sorry, I think I've heard his name but, well, I'm not too into talk radio. I'm a Democrat. I mean, sure, I listen to a little NPR but…"

"Well, that doesn't really matter. The point is…"

Is there a point, I wondered, *or is this guy who looks so well put together really a nut case?*

"You see," Sam continued, "we're about to launch a new show, and we've been looking for some time now for the right person to host it. It's going to be a real departure from the shows we've done in the past—a completely new venture."

"Sounds interesting, but again, what does that have to do with me?" I asked, glancing at my watch.

"I'm sorry to take up your time but I didn't want to discuss this on the phone. Frankly, over the last few months, you've made quite a name for yourself in Philadelphia, and I think you'd be the perfect person to host our new radio show."

"You want me to host a radio show?"

"It's a health and wellness call-in show, specifically for people with relationship issues. No long-term therapy or anything like that. As a matter of fact, I wouldn't call it therapy at all. Just advice, straight from the heart, from a therapist who's single herself and understands the challenges involved in making relationships work," he added.

"You really caught me off guard. I need time to think. Of course, I'm flattered that you'd even consider me to be the host of your show. At the moment, I'd have to say it sounds, well, terrifying, frankly, but I'm definitely intrigued by your offer. It is an offer, right?"

"Absolutely. I know there's going to be a learning curve, as far as the technical end goes, but my team will work with you. How about if I send you some information tomorrow? I can have a messenger bring it over in the morning. If you like what you see, you'll come in and we'll talk turkey. We'd like to start by airing the show once a week—we were thinking Sunday evenings at seven o'clock—but we're hoping to expand to at least twice a week as soon as things get rolling."

"Sure," I said. "Send me some information and we'll take it from there."

As soon as he left, I called Carol; she picked up on the first ring. "I've been dying to talk to you," she said. "Anything new since that interview on *The Morning Show*? Has Oprah called yet?"

"Very funny. Like Oprah would be interested in talking to me. But actually, there is a new development and I wanted to talk it over with you."

"A new development? What kind of new development?"

"Well, I just finished meeting with a new client, a guy named Sam Sloane. The reason I'm telling you his name is that it turned out he wasn't interested in therapy or in being a subject for my project either. He wanted to meet me because he's a radio producer who just happens to be looking for a host for his new talk show, a call-in show for people who have relationship issues. And guess who he's considering for the job?"

There was silence on the other end. "Carol," I said, "are you still there?"

"I don't believe this," she said. "This is too much."

"I don't believe it myself. Sam told me he'd been reading up on me, and he thought I'd be the perfect person to host this new show. He was insistent so I asked him to send me some information and said I'd think it over."

"What's there to think about?" Carol shrieked, almost breaking my eardrum. "This is the opportunity of a lifetime."

"Only if I can handle it. I have no idea if I'm equipped to give psychological counseling to the masses over the airwaves—about relationships, for God's sake. I mean, it's one thing to counsel people one-on-one, but on the radio? What if they find out that deep down I'm a fraud and as clueless as they are about how to find a decent man? Let's face it, Carol—I have my own issues on this topic, as we both know. I'm writing an article on dead-end dates and failed relationships because I've had so many myself. And the bottom line is, I still sleep alone every night."

"Look, whatever the reason, you're becoming the authority on relationships—in Philly, at least. Nobody seems to care whether you're single or married or in a long-term relationship. And you and I both know that you were born to be a radio host. You're funny as hell and you definitely have the gift of gab. Your listeners are going to love you. Who knows where this could lead? Maybe you really will be on Oprah someday. And if you are, I'm coming with you."

"It's a deal," I said. "And, by the way, I have a cancellation at four o'clock. You'd better come in and talk to me, because I think you've lost touch with reality, my friend."

The next day, I was in the kitchen preparing breakfast when the doorbell rang. When I opened the door, there was a man with a WKLR logo on his jacket. He handed me a large envelope; I took it to my office, ripped it open, and read through the documents inside. Everything Sam said was true, and, to be honest, it did sound like an amazing opportunity. I still wasn't sure how I felt about giving advice on the radio, but if Sam trusted me, why shouldn't I trust myself? *I have nothing to lose by giving it a try*, I thought, *except, of course, my social work license, not to mention my self-esteem*. I decided to think it over for a day or two and talk to some of my colleagues about it too. But I already knew that no matter how apprehensive I felt, there was no way I was going to turn it down.

CHAPTER EIGHT

And so I became the host of my very own call-in radio talk show. What Carol said was true—in my heart, I'd always known I was born to do something in the public eye, or, in this case, the public ear. I loved public speaking, and over the years I'd conducted numerous seminars on a wide variety of mental health topics. However, I'd never even dared to dream that I might have an opportunity like this one.

Just a few weeks later, I was at WKLR studios, preparing for my first night on the air. I'd made several visits to the station beforehand, and they'd patiently walked me through the mechanics of the job. It was exciting and everyone was helpful and understanding, even though it was clear that I was not a whiz at the technological side of things. Most of the behind-the-scenes people were guys who looked like they'd finished junior high about ten minutes ago. They kept their distance at first, but I was so nervous, I didn't care. Later, I found out they'd started a kind of office pool, placing bets on how long I'd last with no experience or training in the communications field and nothing going for me except the notoriety I'd gained through Project Ex.

Sam had suggested that I contact my clients to let them know about the show and encourage them to call in that first night. I took his advice and spread the word. However, it took a few minutes for the phone lines to light up after I finished introducing myself. The silence was terrifying, and I thought I'd faint before the first call came through. My hands were shaking so hard that I spilled coffee all over my favorite slacks, but once I started talking, it all felt pretty natural.

Even with all the coaching, I still screwed up some of the technical stuff and disconnected a couple of people in the beginning. I didn't want to be rude, so I let a sixty-seven-year-old man ramble on for what seemed like hours about how women always seemed to dump him when they found out he was unemployed, hadn't seen a dentist in over thirty years, and still lived with his mother. *Gee*, I wanted to say, *can you blame them?*

But the calls really started to pour in after Jeff from Abington phoned in. Listening to his dilemma flooded me with memories of my date with the CyberPsycho whose utter cluelessness about relationships had prompted me to begin Project Ex in the first place.

"Hi, Jeff," I said in my newly discovered radio talk show host voice. "What's on your mind tonight?"

"Well," he said, "I'm thinking about going back to my wife. We separated a few months ago."

"Have you spoken with her? How does she feel about that?"

"Yeah, I called her yesterday and told her I thought I'd be ready to come home soon, but she hung up on me."

"Why do you think she did that?"

"I'm not sure. I mean, when I talked to her last week and told her how much I missed her, she seemed really happy."

"So you think she hung up on you because…"

"I told her I had one more thing to do before we got back together."

"And what's that?"

"I need to go out with just one more woman. I met this great chick last week, and I want to check out the possibilities with her before I go back to my wife."

For a moment, there was silence. Then I said, "Let me get this straight. You told your wife that you miss her and you don't want to be separated anymore. But before you go home and resume your role as faithful husband, there's just one more woman you want to go out with—to make sure you're not missing something."

"Yeah, that's it," he said. "I wanted to be honest with her. Isn't that what marriage is all about?"

I struggled to keep myself in check. It's a good thing that radios can't broadcast your thoughts because mine were filled with a long string of expletives, ending with, *She's better off without you, asshole.*

"What if the tables were turned?" I asked, reminding myself silently about the Social Work Code of Ethics, which said I had to try to help this guy even if I thought he was the biggest schmuck in the world.

"What do you mean?" he asked, suspicion seeping into his voice.

"Well, what if you called your wife and told her you were ready to come home and she said, 'Sounds okay, but can you give me a couple more weeks to make sure there isn't anyone better out there?' What if she was the one who wanted to 'check out the possibilities' before she said yes?"

"That's ridiculous," Jeff said. "My wife wouldn't do that. She loves me. She's waiting patiently for me right now while I decide what to do."

"If she's waiting so patiently," I said, trying to keep the annoyance out of my voice, "how come she hung up on you?"

At that point, the phone lines were blinking like crazy, so I decided to let some of the callers tell Jeff their point of view, which basically boiled down to: *if your wife's even considering taking you back, she's just as screwed up as you are and you deserve each other.*

As soon as I got home, I called Carol. "Well?" I said. "What'd you think?"

"Dr. Phil, move over," she said, and we both giggled uncontrollably. "Lydia, you were amazing. I can't believe how you handled all those callers. I mean, there were a couple of silences, especially at the beginning. And it was funny when you cut those people off. But once you got the hang of it, it was great."

"It was, wasn't it? And you know what—I enjoyed it, even though I was really nervous. I mean, can you believe it? Me, on the radio, giving advice to people about their love life?"

After I hung up, I wandered around the house, trying to decide whether I should go straight to bed—sensible; settle down in front of the TV—boring; or check out the leftovers in the refrigerator—appealing. In the end, I decided to plop in front of the TV with a large Hershey bar—dark chocolate with almonds, of course, full of antioxidants—by my side. I couldn't believe how much my life had expanded in just a few short months, from therapist to researcher, writer…well, almost writer…and now radio talk show host. I decided to go to bed but knew I was much too revved up to sleep.

CHAPTER NINE

It didn't take long for my weekly radio talk show to become a regular part of my life. Facing the challenge of callers who might present any problem or issue made me feel charged, full of anticipation and the excitement of facing the unknown. The staff did an amazing job of screening callers, but occasionally some folks with serious mental health issues slipped through. It was difficult to find a delicate way to say, "Sorry, you need in-depth professional help—more than I could possibly offer in a few minutes on the radio," but most of the time I was able to be empathetic and still get them off the line pretty quickly. I'd also been conscientious in compiling a list of local mental health resources, which included the names of several experienced couples therapists, and had trained a few staff members how to handle the callers I referred to them.

Over the next couple of months, I began to settle into my radio talk show host role. I still questioned myself at times and wondered if I could have or should have asked more probing questions or how I could have provided more thought-provoking answers. However, the feedback from my listeners was overwhelmingly positive, so I figured I must be doing something right. Once I started to relax, I discovered I was enjoying just about every minute on the air. I began to let my sense of humor peek through too; I'd been holding myself back, afraid of hurting someone's feelings or being misinterpreted. I tried to be patient with every caller, but there were times someone pushed my buttons and I allowed my frustration or annoyance to seep through. I was astonished to discover that most of the time, my listeners didn't seem to mind. On the contrary, they seemed to love finding out I had my areas of vulnerability too.

One night at the end of July, I arrived at the station just ten minutes before airtime. I usually gave myself at least half an hour to prepare for each show, but by the time I threw my jacket on the chair and glanced over the memo from Sam on my desk, I had barely five minutes until I picked up the first call.

"You look hassled," my assistant Keith said. "Are you okay?"

"I'm fine," I said, taking several deep breaths and settling into my chair. "I was running late and then my car wouldn't start, so I had to call a cab. I'm feeling a little frazzled, that's all."

"We're on in two minutes. Are you ready for the first caller?"

"No problem." Keith gave me the signal and I did my intro: "Hi, welcome to Sunday nights with Lydia, a unique call-in show where the focus is on building stronger and more loving relationships." The phone calls started coming in and I picked up the first call.

"Lydia, it's Brett Steinmuller. Long time no see, huh?"

Brett Steinmuller. The name sounded vaguely familiar, but I had no idea who he was. "Yes, it has been a long time," I said, praying he'd say something to jar my memory.

"I couldn't believe it when I heard about your radio show. But I wasn't surprised. I knew you were destined for great things."

"You did?"

"Absolutely," he replied. "Even back then, you were pretty damn special."

"Back then," I repeated, rifling my fingers through my hair, willing myself to remember something about this guy.

"Wait a minute—you don't know who I am, do you?"

"As a matter of fact, I don't have a clue. Are you sure I know you?"

"Know me? Of course you know me. We were an item way back when at Camp Timbers."

"Camp Timbers? I haven't thought about that place in about forty years."

"It hasn't been that long, but almost. I think you were about sixteen the last time I saw you."

"Okay, it's been thirty-four years. That's an awfully long time. How could you be so sure I'd remember you after all these years?" My cheeks were burning. Once he mentioned camp, the memories came flooding back and I knew exactly who he was. Brett Steinmuller, the heartthrob of just about every adolescent female camper at Camp Timbers. He'd been a junior counselor, tall, tanned, and muscular, with the hairiest chest I'd ever seen. The first time he pulled off his shirt during swim time, I'd almost fainted. He'd noticed me staring at him and had given me a provocative wink before he jackknifed smoothly off the pier into the lake. I was smitten and he knew it.

"Well, I was your first. Or at least that's what you told me."

I glanced over at the guys in the booth. Their faces were contorted in laughter.

"Brett," I said, "this isn't an appropriate interchange for us to have over the airwaves. I'm going to hang up right now."

"Look," he said, talking rapidly, "I'd love to see you again. As I recall, you were pretty damn cute at sixteen."

"It's time to let go of your adolescent fantasies. We haven't seen each other since we were teenagers, for God's sake."

"Where's your sense of adventure? Aren't you dying to find out what I look like now?"

"The only thing I'm dying to do at the moment," I said, looking at the blinking phone lines, "is end this call."

"Come on," he said, "we had something special. It wasn't just an adolescent fling—we were mature beyond our years."

"Give it up, Brett," I said as I hung up.

Of course, I took some ribbing from the next few callers. "Give the guy a break," seemed to be the consensus. "He's been pining for you for over thirty years," one caller said. Pining, my ass. Once he'd jarred my memory by mentioning Camp Timbers, it hadn't taken me long to figure out why he was calling. My guess was that he'd called in to my radio show because he'd just broken up with his most recent hottie. Even back in the day at Camp Timbers, he'd been known as a notorious flirt and he never could tolerate being without a girlfriend.

Most of my bunkmates had a crush on one of the junior counselors, who were only eighteen or nineteen, not much older than we were. The fact that I was the only one who succeeded in having a fling with one of them made me feel incredibly sophisticated. It was all very exciting, especially because our supposedly clandestine romance was strictly taboo. From the beginning, I knew Brett was going to break my heart, and sure enough, he did. About two weeks before the end of the season, he started hanging out with one of the counselors, a gorgeous twenty-something-year-old with a breathy voice and the biggest boobs I'd ever seen. I was heartbroken and humiliated, so I ripped up all the cute little notes he'd slipped to me throughout the summer and tossed them into the lake, along with the tiny panda bear he gave me after he won it in an arcade game at a local carnival.

I shook my head to clear away the memories and noticed all the phone lines were lit up so I picked up the next call. "I think you were too hard on Brett," Debbie, a mother of three who said she'd married her high school sweetheart, told me. "He could be your long-lost love."

"Look," I said, "I'm really glad you and your husband found each other when you were so young. However, trust me—Brett Steinmuller is not my long-lost love." *If anything*, I thought, *he hasn't been lost long enough.*

The call from Brett had set the tone for the show and had definitely struck a nerve with my listeners. For the rest of the evening, I had to listen to comment after comment about the power and passion of young love. Most of my listeners agreed with Debbie and felt that I'd brushed Brett off too easily and should at least have considered seeing him again.

Judging from my listeners' comments, it had been a great show. However, talking to Brett had stirred up painful memories for me—memories I'd suppressed for a long, long time. I didn't want to think about the fact that for the last thirty-four years I'd been choosing the wrong guys to go out with, but it was true. I'd always been attracted to "complicated" men—men who seemed exciting, mysterious, unknowable. I never imagined myself with the guy next door, the one who wore his heart on his sleeve and presented no challenge. Therefore, many of my relationships had been with difficult men who'd rejected me for reasons I never knew or couldn't understand and left me feeling inadequate, confused, and unfulfilled. Yes, most of them were Jewish, but that was only because my mother had drilled it so deeply into my psyche that I ought to date only Jewish men. Something about shared histories, values, and traditions, which seemed to make sense at one time but no longer seemed so clear-cut, especially when the Jewish ones turned out to be as hopeless and lost as everyone else—including the one I married. Here I was, fifty years old, and I was still confused about how to find a healthy relationship. Maybe that was why I was having so much trouble writing the damn article about Project Ex. There must be a pattern to my past failed relationships—a pattern I really didn't want to uncover, investigate, or acknowledge to others or myself. And if I wasn't capable of changing my own dysfunctional patterns, how could I expect my clients to change theirs?

There was one person I rarely allowed myself to think about, one person whose name was taboo…Rusty Munson. He'd been the love of my life, and I'd turned my heart and my soul over to him. When he made promises—when he swore he'd love me forever—I believed him. And when he broke my heart, I felt like he'd cracked it open with a sledgehammer. I was only nineteen—just beginning my sophomore year—when I met him at the student union at NYU. He was a junior and incredibly handsome, with blonde hair, longish and curling slightly behind his ears, and the clearest blue eyes I'd ever seen. And, most intriguing of all, he wasn't Jewish. I knew my parents would be shocked when they met him and he casually mentioned that he'd been raised Presbyterian but considered himself an agnostic. They'd feel betrayed and bewildered and they'd never understand the attraction. The more I considered that, the more my attraction for him seemed to deepen.

I was a psych major and Rusty's passion was theatre. I envied him because he was determined to be an actor. His parents didn't approve but they didn't try to deter him either. He knew that once I'd dreamed of an acting career too, but I'd caved in when my parents made it clear how they felt about that idea. No way were they going to pay for my college tuition if I was going to end up a starving, two-bit actor, living in a tiny walk-up apartment in Harlem with only a job as a waitress to keep me going financially. Now I could see that I'd projected that dream onto Rusty and lived it vicariously through him.

Stop it, I told myself, shaking my head to push thoughts of Rusty out of my head. Why was I allowing myself to think about him after all these years? Damn that Brett Steinmuller—it was his fault. *I wish I'd never spent that summer at Camp Timbers*, I thought as I stuffed my notes into a manila folder. It was midnight—time to go home. I left the studio and trudged to the parking lot, feeling defeated and acutely aware of being alone.

When I got to the parking lot, I spent ten minutes searching for my car before I remembered it was sitting in my driveway at home. I was close to tears as I pulled out my cell phone and called a cab, feeling humiliated that I didn't have a significant other I could call to pick me up and take me home.

Some relationship expert you are, I thought. I couldn't seem to get Rusty Munson out of my mind. If he hadn't broken up with me all those years ago, everything—everything—would have turned out differently. I'd still be fifty, but I wouldn't be alone and on this ridiculous quest to find true love.

As soon as I got home, I turned on my computer and logged on to Facebook. Then I typed in the name "Rusty Munson" and waited. There were three Munsons, but no Rusty. However, there was a Ryan Munson from Encino, CA. I knew that Rusty's real name was Ryan, but he'd rarely used it in his younger days. He was in his fifties now; maybe he felt his old nickname didn't suit him anymore. I clicked on Ryan Munson and held my breath, squinting at the photo. He looked older, that's for sure. His hair was thinning in the front and looked more gray than blond. But the smile was the same—warm, intimate, and yes, still very sexy. I checked his profile and devoured the few entries he shared. It sounded like he'd made quite a career for himself doing voice-overs, performing in regional theatre productions, and directing too. He'd recently turned to writing and was in the midst of completing his first screenplay.

I felt my heart leap. He might be thirty years older and calling himself Ryan now, but he sounded like the Rusty I used to know. The fact that he lived in California didn't matter. I was open to a long-distance relationship. I imagined myself telling Carol, "Yes, I'm bicoastal now."

The first step was to make him my Facebook friend. I pushed the "Add Friend" button and then wrote him an email. I made sure to keep it brief and breezy, not intimate and intense – *I think about you all the time. Come back to me.* – the way I wanted to write it. This wasn't *Cold Mountain*, after all. *If I take it slowly*, I thought, *I might be able to work my way back into his heart.* I'd heard from one of our college friends that he and his wife had split up a couple of years ago. *With any luck*, I thought, *he's still single, and maybe he's pining for me too. Maybe—just maybe—I'll have the chance to reconnect with him after all these years. And then who knows* what *might happen*, I thought as I headed for bed, allowing myself to feel just a glimmer of hopefulness.

CHAPTER TEN

I was counting the days until the weekend but when it finally came, I still felt brittle and anxious. I decided I needed a break from Project Ex, so I called and cancelled the interviews I'd scheduled for the weekend and my private therapy clients too. I envisioned myself sleeping in the next day and then spending a leisurely day at home, catching up on my reading, chatting on the phone with Carol, and then vegging in front of the TV. *Who knows, maybe I'll even make a pot of soup*, I thought as I tried to remember the last time I'd cooked rather than nuked anything other than a hot dog.

I woke up early on Saturday but didn't even consider getting out of bed. I fell back to sleep immediately and didn't open my eyes again until 9:30. I lay there for a while, feeling decadent and a little guilty about my decision to take the day off. *Screw it*, I thought as I tossed back the covers and got out of bed. I headed for the bathroom, washed up, brushed my teeth and threw on a pair of sweats and my favorite T-shirt, the tie-dyed one Steph and Nate had bought me for my birthday when we were all down the Shore together. *How long ago was that,* I wondered, noticing that the material had frayed near the neckline.

In the kitchen, I poured my favorite cereal into a large bowl, added milk and half a sliced banana, and sprinkled chocolate chips on top. Then I placed the bowl and a glass of water on a tray and carried it up to my bedroom. I put the tray on my bed and then scooted downstairs, opened the front door, and raced down the driveway to pick up the newspaper. On the way back upstairs, I grabbed two more newspapers and the latest issues of *Vogue* and *O!* from the coffee table in the living room. With a sigh of happiness, I threw the newspapers and magazines on my bed, plopped down next to them and began to wolf down the food. When I was finished, I put the tray on the floor and settled back on the pillows. I reached for the newspaper and scanned the index, searching for something interesting. I noticed an intriguing title—"A Retrosexual in Therapist's Clothing" —on a column in the Lifestyle section and grimaced when I saw it was written by none other than the restaurant critic/reporter everyone loved to hate, Jared Abrams. Lately, it seemed Abrams was taking a break from the restaurant beat, but he'd been restaurant critic at the *Philadelphia Globe* for a long time. "Retrosexuals"—that was a term I'd never heard before. *I wonder who he's out to get this week,* I thought as I began to read:

> *Several of my friends, as well as my twenty-seven-year-old daughter, Emily—who's been doing her best to keep tabs on the women I've dated since her mom and I divorced ten years ago—urged me to check out a new radio talk show called "Sunday Evenings with Lydia" that airs on WKLR at 7:00 p.m., so I tuned in last week. The host, Lydia Birnbaum, is a therapist who has recently achieved some local celebrity with a so-called research project she's named "Project Ex," as in "ex-boyfriends," as opposed to "extraordinary gentlemen" or "extemporaneous speaking" or "existential crisis."*

Birnbaum, who turned fifty this year but frankly reminds me of a spoiled teenager who never got past her childish and decidedly antifeminist notions about romantic love, placed an ad on Facebook a few months ago in an effort to locate some of her exes. Since then, she's been conducting interviews with them, gathering data on "dead-end dates and failed relationships." She claims her goal is to write an article based on her findings to be published in a yet-to-be-disclosed journal—one can speculate: People, *or perhaps* Tiger Beat—*to provide guidance to other singles who like herself have experienced "repetitive relationship failures" (which seems to be psycho-babble to explain the fact that she keeps meeting losers).*

After being "discovered" by Philly Now *columnist Beth Murphy, much as drunk drivers have been known to "discover" brick walls, Birnbaum has garnered interviews on just about every local radio and TV show and now she's been dubbed Philly's "relationship guru." Admittedly, I may have a somewhat biased view of therapists based on my own dismal experiences during the tortuous breakup of my own marriage. However, I tried to have an open mind when I tuned in to her radio show last week. Although it seemed more like entertainment than therapy to me, I won't deny that most of the people who called in to pour out their hearts to her seemed satisfied with her off-the-cuff advice. As a matter of fact, although I doubt I'll ever be a fan, I probably wouldn't have written this column if the theme for the evening hadn't been determined by a caller who identified himself as her "first"—a man she met when she was at summer camp when both were teenagers. It was clear she wasn't overjoyed to hear from him, especially when he said he'd love to pick up where they left off over thirty years ago. That's when it occurred to me that it may have been a retrosexual agenda that motivated Birnbaum to launch Project Ex in the first place. By the way, if you're not familiar with the term "retrosexual," you can check it out on the Internet. It has several meanings, including "to mine through past romantic liaisons in order to find a*

Project Ex

current relationship or romantic encounter." Shame on you, Lydia Birnbaum. Why don't you just come clean about the self-serving motivation behind Project Ex?

I read through the column and then read it three more times as I tried to steady my shaking hands. I started pacing around the bedroom and then I did what I always do when I need to vent—I called Carol. The phone rang and rang, and I was about to disconnect when she picked up.

"I was just thinking about you," she said. "There's a huge sale at Bloomie's. Want to check it out with me?"

"You haven't read the paper today, have you?" I asked.

"Nope. I've been busy cleaning out my closets so I'll have room for the new stuff I plan to buy today. Is anything wrong? Has something terrible happened?"

"Nothing catastrophic, if that's what you mean. Just that my radio show is the topic of Jared Abrams' column today."

"Jared Abrams wrote a column about your show? Isn't he supposed to be doing restaurant reviews?"

"He seems to be taking a break from his role as food critic—not sure why. Maybe he's been banned by all the restaurant owners in Philly because of his negative attitude. All I know is, right now his focus is on me and I don't like it."

Just then, I heard the familiar "call waiting" beep but I ignored it.

"What did he say?"

I read her the first paragraph. "That's just the beginning. Did you ever hear anything so outrageous? How could the *Globe* print such bullshit?"

The phone beeped again. "Hold on, Carol," I said. "Someone's trying to reach me. Don't hang up."

I switched to the other call. "Hello," I said.

"Lydia," my mother said, "have you seen today's paper?"

"Of course," I said. "You know I always read the paper, Mother. And yes, I read Jared Abrams' column, but I can't talk now. I'm on the other line with Carol."

"It seems you're always on the other line with Carol when I call…"

"That's not true, but I'm not going to discuss it now. I'll call you later," I said as I switched back to my conversation with Carol.

"Hey, Carol, I'm back. That was my mother. She saw the column, and I'm sure I'll be hearing what she has to say about it soon."

"Lydia, I think you're overreacting. Abrams may be an SOB, but the truth is, he's just doing his job. He's stirring up a little controversy, that's all. In the end, it may turn out to be a good thing."

"I don't know how you can say that. He's trying to humiliate me."

"It's just a stupid column in the newspaper. People will read it and forget about it. Not to mention that you have quite a following now and he's going to incite some people's wrath. I bet he gets plenty of negative feedback about it."

"You don't get it, do you? Can't you see he's out to undermine my professional reputation and destroy my personal life?"

"I think you're getting too worked up over this," Carol, my usually loyal BFF said. "This will blow over. How many people read his column anyway? By next week, he'll move on to a new topic and this whole thing will…"

Just then, my doorbell rang. "Hey, Carol, gotta go. Someone's at my door, and I have a feeling I know who it is. Talk to you later…"

As I expected, it was my mother. She must have called me from her cell phone, I realized. She'd probably been right around the corner.

"Why didn't you tell me you were coming over?" I asked as I opened the door.

"You hung up so fast, I didn't have a chance to tell you anything. Don't worry—I can't stay long. I'm meeting Sylvia and Ethel for brunch."

That's fine with me, I thought, but what I said was, "Come on in."

She followed me into the kitchen and then began to bustle around, filling the electric teapot with water and selecting two tea bags from my stash in the pantry. I sat at the kitchen table and watched her take charge in my kitchen. Although in a way it felt comforting, it also made me feel acutely aware of my shortcomings. As usual when I was around her, I felt a wave of inadequacy sweep over me.

My mother put two mugs on the table and sat down across from me. "Chamomile seems best, don't you think?" she asked. "So soothing." Then she took a paper bag out of her purse and pulled out a huge cinnamon bun.

"I thought you were going to brunch," I said.

"Oh, it won't hurt to have a taste of this first," she said, cutting it in half and then placing both pieces on a plate in the center of the table.

We sat there with our mugs of steaming tea, and I began to devour my half of the cinnamon bun. *This isn't so bad,* I thought. *My mother rushed over here to comfort me as soon as she read that dreadful column.*

I'd barely swallowed the first bite when she said, "I knew I shouldn't have let you go to that summer camp. It's a good thing I never found out you were fooling around with one of the counselors. And I really believed you were a virgin when you got married."

"I refuse to talk about this with you. This isn't what I need right now!"

"And what do you need?"

"I need you to tell me that Jared Abrams is a scumbag—that's what I need," I said. "Even if you don't believe it, that's what I need to hear." And then I burst into tears.

She reached across the table and patted my hand. The wariness in her eyes made me feel sad and guilty. Why was it always so awkward between us? Why couldn't she just come over and give me a hug? "I stopped by because you sounded upset on the phone. I was worried about you. And frankly, I'm still worried. How can you let one newspaper column do this to you? Look at you—you're a wreck."

"You're right," I said, first wiping my eyes and then blowing my nose into my napkin. "I don't know why Abrams' column affected me this way. Carol thinks I'm overreacting too, and maybe I am. But you don't know how hard this is. I don't think I'll ever get used to being under public scrutiny this way."

"I guess you'll have to," she said, "because it comes with the territory. You're a celebrity now and that means you're open game to people like Jared Abrams. You know I didn't approve of Project Ex at first. Frankly, it seemed to me you were looking for trouble, digging up your exes that way. But the truth is, that project has turned your life around. So who cares if you find yourself stirring up some controversy and someone takes a pot shot at you every now and then?"

I just stared at her. When did my mother start using terms like "open game" and "pot shot"? *It must be Irving and his penchant for daytime TV shows*, I thought. *God only knows what stuff they watch together on that relic of hers.*

"Why don't you take the rest of the cinnamon bun?" she said, shoving her plate in front of me. "I have to save room for brunch."

And I wonder why I have issues with food, I thought as I mumbled, "Well, if you insist…"

Ten minutes later she was on her way out the door. I sat at the kitchen table cutting slivers from the remainder of the moist and sticky cinnamon bun, feeling an ache that seemed to spread from my very full stomach to my empty heart. *What's happening?* I asked myself. *Why does my life suddenly feel so out of control?*

CHAPTER ELEVEN

I steeled myself for a brouhaha at work after Abrams' column appeared. Although I took some ribbing about the alleged "retrosexual agenda" behind Project Ex, my colleagues seemed to have grown accustomed to my celebrity status, and to my surprise, the buzz died down pretty quickly. The fact that, like me, they were always swamped and barely had time to go to the bathroom—let alone spread vicious gossip about the pathetic state of my love life, past and present—helped a lot. I knew that I was probably the topic of many conversations behind closed doors, but I reminded myself numerous times a day that I'd be taking a leave of absence very soon— probably by the end of September—and then they could gossip about me all they liked.

At the end of May, when I'd accepted the job as talk show host at WKLR, it had caused quite a stir too. Dr. Parker, the medical director, had called me into his office to congratulate me but also to let me know that my position at the radio station had created a major headache for Briarside Behavioral Health. He said the board of directors felt uneasy about my new celebrity status and wanted to make sure I made it clear to my listeners that the advice and opinions I expressed on the air were my own and were not sanctioned in any way by my employer. I wasn't surprised to hear that the board had concerns about how my new role might affect the hospital, therefore, them. It was clear they didn't want to find themselves embroiled in a lawsuit or anything else that might adversely affect their bottom line. They certainly didn't want to attract any publicity that might have a negative impact on their referral sources or tarnish their professional reputation. Of course, I knew they didn't have anything to worry about. I never talked about my connection to Briarside when I was on the air and, until the fiasco with Brett Steinmuller, my listeners had rarely questioned me about what I now considered my "other" life. They accepted that I was a licensed therapist and showed little interest in my background or training. I guess they figured the powers that be at WKLR had selected me to host the show and that was good enough for them.

Dr. Crenshaw rarely asked about Project Ex or my radio show—both of which he considered frivolous, I was sure. He never mentioned Abrams' column either, although I was sure he'd read it, since he devoured the newspaper every day. I think he was a little nervous about where my radio career might lead, but he never said a word to discourage me. I knew he didn't want to lose me, but he didn't want to stand in the way of my doing what I loved either.

I was still feverishly trying to locate a place Betty Anne and her baby could call home, at least for a while. It turned out she was, in fact, pregnant, eight months now, and seemed to be getting bigger every day. Although she was still psychotic, since we couldn't medicate her, she seemed content to stay in the hospital and had even agreed to sign herself in. Her temper still flared every now and then, but most of the time she was pretty placid. She loved watching TV, especially old *I Love Lucy* episodes, and could sit at the arts and crafts table for hours, coloring books, crayons, and markers fanned out around her.

If Betty Anne had been a drug addict, I wouldn't have had any problem finding a treatment program for her. There were several excellent programs for drug-addicted mothers and their children. However, it was difficult enough to find a decent residential program for patients with serious mental health issues like schizophrenia, let alone for a woman who was about to deliver a child. The fact that she'd never been willing to accept long-term lodging in the past didn't help either.

The County Department of Children and Youth Services would have to step in and place the baby in foster care, unless there was a strong support system willing to take care of both of them. The whole situation was a nightmare. I hated to admit defeat, but I was getting damn close to giving up. *I'll just turn this over to child welfare,* I thought. *This is more than I can handle.*

But I was frustrated and angry because I knew the child welfare system wouldn't have a clue how to handle such a complex situation. In the end, Betty Anne would wind up in a halfway, but in actuality semi-permanent, home for the mentally ill, and her baby would indeed be placed in foster care. Before long, she'd be back on the street again. Why was I putting so much energy into something that couldn't possibly have a happy ending?

As the days flew by, I became more and more anxious about finding a placement for her. Dr. Crenshaw was trying to remain calm, but I knew he was under pressure to move her to a less acute setting as soon as possible. We were treating her for free at this point, since it was tough to convince the insurance company that a patient who wasn't at risk of harming herself or others and couldn't be medicated needed to remain in an inpatient setting.

One afternoon, he stopped by my office with a worried look on his face. "Have a minute?" he asked.

"Have a seat," I said, pointing to the only chair in my minuscule office. One filthy window looked out onto a concrete wall. It wasn't what I'd call an uplifting environment, but it didn't really matter because I never saw patients here.

"I came to talk about Betty Anne," he said. "I don't know what we're going to do with her but we have to act soon. One thing's certain—she can't have her baby on the locked unit. We offer a lot of services, but labor and delivery isn't one of them…"

"You don't have to remind me," I said. "I've been racking my brain trying to figure out where we can send her."

"Do you really think you'll be able to find a place for her, Lydia? I know you've worked miracles before, but finding a place for a homeless schizophrenic who just happens to be eight months pregnant sounds like a challenge even for you."

I gave him what I hoped was an optimistic smile. "You know me, Dr. C.—I never give up."

"I knew you'd say that. Don't ask me how you do it but somehow you always seem to come up with a creative solution. I'll tell you one thing—I don't know how I'll manage without you when you take your leave of absence."

I blushed and felt myself beaming with pride. I'd been working with Dr. Crenshaw for four years and I still thought he walked on water. He glanced at his watch and pushed back his chair. "I'm meeting with Dr. Parker in ten minutes. Do you think I can give our medical director some assurance that it won't be necessary to turn the ECT suite into a delivery room?"

"That would be a different sort of shock than the ones they're used to. Don't worry," I said, watching his face turn pale. "I'm determined to find a place for Betty Anne and her baby, but if all else fails, then Children and Youth will have to take over."

Still looking concerned, Dr. C. rushed to his meeting. After he left, I tried to organize the papers on my desk, but my thoughts kept returning to Betty Anne. How could I pull this off? I glanced at my watch—time to get to the unit for arts and crafts group. I grabbed my phone and headed to the locked unit. Betty Anne was sitting by herself at a table in the corner. There were a few other patients gathered around a table in the middle of the room, cutting and pasting shapes onto colorful paper while they waited for group to begin.

I smiled and waved at them as I approached Betty Anne's table. She was pasting butterflies onto a bright orange piece of construction paper and didn't look up when I scooted into the chair across from her.

"Hi, Betty Anne," I said. "Love those butterflies."

She glanced at me for a moment as she rubbed her hand across a pink and purple butterfly, pressing it on top of one that was red, orange and yellow. "Those are my favorite colors," I said, pointing to the pink and purple splotches.

I was surprised to see tears begin to stream down her face. "What's wrong?" I asked.

"Butterflies are sad," she said, wiping away the tears that had plopped onto her artwork. "No place to go. They fly and fly and then they die. They fly and die and die and fly."

She kept her head down and didn't look up again. Was she trying to tell me something, or was she lost inside her head?

"Do you have some place to go?" I asked, my voice soft. "Or are you like the butterflies?"

She jerked her head up and leaned over, her face close to mine, the tears still glistening on her cheeks.

"I'm not a butterfly," she said. "I have a home."

"I'm so glad to hear that. I really am, because you need a nice home for you and your baby. We just don't know where your home is, Betty Anne. Can you tell me?"

She glared at me. "Peggy's coming soon. When you've got a sister, you've got a home. When the cows come home, she'll come too."

It sounded like nonsense, but maybe it wasn't. I leaned closer. "I could call her and let her know the cows will be coming home pretty soon now. I bet she'd like to know."

Betty Anne snorted. "She knows. I talked to her last night. She knows about the butterflies and the cows." Then she got up, picked up her butterfly picture, tucked it under her arm, and walked away without another word.

I pushed back my chair, but I wasn't ready to get up yet. I sat there, thinking about our conversation, and suddenly it struck me: when was the last time I'd checked on Betty Anne's support system? She'd been in and out of Briarside at least twice a year for the past four years. I hadn't even bothered to review her family history again during this admission. I figured if there'd been anything to dig up, we would have discovered it long ago. But maybe—just maybe—we'd missed something and she really did have a sister who cared about her. Maybe her sister had been looking for her and couldn't find her. I thought about that while I led the rest of the patients through arts and crafts group, encouraging them to express themselves through their designs. After what seemed like hours, the group was over and I rushed to the nurses' station and grabbed Betty Anne's chart. "I'm signing this out for an hour," I told Nancy. "Dr. C. needs it ASAP."

"Okay," she said hesitantly. "But don't forget to bring it back today. You know only docs are allowed to take charts off the unit."

"Don't worry," I said and then I raced to my office. I plunked myself down at my desk and opened Betty Anne's file. I read for about forty-five minutes, ignoring the clock that told me it was time to go home. I was getting discouraged when I decided to flip back to the beginning and review the psychiatric evaluation the admitting physician had completed during Betty Anne's first hospitalization four years ago. Sure enough, the doctor had pieced together a family history. It wasn't extensive—as a matter of fact, there was only one person listed as next of kin. The name jumped out at me and sent shivers up my spine—Peggy Buford-Jackson of Harrisburg, PA.

So it was true—Betty Anne had a sister named Peggy. I sat there for a few minutes, deciding what to do next. *Go home*, I told myself. *Go home and think about this until tomorrow.* That seemed like a good plan although it wasn't what I wanted to do. I wanted to try to locate Peggy right away. I wanted to call her and ask—beg—plead for her to come and pick up her homeless, mentally ill, pregnant and soon-to-deliver sister.

But first, there were ethical issues to be resolved. Should I notify Betty Anne I was planning to call her sister? Was it okay for me to contact her without Betty Anne's permission? I rationalized that it was Betty Anne who'd provided the information. She'd told me her sister was coming to get her. That was enough for me. I closed the chart and pushed back my chair. I'd return it to the locked unit, go home, and try to contact Peggy tomorrow.

But ten minutes later, I was back at my desk. It took only another ten minutes to locate a Mrs. Margaret Buford--Jackson in a little town right outside Harrisburg. It wasn't exactly a common name. Hands shaking, I dialed the number.

"Hello," a resonant voice said.

"Hello," I said. "My name is Lydia Birnbaum. I'm a case manager at a psychiatric hospital in Philadelphia."

"Ohmygod," Peggy Buford-Jackson said. "You're calling about Betty Anne, aren't you?"

"Are you her sister?"

"Yes, I am. Is she okay? Is my baby sister okay?"

"Well, we've had her here at the hospital for some time now. She's doing pretty well, all things considered. You see, she's pregnant."

Peggy sighed. "It's not the first time, you know. She has two children—I ought to know since I raised them! Thank God, they're both fine—perfectly normal, like the rest of us. Our grandmother was schizophrenic. It skipped a generation and I guess it skipped me too, but Betty Anne…" Her voice trailed off.

"She has other siblings?" I asked, intrigued.

"Oh yes, there are six of us. But nobody else will have anything to do with her. She's burned some bridges. I've always taken care of her, though. I'm the oldest. If I won't, who will?"

"Well," I said, clearing my throat, "I'll be perfectly honest. She could use some taking care of at the moment. We've been trying to find a place where we can send her—a place where they'll take good care of her and the baby. Being pregnant and mentally ill—well, it's not exactly a winning combination."

"Tell me about it. Like I said, we've been down this road before. Both her kids are grown now. Her daughter Callie Anne just graduated high school, and her son Jaylen is twelve. He lives with his father's family in Tampa." Peggy sighed again. "My husband and I have had to move around a lot over the last five years, but we've been back in Harrisburg for a few months now. We've had our own problems, and I lost touch with Betty Anne but I never stopped thinking about her. I had a feeling she was in trouble, and I've been at my wits' end trying to figure out where she is."

"Well, she's right here on our locked unit. I don't know quite how to ask but…"

"Will I come and get her? Like I said, she's my baby sister and I've been taking care of her all her life—when I can find her. Just tell me when you're ready to release her, and I'll be there."

"You'll take her home with you for a while, at least until after the baby comes?"

"Naturally," she said. "It's what I've always done when she gets herself into trouble. It's what I'm supposed to do. Don't know how my husband's going to feel about it. We're certainly not getting any younger. But we'll figure something out. Can you give me your phone number? Is it okay if I call you tomorrow to get the address and all that?"

"Sure," I said, giving her my work number. "Do you think you'll be able to come for her by the end of the week? She's doing really well, but she'll need mental health follow-up, of course. I can help you find an outpatient clinic…" "We have a community mental health center just a few blocks away. She went there years ago. She's off her meds now, right? I mean, she ended up with you, plus with the baby on the way now…"

"Right," I said, realizing how savvy Peggy was about her sister's treatment. "No psychotropic meds until after the baby's born."

"And I'll call Dr. Allen. She delivered both of Betty Anne's babies. I'm sure she'll be happy to help out again." Then before she hung up, Peggy said, "You know, I could have sworn I heard her calling me last night. Heard her voice as clear as day. Isn't that something?"

"Sure is," I said, remembering my conversation with Betty Anne earlier in the day. I thanked Peggy again, hung up, and then sat at my desk for a moment before I paged Dr. Crenshaw. I knew I was about to make his day.

PART II—LYDIA ON HOLD

CHAPTER TWELVE

Suddenly my life seemed to be moving forward at breakneck speed. Now that I'd found a placement for Betty Anne, I felt less guilty about my plan to take a leave of absence from Briarside. Reuniting Betty Anne with her family was one of the most rewarding and heartwarming experiences of my career. When Peggy Buford-Jackson arrived to pick up her sister just a few days later, almost every member of the treatment team was there to wish them well. Of course, we all knew we might be seeing Betty Anne again—we had cured a situation but not an illness—but at least her family was involved now, and the baby would have a stable and loving home.

Sam Sloane had promised that in just a few months, my radio show would expand to two nights a week, adding Thursdays, which meant I'd receive a sizeable increase in pay. I was also the would-be author of an article on relationships that, while still mostly unwritten, might open doors to future writing assignments once it was published. My private practice kept growing too, now that my newfound celebrity had provided me with plenty of referral sources, including some Project Ex interviewees who had sent their friends with relationship issues my way. After twelve years of struggling, I was astonished to realize everything seemed to be falling into place. Of course, I was still alone, but I told myself I was sure to meet someone wonderful soon with all this positive karma streaming into my life.

Even though my schedule was jam-packed, I rarely turned down a new client. At the end of August—just a few weeks after Betty Anne was discharged—a guy named Rick Mann left a message on my answering machine. Rick's voice sounded strained and he had just the hint of a New England accent. I was intrigued right away—maybe it was the accent since I've always been a sucker for anyone who sounded even a little Kennedyesque —or maybe it was just the usual curiosity I felt whenever a new client called. He said he'd considered calling in to my radio show but felt he needed more help than I could offer on the air. Since it was only 10:30 and in his message he'd said he'd be up until midnight, I decided to contact him right away.

He answered on the second ring, his voice low and hoarse. "Hello, this is Rick Mann."

"This is Lydia Birnbaum, returning your call. I know it's late, but you said it was okay to call."

"And I appreciate your getting back to me so quickly," he replied, clearing his throat.

"You want to schedule an appointment to see me?"

"Well, yes and no."

"Yes and no?" I felt a tinge of annoyance. I was exhausted and in no mood for crackpots.

"I do want to talk to you. But I really don't have time to come and see you."

And I really don't have time for this bullshit, I thought, but I said, "Well, then, maybe you should wait for a while and call back when you have time for therapy."

"No, you don't understand," he said, a pleading note in his voice. "I have a lot I need to talk about, but I don't spend much time in Philly. I produce corporate films and infomercials and I have a pretty hectic travel schedule. So I thought maybe you could begin by counseling me by phone, cell phone, I mean."

"By phone? You want me to do therapy by phone? Are you looking for something kinky? Because if you are, you're talking to the wrong person." *Geez*, I thought, *is there anybody normal out there anymore?*

Rick chuckled. "I could have called a 900 number for that. No, honestly, I need some professional advice, and I can't get in to see you in person right now. What's wrong with that? And, hey, I'm planning to pay you, of course...which is more than your radio listeners do."

"Well, I'll have to think about this for a day or two. Phones and therapy don't go together as far as I'm concerned." I tried to keep the annoyance out of my voice. Was this guy baiting me or was I just tired? "Therapy is an intense experience and requires your full attention and concentration. I doubt you'll be able to concentrate when you're on the expressway with a cell phone next to your ear."

"I wouldn't drive while we were in session. Don't worry—I'd make sure to pull over. Sorry, I was only joking. I kid around a lot when I'm nervous. Anyway, you counsel total strangers on the radio. I don't see why you couldn't work with me by phone, at least for a while."

"Well, there are a lot of reasons, but I'm not going to discuss them right now. I don't need to explain myself to you," I said, realizing how defensive I sounded and felt. This guy was pushing my buttons and he seemed to be enjoying it.

"Please don't say no without thinking it over."

"I'm not ruling out phone therapy. I've certainly counseled clients by phone before. It's just that I've always had face-to-face sessions with them first."

"I don't need to meet you in person to know I can open up to you. I feel a connection with you already and I haven't even started therapy yet. I've heard you on the radio too, so I know how good you are at what you do, in spite of what I've read about you in the newspaper lately."

Jared Abrams' column. Was there anyone who hadn't read the damn thing? "Well," I said, "I'll think about it. But it's getting late and all I know at the moment is, I'm tired and ready for bed."

"I told you, I'm not looking for that kind of thing…although if you could send me your picture," he said, a teasing note in his voice.

"Maybe you really should call a 900 number," I said, aware I was on the edge of flirting with this man who was making a bid to be my first phone client. What was wrong with me?

"I was just fooling around. I'm tired too," he said.

"I need a couple of days to think about your proposition." Oh God, did that sound sexual? "Offer. Your offer. I'm just not sure phone therapy will work. We need to get to know each other. I mean, I need to look into your eyes and you need to look into mine too."

"We're not going away together for the weekend or anything. I don't feel like I have to gaze into your eyes in order to get help with the issues that are bothering me."

"I didn't say I wanted to 'gaze' into your eyes," I said, horrified. "I'm just not sure this can work. I have to think about it."

"Please give me a chance. I really need help, and I already feel I can talk to you."

"I have to think this over," I repeated. "Maybe I'll talk to some of my colleagues…see what they have to say about phone therapy."

"Do you know anyone at Verizon? I'm sure they'd be happy to make a case for phone therapy," he said, chuckling. "Sorry, I'm not trying to make light of this. I know therapy is a serious thing. I'm just nervous—afraid you'll turn me down."

"Why don't you give me a call at the end of the week," I said. The strange thing was, I was feeling anxious too. *I'm just overtired,* I thought as I hung up and headed for the kitchen. Before I knew it, I was standing at the counter, eating mocha fudge ice cream out of the container. *Where did I put that chocolate sauce?* I asked myself as I began to forage through the pantry for something else to eat.

JARED

Jared Abrams started humming when he hung up as he headed for the small den that served as his home office, his favorite room in his small apartment. Built-in bookcases, crammed with books, newspapers, and magazines, lined the walls. The huge desk where his laptop sat was directly beneath a window that faced onto a courtyard with a tiny garden. He loved his apartment in Old City, right near the heart of historic Philadelphia. Sitting down at his desk, he shoved aside a huge pile of papers, picked up the phone again, and dialed Ben Steiner, his editor. His cat, Millie, sidled up to him, rubbing against his leg.

"Steiner?" he said as soon as he heard the familiar voice at the other end. Millie leaped up into his lap when she heard his voice and began curling herself into a soft ball. Rubbing her behind the ears, he said, "I've got a story for you. It's about that therapist, Lydia Birnbaum. You know who she is—she's been the topic of a couple of my recent columns. For some reason, she's become an overnight celebrity, in Philly at least. I've been doing some research on her, and I'd like to write an exposé—a real juicy one. In fact, we've already spoken. Only, she doesn't know it yet."

Steiner chuckled. "So, you're going undercover again, are you? Well, if you think you can pull it off, then go for it. You could be on to something here."

"Oh, I know I am," Jared said. "Just wait until all her adoring fans find out what a fraud Lydia Birnbaum really is. You know how folks are in Philly—they can love you one minute and drop you like a hot potato the next."

"I hear you," Steiner said. "Go for it."

CHAPTER THIRTEEN

All through the following week, I kept thinking about my phone conversation with Rick Mann. The guy had struck a chord in me, but I didn't know why. Our entire conversation had taken no more than fifteen minutes and yet I kept replaying it in my head, asking myself what I could have said differently. He reminded me of men I'd dated in the past, guys who had left me feeling off-balance, insecure, inadequate in some way I could never quite define. Usually when a man like that broke up with me, I felt there was an underlying message, something he was trying to tell me about myself—something I didn't want to hear.

I agonized and agonized but finally I convinced myself that doing phone therapy with Rick Mann wasn't such a bad idea. So what if he was bringing up some strong feelings about men I'd dated in the past? Therapists expect to experience what we call countertransference. It was perfectly normal for clients to evoke feelings or memories of things that had happened in our own lives. The important thing was to be aware of the feelings, explore them, and make sure they didn't get in the way of our work. As for the phone therapy part, well, it really wasn't such a big deal. I'd certainly conducted some phone sessions with long-term clients who were out of town or in the midst of a crisis. However, they were the exception, and the phone sessions had always been with clients who usually had regular, face-to-face therapy. After thinking it over for several days, I decided to just get started instead of overanalyzing, or should I say, obsessing, over it. I found Rick's cell phone number and gave him a call.

It took him a while to answer. I was composing a voice mail message in my head when he finally picked up. "Rick Mann here," he said. I'd forgotten what a great voice he had, rich and sonorous. I was surprised to feel my face flush, and I got pissed off because just hearing his voice made my knees weak. *Remember*, I told myself, *countertransference is normal. For whatever reason, he's bringing up your feelings about other men who've rejected you. You're transferring feelings about your own past failed relationships onto him.*

"Hi Rick, this is Lydia Birnbaum."

"I'd almost given up hope of hearing from you. I thought you'd forgotten all about me."

Forgotten about him? Was he kidding? He'd occupied way too much space in my head over the last week. "Well, I wanted you to know I've given a great deal of thought to your request for phone therapy."

"I'm glad to hear that," he said. "I hope that means you've decided to take me on as your client. "

"As a matter of fact, I have. I've decided it was a reasonable request, considering your work and travel schedule." I felt the tension in my neck and shoulders and realized how apprehensive I was that he might have changed his mind.

"Thank you. I really appreciate it. Believe me, I don't envy you, having me for a client."

"I'm not sure what you mean by that, but we can talk about it in your first session. Maybe your self-esteem's a little low?"

"I've been feeling down on myself ever since my girlfriend, Mandy, and I broke up a couple of weeks ago."

Girlfriend? For a split second, I felt disappointment wash over me. *Why should I feel disappointed he has a girlfriend?* I asked myself, knowing I didn't want to hear the answer.

"What's your schedule like?" I asked briskly. "Sounds like we should arrange a session soon. How about next Saturday, the twenty-ninth? Will that work for you?"

"Let me think. Saturday... I'll be in New York. Can you call me at noon? I should be free by then. Wait a minute...I think I have a meeting at 11:30. I'm just checking my calendar. No, it's okay—the meeting was cancelled. But I'm supposed to meet my friend, Stan, at the gym at eleven. Can we make it at one instead?"

All this rearranging was making my head spin, and I could feel my blood pressure rising, point by point.

Rick seemed to sense my frustration. "Never mind, how about ten o'clock? I'll make sure I'm available."

"That's better."

"Oh, and I guess we should talk about payment arrangements, right? I'm having an issue right now with my checking account. Would it be okay if I sent you a money order? I could pay for the first month in advance."

A client had never paid by money order before, but it seemed like a reasonable thing to do since he was having banking problems. My bank had screwed up my account once and it had been a nightmare. I told him my fee and he promised I'd receive a money order before his first session.

"And, by the way," I said, "I expect you to call me. If you were coming for a regular therapy appointment, it would be your responsibility to arrive at my office on time."

"Sounds good. I just put the first appointment in my calendar. I got the message—don't call me, I'll call you. I've used that line on more women than I care to remember."

I bet you have, I thought, but what I said was, "Maybe you'll want to talk about that in your first session."

Should I Google this guy and see if I can find out more about him, I asked myself as I hung up. I felt guilty and dismissed the thought as soon as it entered my mind. *I've never checked out my clients on the Internet before, and I'm not going to start now,* I decided.

CHAPTER FOURTEEN

The following Friday—the day before Rick Mann's first scheduled phone therapy session—I was a nervous wreck. I was driving home from work at six o'clock, and I was stuck in rush-hour traffic. The cars just weren't moving and I wanted to scream. I had a standing 6:30 appointment with Kevin Corcoran, who suffered from obsessive-compulsive disorder and who always came not a moment late. As a matter of fact, he was usually early, and he'd probably be waiting on my doorstep, pacing. And then I'd have to hear about it: twelve paces to the front door, four paces to the azalea bush, seventy-five paces to the end of the driveway.

Just thinking about him pacing outside my front door made my heart start to pound. I could feel it in my chest, beating out the rhythm of his paces—faster, faster. Was I having a panic attack? Oh, great—Lydia Birnbaum, local talk show host, acclaimed therapist, stuck in traffic and flipping out. How would Rick Mann feel if he knew the therapist he'd chosen could benefit from some therapy herself?

Rick Mann. I'd be seeing—oops—talking with him tomorrow. Cell phone therapy—what the hell was I thinking when I agreed to that crazy arrangement? Agreeing to conduct therapy sessions with Rick by phone meant I wouldn't be able to observe his body or facial language, and I was concerned about that. I wasn't kidding when I told him I needed to look into his eyes. You learn a lot about a person by watching their responses to your comments and questions—seeing the flicker of doubt or fear or pain in their eyes when they raise a particular topic. But I was a seasoned professional—not someone just starting out in the mental health field—and I had agreed to the phone therapy arrangement, so there was no going back now. That's what I told myself, anyway.

As I pulled into my driveway, I saw Kevin, pacing back and forth, his hands shoved into his pockets. As soon as he caught my eye, he glanced at his watch. I got the message—you're the therapist and you're late. *How can I use his annoyance and impatience with me as a therapeutic issue?* I asked myself as I jumped out of the car and raced to the door.

Kevin was so agitated after pacing outside for ten minutes that I had to start the session off by using visualization techniques to help him calm down. After that, I taught him how to use deep breathing and meditation as a way to keep himself in check. He still looked a little grumpy at the end of the session when it was time to pull out his wallet and pay, but I felt I'd done the best I could, considering that the main thing on my mind during most of the session was Rick Mann.

I went to bed pretty early, but I tossed and turned all night. I woke up the next morning feeling exhausted and on edge. No question about it, Rick had me rattled. Too bad I couldn't incorporate some of those relaxation techniques I'd taught Kevin yesterday into my own life.

I was glad I'd scheduled Rick's session in the morning. I'd get it over with and move on with my day. At 9:50, I was in my office, waiting for the phone to ring. *I bet he won't call on time. That'll give me a reason to put a stop to this arrangement before we go any further. Listen, Rick, I'll tell him, this just isn't going to work. I can't sit around waiting for your calls...*

At that moment—10:02 a.m. on the digital clock on my desk—the phone rang. I let it ring twice then grabbed it.

"This is Lydia," I said.

"And this is Rick Mann, calling right on schedule."

"I never expected anything less," I said, knowing full well it was a lie.

"Really?" Rick asked. "That's not the impression I had from our last conversation."

"What do you mean?" I asked. Barely a minute into the session I was on the defensive already and feeling guilty about lying, too.

"When we spoke last week, you kind of went on and on about how important it is for me to call on time, which made me feel you didn't trust me. I figured you were expecting me to call in late so you could chew me out."

"Rick," I said, my blood boiling and my face burning with humiliation, "I'm sorry if I gave you the wrong impression when we spoke last week. We have a contract, you and I, and you agreed to the terms. What kind of therapist would I be if I didn't believe you?" *A lousy one,* I thought, feeling miserable.

"Well, you told me honesty is the basis of all therapy and that's why I brought it up."

"And I'm glad you did," I said. Another lie. What the hell was wrong with me? *Pull yourself together,* I thought as I asked, "So, how about if we get started? I remember you told me you have a tight schedule today."

"Yeah, I'm feeling pretty hassled already. I have to be at a shoot at two thirty and I still have some stuff to pull together."

"What's on your mind? What do you want to talk about?"

"I don't know. I mean, I've never done anything like this before."

"You've never been to a therapist?"

"No, I don't believe in stuff like that."

"So what made you decide to try it now?" I asked. *And why did you have to pick me? Couldn't you find some other unsuspecting therapist to torture?*

"I'm just not happy with where I'm at right now. For Chrissake, I'm fifty-three years old, with a divorce under my belt and God knows how many broken relationships since then. No matter how hard I try, I always seem to end up with the wrong women." He chuckled. "And from what I've heard—and read in the paper—even though you're a hotshot relationship therapist, you're in the same situation. I have to say I'm kind of intrigued by that. If you know so much about relationships, how come you're still single?"

I was sitting completely still, but the room was spinning around me. Who was this man and why did I let him get to me this way? It was a perfectly logical question—one I expected to hear more often but rarely did, unless you counted my own nagging doubts—but coming from him, it felt like a judgment and a challenge.

"Rick," I said, "you're the one who called and asked me to work with you. If you've changed your mind and want to find another therapist, it's fine with me. Otherwise, I suggest we continue with your session, and let me stress that it's *your* session, not mine. I'm not going to share details of my private life with you."

"Sorry, I didn't mean to push your buttons. It seemed like a reasonable question to me, but I won't ask about your personal life again, you can be sure of that. I have plenty of my own issues to focus on."

"I'm sure you do," I said between clenched teeth,

From that point on, the session seemed to progress smoothly—for Rick, at least. He told me a little about his childhood, which sounded pretty normal until he turned sixteen, when his father ran off with one of his mother's closest friends. When his father tried to contact him five years later, Rick refused to talk to him, and although he still occasionally received emails and phone calls from his dad, he ignored them. He was concerned that somehow the breakup of his own marriage ten years ago was his fault—even though he'd found his wife between the sheets with her art teacher in the bedroom she and Rick had shared for over fifteen years. He wondered whether the dissolution of his marriage and his inability to find a lasting and meaningful relationship since it ended were connected in some way to the fact he'd never had a strong male figure in his life.

When it was time to end our session, Rick seemed eager to schedule another one before the end of the week. Since he was a new client who seemed to be in crisis after the breakup of his most recent relationship, I agreed to biweekly sessions for the first few weeks.

After I hung up, I sat at my desk for a while and then pulled out Rick's file so I could make some notes while the session was still fresh in my mind. Although it hadn't started out too well, things had progressed nicely once he began to share his history with me. I still felt ill at ease but decided that was because I wasn't used to conducting therapy by phone. *It'll get easier once you know more about him and his situation*, I told myself as I finished my notes and filed his folder in my drawer.

JARED

Jared was grinning as he hung up after his first phone therapy session with Lydia Birnbaum. It was going to be a piece of cake to make her believe he was Rick Mann. He had to admit he'd been feeling nervous about pretending to be someone else. But once he started talking to her, it had all come so easily. He'd just used episodes from his own life, changing the names and some of the details. He was getting into the New England accent too. It seemed like a nice touch and helped him feel like someone else. He had a great ear for languages and had always excelled at mimicking other people's accents.

He made a few notes in his computer, humming as he worked. *Wait until my readers find out about the real Lydia Birnbaum*, he thought. *I wonder how all her "satisfied customers" will feel once they find out how easily she can be duped.*

He had a feeling this article was going to turn out to be the best piece he'd ever written—and that somehow or other, his life was about to change. Maybe he was destined for bigger things. *Who knows*, he thought, *I could still end up with my dream job as an investigative reporter for the* New York Times.

He glanced around his study and smiled when he noticed Millie sitting on the windowsill, her tail moving spasmodically as she stared at a cardinal in the cherry tree outside.

He went over and scooped her up in his arms. "Millie, my love," he said, "you're getting some extra treats today. Your daddy is working on something big, and there's no reason you shouldn't benefit too."

He carried her to the kitchen and opened the cabinet where he kept her treats. He put her gently on the counter and she began to pace back and forth, rubbing against him.

Jared took two treats out of the bag and fed them to her, watching her whiskers wiggle as she ate. Standing there, leaning against the counter, he allowed his thoughts to drift again to his phone session with Lydia. Why had he pitched this crazy idea to Steiner, anyway? Why did he feel driven to prove Lydia was a fraud? The idea that she had leaped to local celebrity in such a short time irritated and annoyed him far more than he felt it should. What irritated him the most—infuriated him—was that so many people seemed to consider her the expert on relationships, as if her word was gospel.

When he'd gone through his divorce ten years ago, he and his ex-wife, Madeline, had seen plenty of therapists but no one—no one—had been very helpful as far as he was concerned. Even though Maddy was the one who'd had the affair, he felt most of the counselors/therapists/psychiatrists they'd spent a fortune on had taken her side. He'd felt they blamed him for her infidelity, and that made no sense—no sense at all. Would they be blaming her if he had been the one caught cheating? Now, years later, he could admit their marriage had been on the skids for some time, but he still couldn't understand how—why—Maddy had needed to hurt him that way. He hadn't realized it before, but maybe his drive to write this piece on Lydia had a lot to do with all those therapy sessions. Maybe in some perverse way, and he knew it was perverse, he was trying to get back at the so-called professionals who—in his estimation, at least—had failed to do what at that time he'd believed he wanted them to do—salvage his marriage.

Jared put the cat treats back in the cupboard and bent down to refill Millie's water dish. Millie jumped down and scampered off. Turning the lights off in the kitchen, he headed back to his study.

CHAPTER FIFTEEN

By the beginning of October, I was busier than ever and I was glad I'd decided to finally take the leave of absence I'd been mulling over for so long. I needed time to concentrate on my private practice, my radio show, and compiling data for the article on Project Ex. It was a huge relief—but also scary—to know I'd left Briarside behind for at least a few months and possibly forever.

The phone sessions with Rick Mann seemed to be progressing reasonably well. He definitely knew how to push my buttons, but I tried to keep things on an even keel—as much as that was possible with him. He'd had six more sessions so far and had shared more about his family of origin and his marriage. He had two daughters, both in their twenties, one married, one single. "I may have screwed up my marriage," he'd told me in his last session, "but somehow or other, my kids are pretty healthy. Are your kids normal too? Because you know what they say about shrinks' kids."

"We've already covered this," I'd replied, feeling my muscles tighten. "I'm not going to share anything about my family with you."

"Which means, 'you just hit a nerve, Rick.' What a shame there can't be a little more give-and-take in our relationship."

"Give-and-take?" I'd asked. "What do you mean?"

"Well, let's face it, I'm doing all the giving and you're taking it all in. Are you sure that's therapeutic?"

We seemed to have at least one interchange like this in every session, and it was not only exhausting but troubling.

As the weeks went by, I couldn't shake the feeling that in spite of my newfound career and burgeoning private practice, something was sure to go wrong. One Sunday morning, I sat down at the desk in my home office to check my email and was surprised to find one from my ex-boyfriend, Robert. Curious, I opened it right away:

> *Hey Lydia, I read Jared Abrams' column about you and Project Ex and I've been thinking about it ever since. What a cool way to dig up your old boyfriends. Am I responding too late or could I be one of your research subjects? I think you're on to something. Robert.*

Robert, the musician. How could he have the nerve to contact me after the way he broke my heart? I wasn't ready to see him yet, and I certainly couldn't conduct an interview with him. The feelings were still too raw, too exposed. I decided to ignore his comments about the retrosexual aspects of Project Ex and wrote back right away:

> *Hi, Robert. Thanks for the offer, but I'm not accepting any more interview subjects at the moment. My schedule is full for the next few months. Hope all is well with you... Lydia*

A week later, I got another email, with a YouTube link attached:

Lydia, you inspired me. Check out this link on YouTube. Remember—it's all tongue in cheek. I know what a great sense of humor you have. And, by the way, thanks a lot. I never tried spoof rap before. Robert

Spoof rap? What the hell was spoof rap? I clicked on the link and there was Robert, introducing a new song he'd written— "Lydia B. of Project Ex—Searching for Members of the Opposite Sex." I held my breath, turned the volume up as high as I could, and listened:

I could write an email or send a text
But a song seemed best
For Project Ex
A single therapist name o' Lydia B
Put an ad on Facebook, 'cuz she wanted to see
If some of her exes—men she used to date—
Had any insights they could relate
Did any of them find love and happiness
Or were they still alone and relationship-less?
And I was thinking—this could be conjectural…
But could her motivation have been retrosexual?
Is Lydia searching for a past connection
To move her present love life in the right direction?
Project Ex, Project Ex
Is she conducting a study
Or jonesing for sex?

I sat there, staring at the computer screen. I felt like I was encased in a block of ice. The only thing that seemed to move was my finger, which kept pushing the "play" button as I watched the video over and over. I reached in my pocket with my other hand, pulled out my cell phone, and speed dialed Carol's number. She picked up on the first ring.

"Carol," I said. "You won't believe it."

"Now what?" she asked. "Jared Abrams again?"

"Worse, much worse. You just won't believe it."

"I'm not going to believe anything unless you tell me. What's going on?"

"Turn on your computer. I'm forwarding an email with a YouTube link to you right now."

"Give me a minute. I'm going upstairs to my office. Just hold on."

I put the phone down beside me on my desk and laid my head on my arms. Suddenly I felt exhausted, barely able to keep my eyes open.

"Okay," I heard Carol say, and I picked up the phone again. "I'm opening my email now. You heard from Robert again? Give me a minute… I'm clicking on the link now."

"Turn up the volume," I said.

There was a pause and then I heard the rap beat and Robert's voice in the background. I felt my face getting red.

"Wow," Carol said. "This is big. Really big."

"I don't know what you mean. All I want to do is cry."

"Lydia, where's your sense of humor? This is funny, and not only that, it's big."

"If you say that again, I swear I'm going to hang up right now."

"Just think about it. Thanks to Robert and this crazy rap song, you're on your way to going viral."

"No, you're on the way to going wacko. What the hell are you talking about?"

"Check out how many views this video's gotten already—hundreds! Obviously the people who've viewed it have sent it on to their friends—Facebook friends, I mean—and their friends are going to keep forwarding it to their friends until…who knows? I never heard of 'spoof rap' before, did you? It's actually kind of cool…"

"Cool?" I said. "I've never been so humiliated. Why did he have to put this on YouTube?"

"He wanted lots of people to hear it. It's all tongue in cheek, Lydia. But it's clear you and Project Ex had an impact on him. You've made a difference in lots of people's lives. Maybe it's time for a 'Fans of Lydia' page on Facebook. Who knows where it could lead? Before you know it, your talk show could be syndicated. People all over the country will be calling for your advice."

"Sam suggested a fan page on Facebook, but I told him I wasn't ready for that yet. I never expected anything like this. I never expected anything except to find some ex-boyfriends and maybe figure out where I've gone wrong with men. The only thing 'big' about all this is the feeling of humiliation that's washing over me. How could Robert do this to me?"

Carol sighed. "I give up. Why don't you give him a call and ask him yourself?"

The last thing I wanted to do was talk to Robert, or anyone else for that matter. Suddenly all I wanted to do was hibernate.

"Gotta go, Carol. This is all too much for me. I need to take a break for a little while."

"I understand. Why don't you take a walk or go to the gym? You need to clear your head and get your sense of humor back."

"Maybe," I said, but I was thinking about the chocolate *rugelach* I bought yesterday at the Bakery Shack on my way home from work. *Stop it*, I told myself. *This isn't about food.*

But it was. It was about how much I wanted to eat something to comfort me and make me forget about everything else. What was happening to me? I trudged to the kitchen and forced myself to make a bowl of instant oatmeal. *This will stick to my ribs*, I thought as I scooped most of it into my favorite, giant-sized purple bowl and added walnuts, cranberries, raisins, and honey on top. I sat down at the table and wolfed it down, savoring the crunchiness of the nuts and the sweetness of the cranberries and the honey. When I was done, I looked around and saw the *rugelach* I'd been craving. Before I knew it, I was standing at the counter, shoveling one sweet pastry after the other into my mouth

CHAPTER SIXTEEN

I was so thankful I wasn't at Briarside anymore and wouldn't have to listen to my colleagues' comments about the YouTube video. It was unbelievable how many people had seen that damn spoof rap. I'd prayed it would be one of those YouTube videos that have their five minutes of fame and then recede into obscurity forever, but no such luck.

As Carol had predicted, Sam Sloane was overjoyed that the phone call from Brett Steinmuller had stirred up so much controversy—and garnered so much free publicity. The ratings for my show had skyrocketed since Abrams' column had appeared and spiked even higher after word got out about Robert's spoof rap video. And, although I insisted that my private life was off-limits as a topic for discussion on my radio show, my listeners had become obsessed with finding out more about what Abrams had labeled my "retrosexual" agenda. In the past, only an occasional caller had questioned my track record with men, but now more and more of my listeners seemed to be asking questions—which I always sidestepped, of course—about my private life. Did I have a particular "ex" in mind, they wondered, when I placed that ad on Facebook eight months ago—someone I was yearning to find so I could rekindle an old, but still smoldering, flame? I received a slew of emails every day, most of which received canned replies from one of the interns at the station.

Even though I had more free time to work on writing the article with the findings based on my Project Ex interviews, it was getting harder and harder to concentrate. It was almost impossible not to think about Robert's spoof rap—which was racking up hits on YouTube every day—and sporadic digs from Jared Abrams that appeared in the *Globe* from time to time. Abrams had found out about Robert's spoof rap, of course, and had touted it as further proof of Project Ex's retrosexual underpinnings.

When Carol made her daily calls to check up on me, she made it clear she thought I was taking the spoof rap backlash too much to heart. "The two of us need to get out again and have some fun," she reminded me over and over. Of course, I knew what she meant: it was time for us to get back out on the singles scene again. Ever since her boyfriend, Jeff, had broken up with her a couple of months before, she'd been dying to meet someone new. She wasn't just thinking about dinner and a movie, and I knew it. She'd been making it clear for some time that she felt I'd removed myself from the dating world for much too long.

After a couple of weeks, I felt my mood begin to lighten up and realized my sense of humor was back. Carol noticed right away that I was on the upswing and wasted no time in using it to her advantage. "Hi Lydia, what's doing?" she asked when she called me one Saturday afternoon in mid-October. "How about if we go out tonight and look for some guys? It'll be just like the good old days."

"Sure, the good old days… Could you remind me again when they were, or did I happen to miss them somehow?" I said, amazed to feel myself in a bantering mood. "Anyway, I've told you and told you that I've given up on men—for now, anyway."

"You may have told me, but I don't believe you. You're the guru of singledom, remember?"

"Okay, maybe I shouldn't have said 'given up.' Let's just say that I think it makes sense for me to take a break from dating for a while. Project Ex, my radio show, and my private practice are all I can handle right now. My current focus is on relationship issues—other people's relationship issues. Honestly, Carol, I may be starting to feel better, but I don't think I have the emotional energy to start dating again."

"That's the biggest bunch of crap I've ever heard. I understand you're busy with your radio show and your research project and all those new private clients. If I'd known you had some ridiculous idea about cutting yourself off socially to save the singles world, I would have been banging at your door a long time ago. I think you should give your therapist a call. You're losing it, my friend."

I hadn't seen Gwen in almost a year and Carol knew it. She also knew that any suggestion I might be in need of therapy again would set me off. "Maybe you're right and I haven't thought this thing through. But tell me—what did the dating scene ever do for me? Or for you, for that matter, except cause us pain and torment? And a lot of eating binges, which my hips are still recuperating from, thank you very much."

"Oh, really? Those extra ten pounds you've always complained about are a direct result of your frustrations with men? Boy, talk about blaming somebody else for your problems. You really do need to give Gwen a call, Lydia. You've gone off the deep end."

"I don't need my therapist to tell me that if I put myself out there again and meet the same kind of losers I met before…"

"Your research project will continue to grow by leaps and bounds. If you'd had success with men all these years, where would you be now?"

"Blissfully married and enjoying a luxurious vacation on the French Riviera?"

"Lydia, don't play games with me. I know Jared Abrams' columns and Robert's stupid spoof rap threw you into a tailspin for a couple of weeks. But hey, this should be the happiest time in your life. So let's get out there and party again, like we used to."

I was quiet for a few moments. Carol was right and I knew it. I had completely transformed my life and I ought to be jubilant.

"Okay, you got me, and you're right. I'm trying to put everything in perspective and appreciate the amazing things that have happened since Project Ex took on a life of its own. But it's all happened so fast and, well, I guess I'm feeling overwhelmed."

Carol's tone softened. "Let's go out and have some fun tonight. We'll go to a club and see what happens. We could meet a couple of terrific men. At the very least, it'll be an adventure."

"An adventure or another fiasco? All right, all right…anything you say. You pick the place and tell me what time to meet you. I'll be there."

"Oh no, I don't trust you. I'll pick you up at 9:30. And don't try to cancel either. I'm taking my phone off the hook and turning off my cell phone."

"Nine thirty? I'll be ready for bed by then."

"Lydia, my God—get a grip. You're fifty, not ninety."

"But I have nothing to wear."

"You have nothing to wear? How about that sexy number you wore for that interview last week on *Ten at Ten?*"

"That old thing? I guess I could wear that—if it's not at the cleaners, that is."

"I'm calling that shrink I saw last year when I thought I was having a nervous breakdown. You're driving me nuts."

"Which nervous breakdown was that? The one you had after your mother ran off with your hairdresser, or the one you had after you found that schmuck you were dating in bed with that other schmuck you used to date? I'm going, I'm going. I just wanted to give you a little grief, that's all."

"I'll be there at 9:30, and don't try anything funny like turning out all the lights and pretending you're in bed. Remember, I have your key."

"I remember, and I give up. I'm hanging up so I can start getting ready. It's going to take me a while to get myself together—mentally and physically."

"I hear you on that one. See you later," Carol said before she hung up.

I sat there, the phone still in my hand. It had been months since I'd answered any personal ads on the Internet, and I couldn't remember the last time I'd had a date or been at a club with my friends. There was a part of me that was relieved to be going out again, after all the months of staying home alone. That part was saying, *You have a lot to do. Get moving.* The other part of me—the part that was terrified of yet another rejection—was saying, *Do you really need to keep demeaning yourself like this?*

I trudged upstairs to my bedroom where I peeled off my clothes and then headed into the bathroom for a long, hot shower. *Enough agonizing—time for action*, I thought. Carol was right—it was time for an adventure.

CHAPTER SEVENTEEN

At 9:25, the doorbell rang. I glanced longingly at my bed before heading downstairs to open the door.

"Who's there?"

"Cut the crap," Carol said. "Just open the damn door."

"Oh, it's you," I said, letting her in. We hugged each other and then I looked her over. She was wearing a short red dress with ruching that accentuated her tiny waist. "Love that dress. You're going to knock 'em dead tonight."

"And a lot of good they'll do me after they're dead—although I haven't had much luck with the live ones either."

"It really is good to see you. It seems like so long since I've been out with any of my friends."

"Hey, you're looking pretty good yourself." Carol drew back and gave me a long look. "That dress looks even better in person than it did on TV."

"Well, since we both look so gorgeous tonight, we may as well get out there and find some guys," I said, surprised but pleased that I was beginning to feel adventurous.

"Get your coat and let's go. I heard about this new place, the Oasis, in Center City that just opened up a couple of months ago. It's supposed to attract an older crowd. My friend Jan went there last week and said there were lots of guys around our age at the bar."

"Around our age? Ancient, you mean?" I asked, dodging as she leaned over to hit me.

"We may be fifty, Lydia, but we don't look a day over thirty-eight—especially at night when we're in a room full of men who've been drinking."

"As a therapist, I would have to say you're living in a fantasy world and should seek professional help. However, as a desperate single woman who hasn't had sex for almost a year, I'm willing to buy into your fantasy and pray that you're right."

I was putting on my coat when my cell phone rang. I rummaged through my purse, trying to locate it.

"Don't answer the damn phone," Carol said just as I plucked it out and was about to accept the call. "We're out of here." She tried to grab it out of my hands, but I swung it over her head and plopped myself into the nearest chair while I picked up the call.

"Lydia, I didn't know if you'd answer or not. I'm so glad you're there," Rick Mann said.

"Rick, what's going on?" He'd never called me in between sessions before. Not to mention that for some reason I imagined him as drop-dead gorgeous—definitely not someone who would be home with nothing to do on Saturday night.

"I need to talk to you. Do you think we could have an emergency phone session now? I know it's an imposition, but I'll pay you extra—whatever you ask."

"Lydia," Carol said, leaning over me. "Tell whoever it is that you'll call back tomorrow and let's go."

"Just give me a minute. I'll be right back." And before she could say a word, I went into my office, shutting the door behind me.

"Hey, are you on your way out? It never occurred to me you might have a date," Rick said.

"Oh, really?" Even when he was in crisis this guy could pull my chain. "Actually, I do have plans this evening. But I can talk with you for a few minutes."

"Thanks. I hated to call, but I really need to talk."

I sat down on the couch, ignoring Carol, who opened the door, peered in, and pointed to her watch while she gestured in the direction of the front door. I slipped off my jacket and nervously crossed my legs.

"It's Mandy, my old girlfriend. She's back in town. Not only that—she's on her way over to my place now," he said, a slight quiver in his usually solid voice.

"You asked her to come over?"

"Not exactly. She kind of invited herself..."

"How do you feel about seeing her?"

"Well, there's a part of me that really wants to..."

"Which part is that?"

"The part that's tired of being alone. It's a hassle going out every weekend, trying to meet new people."

Tell me about it, I thought.

"And the other part of you?"

"Hell, the other part of me keeps repeating things you've told me in our sessions, like, 'It's okay to be by yourself for a while. You're not going to die if you don't have a woman in your life right now.'"

"So you're in conflict..."

"And you know how much I hate conflict, even inner conflict. But damn, it's been three months since I've had sex. Why shouldn't I go to bed with Mandy tonight if that's how things turn out? Why shouldn't I?"

"You know the answer to that question, Rick. You didn't need to call me to hear it. It was the issues in your relationship with

Mandy that brought you to me in the first place. So, tell me—is there any reason why you shouldn't see Mandy tonight?"

"Because I don't care about her anymore. It's been weeks since I've thought about her. If I see her tonight, I'll be backtracking."

Just then, the door opened and Carol walked into my office. "Lydia," she said, "we'll never get a parking spot if you don't hurry up. The Oasis is going to be mobbed tonight."

I shot her a withering look and she retreated to the other room.

"Hey," Rick said, "are you going to the Oasis tonight? I heard it's one of the hottest singles bars in town."

"I'm not going to discuss where I'm going tonight, Rick. We've been through this before. Your sessions are supposed to be about you, not me, remember?"

"I don't want to hold you up, although it is kind of nice to know you're probably just as desperate to meet someone as I am. For some reason, that makes me feel a whole lot better."

As soon as I hung up, trying not to be embarrassed for myself and to recover some sense of the adventurousness I'd had seven minutes before, Carol grabbed me and practically dragged me out the door. It took just under half an hour to get to the Oasis. After circling the block twice, Carol and I decided to park the car in a garage. As we walked into the club, I glanced around. I was glad it was dark in there, because my cheeks were flaming. *Nothing has changed*, I thought. *I'm still expecting a decent man to turn up in a place where no self-respecting human being would ever show his face.*

There were huge planters scattered around the room, filled with cactus plants. I'd never seen so many cacti in one place before. I'll tell you one thing—they didn't make the place look inviting. As a matter of fact, nothing about it appealed to me, except for a man at the bar who caught my eye. He was sitting there by himself, but I figured he wouldn't be alone for long because he was cute—really cute—with dark, curly hair, a boyishly handsome face, and luminous eyes that were staring at me with an intensity that made me feel uncomfortable and incredibly desirable all at the same time. I felt a strong force pulling me toward him, even though, truthfully, I couldn't see his features all that well.

Carol kept up a running commentary as her eyes swept like a searchlight over the men in the room. "That guy's kind of cute," she said, pointing to the other side of the room. "From what I can tell from here," she said modestly—knowing full well that hardly anyone could match the "eligible-man-sighting" skills she had fine-tuned after years of practice, "he looks about forty-five. And," she said, squinting and scrutinizing his left hand from across the room, "he's single. I bet he's Jewish, and I'm guessing he left his wife within the last three months."

"That's ridiculous. You can't tell all that from across the room," I said as I turned to check out the guy at the bar once more. I stared at the place where he'd been just a few minutes before. The barstool he'd been sitting on was empty. *Just my luck*, I thought. *He's gone and I'll never see him again.*

The evening went downhill from there. Carol pulled me over and introduced me to a couple of guys she seemed to find fascinating, but I found just plain boring. I kept yawning and looking at my watch, but she ignored me until, at 1:15, I leaned over and whispered, "When can we leave? I saw five clients today, and I need to get some sleep." She gave me a dirty look but agreed to leave ten minutes later, after she'd given her phone number to both men. *How did she pull that off?* I wondered.

I slept fitfully that night and forced myself to stay in bed until almost noon the next day. Feeling sorry for myself, I made a huge bowl of microwave popcorn and settled into the comfiest chair in the living room, my feet curled beneath me. No sooner had I popped the first kernel into my mouth than the phone rang. I stared at it, reminding myself once again that I ought to break down and get Caller ID. I knew that I never would. Why should I pay for something to tell me who was on the phone when all I had to do to find out was pick it up myself or wait for my answering machine to screen the call?

I'll tell whoever it is I'm busy and get off in thirty seconds, I told myself as I pressed the talk button.

"Mom?" my daughter Stephanie said. "I can't believe you're home. You're never around these days."

And am I supposed to be around waiting for your calls while you're out every night having fun with your boyfriend? I wanted to ask. *Oy,* I thought, *I'm turning into my mother.*

"Yes, sweetie, I'm home today," I said. "What's up?"

"Well," she said, "I've been feeling kind of down."

"Everyone gets a little blue every now and then. Is this just a little funk or should I get concerned?" As usual, I began to review in my mind all the ways I might have damaged my beautiful daughter with my less-than-perfect parenting skills.

"Nothing's going right," she said with a sigh.

"But when I spoke with you last week, you sounded so happy… excited about your raise and your new apartment and…"

"And what I forgot to mention is that you are ruining my life."

"I'm ruining your life?" For once, I couldn't think of anything else to say.

"You've got to find another career, Mom, or at least go back to being a plain old therapist like you used to be."

"Would you mind explaining how my career is ruining your life? I'm afraid I just don't get it, Steph," I said, trying to keep the hurt out of my voice. "I really don't appreciate your blaming me for your problems, whatever they are." Was it possible I was so focused on Project Ex and my radio show that I'd lost touch with what was going on in my own family?

"Come on, Mom, how would you like it if Grandmom suddenly became the authority on relationships? How would you feel if she was telling people on the radio about her sex life?"

"I am not talking about my sex life on the radio, Stephanie." *Not yet, anyway*, I thought. "If you tuned in to my show every now and then, you'd know that. Come on, you're twenty-seven years old. I put plenty of time and energy into raising you and your brother. Don't you think I'm entitled to have a life now?"

"You can have a life, Mom, but is it fair that you're destroying mine?" she asked as she began to cry.

"That's the second time you've said that," I said, taking another deep breath. "I'm not sure what's going on, but whatever it is, it seems to me you're overreacting."

"Thanks, Mom," Stephanie said. "Did it ever occur to you that maybe you're underreacting because you're only thinking about yourself right now and you don't want to face the fact that you're making a fool of yourself and your entire family? I mean, haven't you gone far enough with Project Ex? And, by the way, do you know how embarrassing it is to have a spoof rap about your mother on YouTube? I can understand that you want to get back at your old boyfriends, but have you ever considered what Nate and I think about all this?"

I opened my mouth to respond, but nothing came out. I felt as if she had punched me—hard—right in the center of my chest.

"Mom? Are you there?"

"I'm here, Steph," I said. I regained my voice as I struggled with the pain that I knew wouldn't go away for days. "Why shouldn't I be okay? My daughter just accused me of being a selfish, vengeful bitch, but I'm sure I'll be just fine."

"Oh, stop the drama, Mom. I'm not accusing you of being a bitch. I'm telling you how I feel—just like you always ask me to do. But of course, as usual, when I don't tell you what you want to hear, you freak out. And, by the way, I know you don't like Les. You may as well just come out and say it, since we're laying stuff on the table."

"If you want to know the truth, I don't think he's right for you. He's a passive, unexciting guy, and I think you put up with him because you know you can get him to give you whatever you want. Something, I might add, it seems your mother isn't able to do."

Shocked by my honesty, I added, "You could do better, Steph."

Now both of us were silent. I was struggling with the guilt and shame that were washing over me in waves.

Steph spoke first. "You've said enough, Mom."

"Steph," I said, "I guess both of us have gone too far and it wasn't right. Sometimes when you love someone and you're really, really close to them, you allow yourself to hurt them in a way you'd never, ever hurt anyone else—even a complete stranger."

"I don't know, Mom. I'm not a therapist like you, and I don't analyze every single thing that happens like you do. All I know is that I need to hang up right now. I'm not angry or anything. I just need to go now."

"I guess both of us are feeling hurt and maybe ashamed too. I know I am," I answered, my heart feeling brittle.

"No matter what, I love you, Mom. I don't understand what you're doing, but I still love you," she said before she hung up.

"Love you too," I said to the click of the phone in my ear.

I laid the phone down beside me on the couch and began to sob. I was destroying my daughter's life. I was the mom and therefore supposed to structure my life around her—to think about how anything I did might affect my children. Now I had hung my dirty laundry out on the line for everyone to see, and my own daughter was embarrassed and ashamed.

Ashamed of what? I asked myself. *What did I do that was wrong?* Was it my fault that Robert had written that stupid rap song and posted it on YouTube? Did I know when I launched Project Ex that it was going to catapult me to local celebrity as the host of my own radio talk show? And wasn't it a good thing, doing what I loved? Stephanie was all grown up now. Wasn't it my time now to do the things I'd always dreamed of, have the things I yearned for, without worrying about what my children might have to say about them?

As I was getting up to find some tissues, the phone rang again. I picked it up on the first ring and heard my son's voice on the other end.

"Hi Mom," he said, his voice deep and rich. "How ya doing?"

Oh, great, I thought—*a double header. What now?*

"Well," I said, sniffling, "I just hung up with Steph, and I must say that I've been better."

"Are you crying? Is she okay?"

"Have you talked to her lately?"

"Yeah, I just spoke with her—yesterday, as a matter of fact," he said, a defensive edge in his voice.

"How did she sound to you?"

"She sounded fine, same as usual, anyway. Except that she's pissed at you, but that's nothing new, is it?" He chuckled.

"She's pissed at me? What have I ever done to piss her off—that's what I'd like to know." I knew very well what I'd done and hoped my son would be on my side.

"She's mad because you're talking about us on the radio. She told me how Robert wrote a rap song about you that's gone viral on YouTube. Way to go, Mom."

"Well, Stephanie didn't seem to think it was the way to go," I said.

"Hey, Mom, why don't you talk to Steph about it if you're upset? Isn't that what you always told me, 'If you're mad at your sister, don't tell me. Tell her.'?"

Now both my children on the same day—within minutes of each other, I might add—had thrown my own advice right back at me. I wished I'd kept my mouth shut more often over the years.

"I know, I know. You're right. I'll give her a call in a couple of days when she's calmed down a little. Are you angry with me too?"

"No offense, Mom, but I don't spend a lot of time thinking about family stuff the way you and Steph do. I mean, I never listen to your radio program, and I've never seen you on TV either. You know me—my theory about most of this stuff is...whatever. Anyway, I didn't call to talk about Steph."

"Well, what do you want to talk about? Is everything okay?"

"I'm fine. It's my car that has a problem."

"Your car has a problem and you're calling me? Now, you know I don't do 'car therapy.' Why don't you call Dad? He knows about stuff like that."

"I don't need any advice about my car, Mom. I know what's wrong with it. The window's stuck halfway down and it won't go up."

"Sounds to me like you'd better get it fixed." *No rocket science in figuring that out*, I thought.

"Well, I took it to a couple of places and they said it's a big deal to fix it. It's going to cost about $200."

"Two hundred dollars? That sounds like a lot. But you don't really have a choice, do you? You have to get it fixed before winter comes or we have a hurricane or something." *Listen to me—one brilliant statement after another*, I thought.

"Whatever," he said. "Winter's still at least a couple months away, and I don't think we're expecting any hurricanes, Mom."

"I don't like the idea of you driving around with a window that won't close. You'll get soaked."

"Hey, I don't like it either. I have a cold already. I don't want to catch pneumonia," he said, my hypochondriacal son who surfed the Internet searching for new illnesses that—thank God—he didn't have.

"Do you need money?" I asked at last, capitulating as I pictured my adorable son—my baby—in the intensive care unit of a hospital, his fingers and toes blue with frostbite. *"My mother wouldn't help* me," I heard him telling the doctors. *"When I told her about the broken window, she said, 'Whatever.'"*

"Well," he said, his voice suddenly stronger, "if you and Dad could each pitch in a hundred, it sure would help."

Help, I thought. *It'll damn well pay for the whole thing.*

"I think I can do that. Will you call Dad?" I asked.

"Can you call him, Mom? He says I only call to ask for money."

The man has a point, I thought, but what I said was, "Of course, honey. I'll see what I can do." I took a deep breath and then asked, "Do you think you'll be getting a 'real' job soon? You'll be twenty-five in a couple of months. It would be nice if you were self-sufficient."

"Mom, I just got a beep… Gotta go. Do you think you can send that express mail? The rainy season's just around the corner, you know. Love you."

For the second time that day, I heard a click in my ear as I said, "I love you too."

I put the phone on the floor and picked up the bowl of popcorn that I'd barely started half an hour ago. I began to shovel the popcorn into my mouth, hoping that the pain, annoyance, and frustration I was feeling would go away. *No, I'm going to need more than popcorn to stuff these feelings*, I said to myself as I got up from the couch and headed for the kitchen to find my emergency stash of peanut M&Ms. I went straight to the canister I kept hidden behind the glasses over the sink. *Why do I need to hide this stuff?* I asked myself as I poured a couple of cups of M&Ms into a large bowl. *Nobody's here to find it, and even if they did, so what? I must give that some thought when I'm not feeling as rotten as I do right now*, I thought as I padded back to the den in my soft, fluffy slippers.

CHAPTER EIGHTEEN

My radio show was still doing phenomenally well and I had more private clients than I'd ever dreamed possible, but did all that really matter if my children—or my daughter, at least—were ashamed of me? I reminded myself every day that I should feel happy and fulfilled, but instead I was feeling lonelier and more restless than ever. I was getting tired of my celibate lifestyle and feeling sorry for myself because twelve years after my divorce, I was still alone. Even having my own radio show didn't excite me the way it had a few months ago.

Every time I sat in a session these days or picked up a call during my radio show, I felt hollow inside. I listened to my clients and my radio listeners and gave advice—wonderful, nurturing advice, or so I was told over and over and over again. When one of my clients or listeners said, "I'm so glad I talked with you. Now I really believe my girlfriend and I can work this out," or "Now I know what I need to do to get my life back on track," I wanted to scream. I wondered what would happen if I broke down one day and suddenly said to one of them, "Shut up already. I'm sick to death of talking about you. Let's talk about me for a change. I'm the one who needs help. I haven't had sex in almost a year."

It would cause quite a stir, I'm sure. I bet the sponsors of my radio show would sue me or fire me on the spot. Not to mention that all the clients I've helped would discover the truth: that I really am just as vulnerable—not to mention clueless—as they are. And my entire practice and my newfound career as radio talk show host would go down the drain.

I felt pretty confident that my clients had no idea that sometimes my thoughts were just as negative as theirs. As they droned on about all the problems in their relationships, I found myself with the crazy thought that even a dysfunctional relationship was better than no relationship at all. Some therapist I was. I knew what would happen if a mind reader like The Amazing Kreskin came in for therapy. As soon as he read my miserable thoughts, he'd run in the other direction as fast as he could. Probably right to the office of Jared Abrams, who would be only too happy to write another negative piece about my shortcomings as a therapist.

What was wrong with that damn Abrams anyway? Why did he hate me so much? I imagined him coming in for therapy, pouring his heart out about all the therapists in the past who had done him wrong. Wait a minute—why would I want to even consider helping him to ease his pain when he had caused me so much?

Meanwhile, the phone sessions with Rick Mann were more and more cause for concern. I was beginning to feel like he was leading me on a convoluted wild-goose chase. *Why*, I asked myself for the umpteenth time, *didn't I just tell him to find another therapist—or wife or guru or whatever it was he was looking for*? For some reason—and it annoyed me beyond belief that I couldn't figure out what the reason was since I was the psychotherapist—I couldn't seem to get rid of him. No matter what I did or what I said, he hung on and I let him hang, so what did that say about me?

I answered a few emails, but I was exhausted and on edge. At ten o'clock, I fell into bed, still feeling wired. Thankfully, I slept but I woke up the next morning at five. When I opened my eyes and saw the clock, I decided it was much too early to get out of bed, so I turned over and went back to sleep. I slept fitfully and had an incredibly vivid dream: I was upstairs in my bedroom, fast asleep, when the doorbell rang. I had the sense it was late at night, because I was frightened and acutely aware that I was alone. I ran to look out my bedroom window, which faces my front walk, and gasped in astonishment. There was a line of men outside my front door, each with a brightly colored, Day-Glo tag draped around his neck like an ID badge. The numbers were so bright that the men's faces beamed with an eerie iridescence. The doorbell rang again, but I couldn't move. I watched, transfixed, as they crowded toward my front door. "Where is she?" I heard the one in front yell. "I'm getting tired of waiting out here." The others began shouting too. They pushed forward, pinning the poor man in front right up against the door. He began to scream, "Let me in, you bitch. Let me in, you bitch." The others joined in, surging forward. I heard a tremendous crash and realized they'd stormed inside, shattering the door. Frantic, I looked around, searching for an escape route. But it was too late. The line of men had turned into a huge serpent, winding its way up the steps with a radioactive glimmer. I opened my mouth and tried to scream, but no sound came out. I heard the hoarse scraping sounds that should have been my voice and felt terror seep through me. Just as the serpent reached the top of the stairs, I woke up, trembling, drenched in sweat.

I lay there, still immersed in the dream, trying to quell my rising panic. *You shouldn't eat Chinese food right before you go to bed*, I chastised myself, remembering the container of Shanghai noodles I'd polished off right before I went to sleep and the demonic snake on the box. I tried to slough off the ridiculous dream, but I felt unnerved and out of sorts. I remembered the comment I'd made to Carol about Project Ex having a life of its own and shuddered again.

"Stop it," I said out loud as I pushed off the covers and headed for the shower. "It was just a dream."

I threw my clothes into a pile on the bathroom floor and turned on the shower. I waited until the water was steaming and stepped in, allowing the moist heat to seep through me. "It was just a dream, it was just a dream," I repeated over and over, but somehow I couldn't quite convince myself it wasn't real.

I had a whole day ahead of me before I headed to the studio for my radio show. I forced myself to clean out a kitchen cabinet and then vacuumed and dusted the living room. When I checked my watch, I was shocked that only an hour had gone by. I returned to the kitchen, whipped up a healthy snack—Ezekiel bread with peanut butter and jelly—and then curled up on the couch in the living room to finish the novel I'd been reading for the last three months. But I couldn't concentrate, so finally, I decided to take a nap. It took all my energy to drag myself upstairs to my bedroom and climb into bed.

I woke up at three o'clock, feeling groggy, hungry, and out of sorts. I got up, splashed some cool water on my face, and headed to the kitchen for some lunch. After I'd wolfed down a tuna salad sandwich, a pile of chips, and several squares of Hershey's Extra Dark, I felt better but still too unfocused to do anything constructive, so I spent the next couple of hours watching reruns of *Will & Grace* on TV. Finally, a successful relationship! *It was season four.* At 5:30, I was back in the kitchen again, nuking a cup of minestrone soup with turkey meatballs for dinner. Then I forced myself to put on some makeup, changed into a clean sweater and a pair of jeans that felt tighter than they used to—*not a good sign*, I thought, pushing that thought out of my mind immediately—and left fifteen minutes earlier than usual.

As soon as I arrived at the station, I began to perk up. I stopped by Sam's office to shoot the breeze for a few minutes then said hello to Keith and the gang and scooted into my booth at 6:55, ready to sign on. The phone lines lit up as soon as I finished my opening spiel, and I felt some of the tension inside me slip away. Time to let Lydia the radio talk show host take over.

The show was going well, and after the first hour, I felt myself begin to get in the groove. It had been a terrible day, but at least I was still on top of things at the radio station. There were only about fifteen minutes left when Keith said, "Someone's on the line who says he knows you." I pushed the button on the console and picked up the call, feeling my stomach tighten. *I wonder what this is about*, I thought, remembering the fiasco with Brett Steinmuller.

"Lydia?" a familiar voice said. "This is Larry K. I just found out you have your own radio show, and I wanted to call and congratulate you."

"Larry, it's great to hear from you. Do you mind telling my listeners how we know each other?"

"Not at all," he said. "I'd be happy to introduce myself. I'm one of the Project Ex'ers who responded to your ad on Facebook. And boy, am I glad you placed that ad. My meeting with you changed everything for me."

"What do you mean?"

"You helped me understand it was time to let go of the past and move on. After we met, I spent a lot of time thinking about my life and how much time and energy I spent feeling angry about things that happened a long time ago."

"So, what happened?"

"Well, the long and short of it is… I finally got up the nerve to join an Internet dating site. And a few weeks later, I met a wonderful woman—her name's Michelle. Now, instead of being angry all the time, I feel happy. Really happy. It's a strange feeling for me, but I have to say, I'm getting used to it."

I grinned so wide my cheeks hurt. "Larry, that's great news. I'm happy too."

"I knew you would be. Well, that's about it. I don't want to take up any more of your time. I know lots of people need your help. I just wanted you to know that Project Ex inspired me to take a long, hard look at my life, and I wanted to thank you for being so honest with me."

"Enjoy your new relationship. I hope I get to meet Michelle some time. And thanks for calling. You made my day." And I meant it.

I glanced over at Keith, who was beaming too. The guys in the booth gave me a thumbs-up. Heart thumping with pride, I was flying high when I picked up the next call.

"This is Mitch," a man said. He spoke so softly I could barely hear him.

"Can you speak up, Mitch?" I asked. "Why are you whispering?"

"I'm not whispering. I'm just worn out. Truthfully, I don't feel much like talking."

"Then why did you call?"

"I called because my girlfriend just broke up with me."

"'Just,' as in within the last few days?"

"'Just,' as in ten minutes ago."

"Your girlfriend broke up with you ten minutes ago? Where is she now?"

"She's exactly where she was ten minutes ago, I'm sure—at her place in South Philly."

"And where are you?"

"I'm sitting in my pickup truck in the Walmart parking lot, wondering what the hell I'm going to do."

"So, she broke up with you by phone?"

"That's exactly what she did, the damn bitch," he muttered under his breath.

"Hey Mitch, watch your language. You can't talk that way when you're on the air."

"Well, what would you call her? We were together for three years, and she just called me on my cell phone and dumped me. Does she sound like Mother Teresa to you?"

"Look, I don't even know your girlfriend, but I can tell you're hurting. Why don't we focus on you and your feelings instead of on what she did?"

"My feelings? How would you feel if your boyfriend called you on your cell phone to dump you after you were together for four years?"

"Four years? I thought you said it was three."

Keith was waving a note in my face: "Pick up line two. It's the girlfriend."

"Hold on a minute, Mitch. Your girlfriend's on the other line."

I switched to the other call. "This is Lydia," I said. "Are you Mitch's girlfriend?"

"Well, I was his girlfriend until I dumped him ten minutes ago. Just like he said on the radio."

"Why don't you tell me your name and then tell me what happened."

"My name is Melanie, and actually, Mitch and I were together for exactly two years. Guess it felt a lot longer because you invested so much of yourself in it, Mitch."

"Hey Melanie, I know you're angry but try to stay away from sarcasm. It's never helpful," I said.

"You're right, I guess. I was just so mad when I heard his voice on the radio. How dare he call you up and act like the victim when I'm the one who's been hurt over and over again?"

Keith stuck another note under my nose: "Mitch wants to talk too."

"Listen, Melanie, my assistant just let me know that Mitch has some things to say too. Should we conference him in on this call?"

"Absolutely not. I don't want to talk to him again—ever!"

I was getting a little tired of this *ménage a trois*, with me being the one in the middle. "Look, if you two have no intention of getting back together, maybe there's no point in going on."

"That's it," Melanie said as she began to sob. "He was so hateful, so insensitive, so self-centered, there was just no point in going on."

"And sometimes that's the way it is. Sometimes you just know it's over and you have to start again," I said. A wave of sadness washed over me and a feeling of hopelessness. How many times had I started over with someone new, only to find myself at another dead end?

"Do you know what he did to me? Do you know what he did after I devoted two years of my life to the son of a bitch? He ignored my birthday—that's what he did. He deliberately ignored my 40th birthday—no card, no flowers, no present, nothing. That was the last straw. I mean, if someone loves you, they should want to celebrate the day you were born, right? Isn't that how it should be?"

Keith put another note in front of me: "Mitch has something to say."

"Hold on, Melanie," I said, as I switched to the other line.

"Thanks for letting me get a word in," Mitch said. "You may have forgotten, but I'm the one who called first, and it's my pain we're supposed to be focusing on."

There was a stirring inside me, a seismic stirring of red-hot fury, and at the moment, all of it was directed at this Neanderthal who was sitting in his pickup truck in the Walmart parking lot, asking me to feel his pain.

"Stuff it, Mitch," I blurted out and then managed to add, "Way to go, Melanie," before I hung up. Keith just stared at me, with a look I'd seen before. It was a look that said, *And you're supposed to be a therapist?*

"Sorry, listeners," I said, "And Mitch, I guess I was a little abrupt with you. Sorry I cut you off, but you were sounding kind of needy and not the least bit open to hearing what Melanie had to say. What I'd recommend is that both of you seek professional help, and I can transfer you to someone right now who can help you find it." I glanced over at Keith, who had a tentative smile on his face.

I fought back tears as I wrapped up the show with my usual sign-off: "Remember to be kind to yourself this week. If you're kind to yourself, it's a whole lot easier to be kind to other people too. And isn't that what relationship is all about?"

What's happening to me? I asked myself later as I drove home. Then I remembered my bad dream and the rotten feeling that had been haunting me all day. *You're exhausted,* I told myself. *You just need a good night's sleep.* But I knew it was more than that—much more.

CHAPTER NINETEEN

I was thankful my schedule over the next few days was so busy that I barely had time to think. I still felt humiliated that I'd lost my cool during my last radio show—something that had never happened before. I was also determined to stop obsessing over the fact that Rusty Munson had not replied to my email. I checked my email and my notifications on Facebook every day, but it was no use. He wasn't going to reply and I knew it. I felt like a fool for allowing myself to believe I could reignite a flame I knew had died, for Rusty anyway, a long, long time ago.

I began eating dinner each night in front of the TV, plodding back and forth to the kitchen to pile the dirty dishes in the sink and then forage in the pantry to find more snacks to munch on while I watched reruns of my favorite shows. I was lolling on the couch one night, a half-empty box of Whitman's buttercreams on the coffee table, when the phone rang. I was sorry I'd answered it as soon as I heard Rick Mann's voice.

"Lydia, I'm glad you're there," he said. "I was afraid I wouldn't catch you."

"Is everything okay?" I asked as casually as I could, although I felt a bit uneasy. Why was he calling me tonight when he had an appointment for phone therapy in the morning? This was the second time in the last couple of weeks he'd called between scheduled appointments. What was going on that couldn't wait?

"I know I have an appointment to talk to you tomorrow morning, and I'm really sorry to bother you, but something's come up and I had to call you right away."

I gulped but waited for him to go on, glancing longingly at the chocolates within arm's reach on the coffee table.

"I've got an idea," he said, "an amazing idea. And I just couldn't wait to share it with you."

"You sound out of breath. Are you okay?"

"You won't believe where I am. Want to guess?"

"Rick, we've been through this before—therapy is not a guessing game. Sometimes I wonder if you're really serious about therapy."

"Oh, I'm serious all right. Very serious. My idea—believe it or not, it's a business proposition—could make both of us rich."

"A business proposition? You can tell me about it," I said, my curiosity boiling over, "but it could never work since—in case you've forgotten—I'm still your therapist."

"Oh, I think we could work that out. But anyway, I can't give you any details about it right now. I'm in a public place and…"

"That's enough. First you call me up and act like you have something urgent to tell me. Then you say you can't talk about it. If you can't talk about it, why did you call me in the first place? I'm ending this call now. I've had quite enough of this," I said, annoyed he was playing this game with me and I'd taken the bait.

I hung up and popped an orange buttercream—my favorite flavor—in my mouth while I sat there, fuming. An instant later, the phone rang again. I picked it up, heard a whirring noise in the background and then the deep voice of Rick Mann. "Hello again. Are you still mad at me?" he asked.

"I'm not angry with you," I said, louder than I intended.

"If you're not angry, why are you shouting?"

"Listen Rick, I'm a therapist, not a mind reader. I'm not going to play games with you."

"You are angry with me, you know. Aren't therapists supposed to be in touch with their feelings?"

"You're right. I am angry. It's clear you're trying to push my buttons, and frankly, you've succeeded. That may be therapy of a certain kind, but it's not the kind I consider healthy or helpful."

"But you have helped me. You do help me. I didn't mean to upset you. I swear I didn't. Although, to be honest, I'm not sure I should be so focused on your feelings, since I'm the patient or the client or whatever. But somehow or other, I do care about how you feel and it wasn't my intention to make you angry."

"I think we've taken this phone therapy thing about as far as it can go—about as far as I'm willing to go. This just isn't therapeutic anymore. You're going to have to find time in your schedule to come in and meet with me in person or I'm resigning as your therapist right here and now."

The whirring noise became less pronounced and then stopped. The only sound between us was our breathing, which suddenly seemed heavier.

"You can do that—resign as my therapist? Don't I have any say in this? I want to share my idea with you. I need to hear what you think about it."

"The only way I'll hear it, Rick, is if you come in and see me in person. What do you say? Otherwise, I'm going to end our arrangement right here and now."

There was a pause and then he said, "Well, I guess you've got me where you want me. I'm not ready to end, so what choice do I have?"

"None. So, when would you like to come in for your appointment?"

"Next week. I think Wednesday will work, but I'll call you."

CHAPTER TWENTY

Two days later, Rick called and left a message on my answering machine. "Wednesday won't work," he said. "I have to be in Chicago for a production meeting. Actually, my travel schedule looks pretty hectic for the next few weeks, so I don't think I'll be able to see you anytime soon. I'll let you know when I'm in town again. Take care and try not to miss me too much. Only kidding."

There was another message, recorded just a few minutes after the first one: "Hi, it's Rick again. You know, I was thinking… Since I'm technically not in therapy anymore—I mean, since you said I can't continue to be your client unless I come to see you in person and since I can't get in to see you—how about if you give some serious consideration to becoming my business partner? This idea I have could take off—I just know it. I'm going to send you an email explaining everything. And don't worry about me, all alone out there in the world without a therapist to guide me. Just thinking about getting rich has made me feel much better. So long… partner."

I sat there in my office, playing the message over and over. I knew Rick was a shrewd businessman. He didn't seem like the kind of guy who would consider getting involved in a business deal without carefully considering every angle. And yet, he seemed to have come up with this idea overnight and wanted to run with it—now. Of course, I was dying to find out what it was all about and why he was so convinced it was going to be a huge success. But what puzzled me most of all was, why in the world did he want me as his business partner?

I thought and thought and thought some more, but all I ended up with was a headache. I knew one thing for certain: I was curious—so curious that I finally decided it wouldn't do any harm to read his email. I went to my office, turned on my laptop, and logged in to my email account. I spotted the one from Rick right away. Just reading the subject line—"Do I have a deal for you"—made my blood boil. How did it even elude my spam filter? I almost deleted it without reading further, but of course I couldn't stop my eyes from scanning down the page:

Hi Lydia,

I suppose you're wondering how you and I could possibly collaborate on a business deal.

You're right about that, I thought.

You probably think we're unlikely business partners. But when you read about my business proposition, I think you'll understand. You asked where I was when I called you the other day. The truth is, I was at the gym, walking on the treadmill. That was the noise you heard in the background.

All the treadmills at my gym have little TV sets attached to them. There was nothing special on TV and I was bored as usual. I was thinking how ten minutes feel like an hour when you're on the treadmill when suddenly I got this great idea. Everyone goes to the gym to feel physically fit, right? But what if you could give your psyche a workout at the same time? Wouldn't it be amazing to have a series of videos available with advice from a hotshot therapist? Each video could focus on a different issue—relationships, finances, work, etc. Maybe this therapist could be available for in-person consultations too, but her primary responsibility would be to create a line of self-help videos which would be available for loan or purchase only by gym members.

Now, I happen to know from personal experience that you're the perfect person to create these videos, and I'd be happy to provide all the technical and marketing support you need. I'll be back in town on Thursday, and I'm hoping we can get together to talk about everything over dinner that night. I know you have your reservations about partnering with me in a business deal, but hopefully you'll hear me out. I think you're making too much out of the fact that you used to be my therapist. The main thing is, I'm not your client anymore, so really, what's the problem?

I hope you'll agree to this impromptu dinner meeting—you owe me that, at least.

Your prospective business partner,
Rick Mann
P.S. I won't take no for an answer.

And you, Rick Mann, are the biggest bullshit artist around, I thought, but I saved the email before I shut down my computer. However, his business proposition sounded intriguing—so intriguing I had trouble getting it off my mind.

It's not for me, I told myself. I might be willing to meet with him just to hear what he had to say, but Rick Mann as my business partner? No way.

I filled the rest of the day with a frenzy of activity, determined to forget about Rick and his business venture for a while. Hadn't he told me he was swamped at work and had no time for therapy? If he couldn't find an hour a week for therapy, it was doubtful he'd be able to squeeze a business meeting with me into his hectic schedule.

The next morning, I woke up early and was feeling pretty good until I checked my calendar. About a month earlier, my mother had asked if I could take her to the podiatrist at four o'clock. I'd scheduled five therapy sessions, four with new clients, between 9:00 a.m. and 3:00 p.m. Five back-to-back clients and then my mother—what a day. I considered calling her and telling her I couldn't make it. I could even offer to pay for a cab. It wouldn't take more than ten minutes to get to the podiatrist's office by cab from her apartment. It would take me twenty minutes just to get to her place. By the time I got through ferrying her back and forth, it would be dinnertime, and I knew what that meant. If I didn't offer to take her to dinner before dropping her off at her apartment, she'd say, "Well, I suppose I can always heat up a can of Campbell's soup for myself."

I knew I didn't have the nerve to back out at the last minute. If I did, I'd never hear the end of it. I glanced at the clock; it was 8:45. *She should be calling any minute now,* I thought.

At that instant, the phone rang. As I pushed the "talk" button, I said, "Don't worry. I'll be there no later than 3:30."

For a moment, there was silence at the other end. I held my breath. What if it wasn't my mother after all? It could be Meri Bowen, my nine o'clock, calling to cancel, or get directions, or...

To my horror, I heard a laugh, followed by the voice of none other than Rick Mann. "Three thirty, huh? That doesn't give me much time to get back to Philly, but I'll try. It'd be nice if you could pick me up at the airport. We could have an impromptu meeting before our official business meeting tomorrow night."

"Our...meeting? What meeting?"

"Didn't you read the email I sent you last night?"

"Rick, it's not even nine o'clock. I haven't checked my email yet," I said. "And, by the way, I thought you were my mother."

"Well, that's an issue you'll have to take up with your shrink. That's called transference—I thought you knew."

"Obviously I was expecting a call from someone else."

"That's the story of my life. Women always seem to be expecting a call from someone else."

"Rick, I'm not your therapist anymore, remember? You'll have to take your neuroses someplace else."

"Now, that's a line I've never heard before. I guess that's the kind of stuff you hear when you get involved with a shrink."

"We are not getting involved."

"I meant that purely in a business sense. Don't worry, I wouldn't think about getting involved in any other way with someone who can't handle my neuroses. Although frankly, I thought you'd be one person who'd know what to do with them."

"I have to hang up now. I just got a beep. It must be my mother... I have to go."

"Your mother again, huh? There are some shrinks who specialize in that kind of thing. In the meantime, don't forget to check your emails. I'll call you tonight."

I quickly switched to the other call.

"Lydia? You didn't forget about me, did you? I've been looking forward to seeing the podiatrist all week," my mother said.

Yes, I thought, *I know that your podiatrist is one of the central people in your life. He's perfect for you because he spends all his time at your feet.* Just thinking about my mother and her feelings about her podiatrist made me giggle. "No, Mother, I didn't forget. I'll pick you up at 3:30."

"There could be a lot of traffic at that hour."

"In case all the roads in Philadelphia suddenly buckle and crack from the sixty-degree heat wave we're having? No, Mother, I think 3:30 will be just perfect."

"Listen, I'm still your mother. I may be old, but I'm not senile. It wouldn't kill you to spend an extra ten minutes with me, you know. I never get to see you anymore, now that you're a celebrity."

I ignored the dig and said, "I'm just busy—too busy. Do you think there's a chance that Irving could take you?" I knew she and Irving had become quite an item. However, he never seemed to take her anywhere. He liked hanging out at her place, eating home-cooked meat loaf and watching *Seinfeld* reruns on her twenty-year-old TV set with the rabbit ears on top.

"You know very well that Irving can't take me. I told you he watches his grandson after school. His schedule's always full."

I'm sure your eighty-year-old, retired boyfriend's schedule is much more hectic than mine, I thought. But instead I said, "See you later," and then I hung up.

The day flew by, and before I knew it, I was on my way to pick up my mother. I tried to get there on time, but there was a lot of traffic and I was ten minutes late. She was fuming but calmed down a little when I managed to pull up right in front of Dr. Edelstein's office at 3:58. "Are you going to wait for me?" she asked as I sighed and parked the car.

Of course she had to wait until 4:30 but she didn't mind, especially since by the time her appointment was over, it was 5:15 and time for dinner, in her opinion, at least. So I took her to her favorite Chinese restaurant—the one that still served chicken egg foo yong and had early-bird specials until six o'clock. I was just thankful I didn't have to take her podiatrist too. The way she talked about him, you'd think he was ready to ask her to marry him. Then, when dinner was over, I dropped her off at her place and headed straight to the gym. It was either the gym or a stint at the nearest mental hospital, and I wasn't really sure they could help me, anyway. If they put me into group therapy and asked me, "Now, how do you really feel about your mother?" I'd probably tell them and then I'd be committed for murderous intent, so I decided it was probably best just to opt for the gym.

I'd joined a new place a few months ago and I loved it. It was all women and everybody worked out in plain old sweats and looked pretty grungy. That was fine with me, and I was happy to join them in their grunginess. Even though some of the women were young and gorgeous, I still didn't envy them as much as I would have if they were dressed in the latest hot gym apparel, with their tight bodies bursting out of their halter tops and tighter shorts.

You do need help, I told myself as I changed into the sweats I always kept in my trunk for "emergencies" like this—used mostly after being with my mother. *Thank God my clients can't read my mind*, I thought. *Then they'd know I'm just as neurotic as they are.*

Thinking about neuroses—not a new topic for me, that's for sure—made me remember my comment to Rick Mann earlier in the day. Had I really told him to "take his neuroses someplace else?" And more importantly, did I really mean it?

I got home from the gym around eight o'clock. I was tired and ready for a snack, so I went to the kitchen, stopping briefly in the bedroom to shed my sweaty gym gear. Usually going to the gym cleared my head and made me feel a lot calmer, but tonight I was still on edge.

That's what spending time with my mother does to me, I said to myself as I opened the refrigerator door and poked my head inside. It was such a familiar location—cold yet comforting. I wondered what I would say to a client who considered her refrigerator a place to hang out—a beloved vacation spot she returned to time and time again.

I checked out the freezer and found some low-fat brownies I'd forgotten about. There was some Cool Whip too. And a package of egg rolls from Trader Joe's I hadn't even opened yet. I could have an egg roll—only ninety calories according to the package—and then have two brownies with Cool Whip for under 500 calories. *Thanks, refrigerator, you've come through again*, I thought. *I must be off the wall, thinking about my refrigerator the way I do.* I was about to diagnose myself yet another time—one of my favorite activities lately, it seemed—when I heard the phone ring.

I glanced at the brownies and then headed into the den to find the phone. *No, I left it in the bedroom,* I thought, dashing upstairs. I winced as I tripped on one of the sneakers I'd tossed on the floor when I got home. I found the phone on my bed, buried under the gym clothes I'd peeled off earlier. As I rushed to grab it, I stubbed my toe on the metal bed frame. Bending down to rub my injured toe, I pushed the "talk" button and half-said, half-shouted, "Hello?"

First there was a pause, and then I heard the familiar voice. "Were you expecting your ex-husband? The IRS, perhaps?"

"No, Rick," I replied, hopping around and rubbing my toe, "I was sitting here by the phone, waiting for your call."

"Well, if that's how you answer the phone when you're expecting a man to call, it's no wonder you're still single."

"Is this your usual sales pitch when talking to a potential business partner?"

"No, only with a potential business partner who used to be my therapist. Everything I usually repress seems to come to the surface when I talk to her."

"This therapist is pretty damn sure this business venture isn't for her."

"Are you willing to talk about it, at least?"

"I don't know…"

"Tell you what—how about if we meet for dinner tomorrow night—strictly business, of course. Then I'll be able to give you all the details, and you'll be able to figure out whether you want any part of it. If you don't, that's okay. Just give me the chance to put everything on the table. Fair?"

"Sounds fair," I said, still unsure.

"Why do you sound so hesitant? I promise not to take up too much of your time."

"No, it isn't that. It has nothing to do with time at all. I'm still sorting through the ethical issues in my head, and I don't see how

I could consider forming a partnership—a business [partnership] that is—with someone who used to be my client. And [by] 'used to be,' I mean, like five minutes ago."

"Why not? I think it gives you a real advantage—yo[u know a] whole lot more about me than I do about you. I kind o[f like the] idea of having a partner who knows me inside out—if yo[u get] my drift."

"Yes, I think I do, and that's what worries me. If I becam[e your] business partner—and I emphasize the word 'if' because [I sin]cerely doubt it's going to happen—we'd have to find a way t[o put] our client/therapist relationship aside, and frankly, I'm not s[ure] we could do that."

"Oh, I'm past all that. Those therapy sessions are behind m[e.] I'm ready to move on with my life."

"Look, it's been a long day and I'm really tired. I just don't have the fortitude to resist your onslaught any longer. So yes, I'll meet you tomorrow night. No promises about business deals or anything like that. Let's meet and talk and then we can take it from there."

"Great! How about eight o'clock at Stella's Café at 20th and Christian? It's a new place, kind of out of the way but very nice, I hear. I can send you the address. Does that work for you?"

"Yes," I said, checking my calendar. "That's fine." *What are you doing?* I asked myself as I wrote the time and date in ink in my calendar.

"So we'll finally get to meet face-to-face," I said. "How will I know you, anyway? I have no idea what you look like."

"Don't worry," he said. "I've seen you on TV, remember?"

"Okay, then. Eight o'clock, tomorrow night."

"You won't regret this, Lydia," he said before he hung up.

CHAPTER TWENTY ONE

    tried on almost everything I owned and rejected each and every item. I decided I hated my entire wardrobe and was ready to throw the huge mound of clothing I had tossed on my bed directly into the trash. I glanced at the clock on the night table and panicked when I saw the time—7:15. Here I was, still in my bra and panties, and I was supposed to meet Rick Mann in an hour. I had no more than ten minutes to find an outfit and get out the door.

    This is insane, I told myself as I rushed to my closet for the third time and began sorting through the remaining pants, dresses, skirts, and tops I hadn't already tossed into the reject pile on the bed. *No wonder I can't find anything in here. I have nothing to wear. Oh my God*, I thought. *I'm having a manic episode.* I leaned against the wall inside the closet and closed my eyes, trying to remember the DSM-IV criteria for mania. *Take a deep breath*, I told myself. *You must calm down. You're not having a manic episode; you just have yourself in a state.*

    What's wrong with me? I asked myself. *Why am I so worked up over tonight? This isn't a date. It's not even a real business meeting. I'm just going to talk to Rick Mann and let him know I can't be his business partner. Then I'm never going to talk to him or see him again.*

"Yes," I said out loud. "I won't have to deal with him anymore." I marched back to the bed and sorted again through my now-rumpled clothes.

I grabbed the dark green blazer I'd picked up last week at Marshall's and the brightly colored Donna Karan scarf I'd splurged on at Nordstrom's. I pulled on a pair of black pants and tied the scarf loosely over a deep V-necked black sweater as I looked in the mirror. *Not bad*, I thought.

I looked at the clock—7:25. It was time to leave.

I dashed out the door, grabbing my coat and keys from the table in the front hall. As I pulled out of the driveway, I remembered I'd left my cell phone on the kitchen counter.

Oh well, I thought, *it doesn't really matter. If anyone wants to reach me, they'll have to leave me a message or call back later.* I smiled as I realized that I actually liked the idea of being without my phone for the evening. It made me feel free somehow—reckless even. No one—except Rick Mann, of course— knew where I was going or how to reach me. I felt a small twinge of guilt as I thought about my clients but decided none of them seemed to be in crisis at the moment. I'd be gone for only a few hours, and anyway, the recording on my answering service provided the phone number for the psychiatric emergency hot line.

There was no traffic and at a few minutes before eight, I was just blocks away from the restaurant. As I searched for a parking space on the street, it occurred to me I might be too early. What if Rick wasn't there yet? If I got there first, should I wait for him near the door or ask to be seated at a table?

I decided it would definitely be better if he had to wait for me. Not for long, of course. I would sit here in the car for the next fifteen minutes and listen to some relaxing music. At around 8:15, I'd stroll over to the restaurant, where I'd probably find him at our table, anxiously glancing at his watch and waiting for me. I liked that scenario. The more I thought about it, the more strongly I felt that the person who should be waiting was Rick Mann.

After circling the surrounding blocks three times, I found a space around the corner from the restaurant. I checked my make-up in the rearview mirror and carefully reapplied my lipstick. I took a few deep breaths—why was I so nervous?—and looked at my watch again. It was almost 8:15.

I'm finally going to meet Rick Mann, I thought, as I felt my heart give a few thumps in my chest. I wondered what he looked like and if I would find him attractive. *Why should you care what he looks like?* I berated myself. *You're going to discuss a business deal—one you're going to turn down.*

As I turned the corner, I saw the restaurant just half a block away. I felt my heart flutter again and heard a rushing in my ears. I stopped for a moment and tried to take another deep breath. *It's just Rick Mann*, I told myself. But saying his name only seemed to make my heart beat faster.

I calmed down a little when I got inside the restaurant. As soon as my eyes adjusted to the dim light, I began to look around. It hit me suddenly that I felt exactly the way I used to feel when I was about to meet a man whose ad I'd responded to via the Internet.

I felt ridiculous and so very vulnerable, standing there, peering around. At least when I was meeting a date, we would discuss beforehand what we looked like, or sometimes exchange photos. Rick had a definite advantage—he'd seen me on TV. It should have made me feel calmer to know he'd be able to recognize me, but it only made me feel angry and insecure. There it was again—the uncomfortable but by now familiar feeling that most of the time he seemed to have the upper hand.

No one approached to greet me and lead me to a table. I glanced down at my watch. It was 8:25. Panic surged through me as I reassessed the situation. Obviously my little plan wasn't going to work. Once again, he'd caught me off guard.

I sorted through my options: I could wait here for a few more minutes, looking and feeling conspicuous. I could ask to be seated and let the waiter know I was expecting someone. I could go to the ladies' room and freshen up again. Or, I could just leave and let him wonder whether I'd been here at all.

Why hasn't he called? I asked myself. I began rummaging through my purse, looking for my cell phone, when I remembered I'd left it at home. *"Damn,"* I thought. *Why didn't I go back and get the stupid phone?*

A young man in a crisp white shirt approached me with a quizzical look on his face. "Are you waiting for someone?" he asked. I saw the pity in his eyes and knew what he was thinking—*stood up again.*

I paused, still deciding what I should do. *Rick is probably tied up in traffic or looking for a place to park,* I thought. *I'm making too much out of this. I'll get a table, sit down and wait for him. He'll probably be here in a few minutes.*

"Yes," I told the good-looking manager. "I'm waiting for a business associate, Mr. Mann. Did he reserve a table?"

I could tell he didn't believe I was there for a business meeting. I had the words "blind date" written all over me and I knew it. But somehow, at that moment, I needed him to pretend he believed me, to pretend he didn't know what I already felt in my heart—I'd be eating dinner alone again.

JARED

The day had flown by and now it was almost time for the meeting with Lydia. Jared checked his watch again. In just fifteen minutes, he'd be leaving home and heading for the restaurant where they'd agreed to meet. He'd picked a small but cozy restaurant in Southwest Philly, counting on the fact that none of his friends or colleagues would be there at eight o'clock on a weeknight. Hell, he was pretty much a loner these days anyway. The few people he hung out with at work usually went straight home on weekdays.

He was also counting on the fact that Lydia had no idea what he looked like. Of course, if she had Googled "Jared Abrams," she could have found a recent if blurry and hardly flattering photo of him delivering a lecture at an underpromoted and underattended Jewish Journalism Foundation awards banquet. But she hadn't; in fact, she'd mentioned to him once in the context of his needing to deal with criticism more positively that it was a good thing she didn't know what Jared Abrams looked like, because if she ever met him, she'd probably be unable to resist an uncontrollable urge to clobber him. But as she'd added quickly, "having the urge to do something and doing it isn't the same thing."

His hand was on the doorknob when the cell phone he always kept in his pocket began to ring. He glanced at his watch as he pulled out the phone.

His heart sank when he heard the voice on the other end. "Jared, I need you to handle something right away." It was Steiner, his editor, and he sounded ornery.

"Right away?" Jared asked. "As in right now?"

"No, as in next week. What the hell is wrong with you? I mean, right now, tonight—this very minute."

"What's going on?" Jared asked. "Are you okay?"

"No, I'm not okay. I'm not okay at all. My ass is on the line and I need you to save it. There's a problem with one of the *Style* pieces. Is that urgent enough for you?"

"Sounds pretty urgent to me," Jared said, but what he was thinking was, *I'll be saving your ass but mine will be in a sling when I have to call Lydia and cancel at the last minute.*

"Are you sure you meant to call me?" he asked. "I mean, I really don't know much about the *Style* section."

"Really?" Steiner said. "Thanks for telling me." He paused then added in an icy tone, "I know what you do, Abrams. I hired you, remember?"

"Yeah, sure," Jared replied. "I remember. I was only kidding around—just yanking your chain a little."

"Well, my chain's been yanked enough today, and I don't need any bullshit from you, so just shut up and listen to me," Steiner roared.

"I'm all ears," Jared said, his jaw tightening.

"I know you hate the damn society stuff, but Lauren's away and there's nobody else who can make a story out of this one. There's a huge event at the Bellevue tonight honoring Catherine Scanlon-Jones. You know who the Scanlon-Joneses are, don't you?"

Jared nodded, forgetting for a moment that Steiner couldn't see him. "Yes," he said after a pause. "I know about the well-connected Scanlon-Jones family."

"Well-connected and fucking loaded," Steiner said. "And I promised Catherine a long time ago we'd do an exclusive interview with her so she could talk about this new cause she's into…"

"Which is…?" Jared asked.

"Which is pure bullshit, I'm sure, but we have to cover it," Steiner shouted into the phone. "Orphans, animals, Appalachian hillbillies—frankly, I don't fucking care what it is. I just need to know your ass will be there tonight, and I'll have the story on my desk in the morning."

"Yes, sir," Jared said. "At your service, sir."

"Don't pull that shit with me, Abrams," Steiner said. "I've been pretty easy on you lately and you know it. Or do I have to remind you the piece about that shrink is at least a month overdue…"

"Okay, okay, I'm on it," Jared said. "Don't worry—I won't let you down."

"Oh, I'm not worried," Steiner said. "As a matter of fact, I'm heading over to O'Riley's now. I'm going to have myself some ribs and a couple of beers."

"See you tomorrow," Jared said. "You son of a bitch," he added softly after he hung up.

Jared shoved his cell phone in his pocket and pulled out his car keys. He felt miserable. He had no choice but to cover the story, and he knew he had to get on it right away.

I'll call Lydia from the car, he thought. He looked at his watch and tried to figure how long it would take him to get to the Bellevue as he loped down his front steps and headed for his car, which was parked across the street. *Damn, I'm going to lose my parking space too*, he thought.

Jared lived in Old City, and it was no easy task finding a place to park his car every night. He was too cheap to pay the exorbitant monthly fee to park it in a garage, so every night he played the game of roaming nearby streets, seeking out a space to call his own. Now he'd be getting home late, long after everyone else had returned from work and parked their cars for the night. He'd probably have to park blocks away and scurry back to his house with the chilly autumn air biting his face.

"It's my own fault," he mumbled to himself. "I should have told Steiner off—told him to go screw himself." He pulled his gloves out of his pocket and buried his chin deeper into his coat.

"It's frigging cold out here," he muttered as he reached his car, unlocked the door, and got inside.

Shivering, he turned the key in the ignition but heard nothing but a whirring sound. He tried again, praying for the familiar hum of the engine. Nothing. All thoughts of Lydia flew from his mind as he jumped out of the useless car and started jogging toward Chestnut Street. *I need to find a cab—fast*, he thought. He knew his chances of finding a passing cab on his quiet street were slim to none. It was well past eight o'clock and he doubted any cabbies were sitting around waiting for him, especially on this unseasonably cold night.

He pulled out his cell phone and dialed information. "In Philadelphia," he said to the recording. "I need the number of a cab company."

"No," he said a few moments later to the operator who picked up the call, "I don't care which one. Look, it's urgent. Can you hurry?" He realized he was shouting, but he didn't care. Damn it, he was pissed.

He was supposed to be at Stella's Cafe right now, convincing Lydia why she should become his business partner. Even if she refused to go along with his outlandish business proposition, he still had her where he wanted her. What kind of therapist was she if she was considering going into business with someone who, in her own words, had been her client "just five minutes ago?"

He had almost all the material he needed to write a scathing exposé, revealing her vulnerabilities and her flaws. And now, here he was, all alone, freezing his ass off while Steiner sat at O'Riley's, a beer in his hand, and Lydia sat alone at the restaurant, cursing the day he was born.

He suddenly realized that, in the rush to find a cab, he'd forgotten to call her. He pushed the button on his cell phone again and began searching for her cell number. Suddenly he heard the familiar beeps and saw the low battery warning on the display. "Shit," he yelled, shoving the phone into his pocket again. A woman who was approaching him, her Yorkie cuddled in her arms, glanced in both directions and rushed to the other side of the street.

He stopped for a minute to catch his breath. *What's important here?* he asked himself. *What do I need to focus on? The story,* he heard Steiner's voice boom in his head. *Get the story.* He could explain everything to Lydia tomorrow.

Just as he turned the corner at Third and Chestnut, he saw a cab whizzing toward him. He waved his arm frantically and was shocked when it slid to a stop at the curb. He jumped in before the cabbie could change his mind. "The Bellevue," he said, his heart pounding. "And step on it."

CHAPTER TWENTY TWO

The manager had seated me at a pretty decent table, considering he knew damn well I'd be eating alone. I had a good view of the entrance and had already watched a few couples walk through the door. A couple of single men had come in too, but they'd headed straight to the bar.

At 8:40, I asked if I could use the phone and called my voice mail. One message. *At least he called*, I thought. *Maybe there'd been an emergency, like a car accident, or worse.* I held my breath as I listened but swore out loud when I heard my mother's voice: "Lydia, I hope you haven't forgotten about the Kornblatt bar mitzvah this weekend. I've been looking forward to it for weeks. Call me tomorrow. I'm going out to play mah-jongg tonight. Where are you, anyway? I couldn't reach you on your cell phone."

How could I forget about the damn bar mitzvah when my mother left reminders about it on my voice mail just about every day? But my annoyance with her was nothing compared to other feelings—feelings of humiliation, shame, disappointment, and pure rage—that were washing over me.

Rick Mann hadn't called. It was then I felt it in every fiber of my being—the manager's estimation of the situation had been correct: I'd been stood up.

Something else could have happened, I told myself. *Something catastrophic.* I began to sort through the possibilities: maybe someone in Rick's family had died suddenly or…

While I was in the midst of this reverie, I glanced again toward the door and saw to my horror that Harvey Schwartzbaum had just walked into the restaurant. Harvey Schwartzbaum: a missing data point for Project Ex, although he wasn't missed one bit as far as I was concerned. Even more to my horror, I saw he was with an absolutely stunning woman who seemed to be hanging on his every word. I grabbed the menu and buried my face in it, but it was too late—Harvey had spotted me and was heading directly toward my table, a huge grin on his smug but decidedly ordinary face.

"Lydia," he said, bending over to give me a peck on the cheek as I tried to ward him off with the menu. "How are you? Long time no see."

Beaming, he turned toward the decidedly younger woman at his side and said, "I'd like you to meet Monica, the love of my life."

As I struggled with the urge to vomit on my salad plate, I smiled wanly and said, "Hello, Monica. It's nice to meet the woman who's the love of Harvey's life."

She beamed back at Harvey, her gorgeous face glowing with pride. "It's nice to meet you too, Lydia," she said. "We're so lucky to have found each other."

"And," Harvey added, a nauseating smile on his face, "I'm so lucky to be getting married to this wonderful woman."

I stared at them and felt my jaw drop. Harvey was getting married? He'd been one of the most commitment-phobic—not to mention annoying—men I'd ever dated. Monica must be a miracle worker if she was able to mold him into marriage material. *Maybe she's pregnant,* I thought, glancing furtively at her flat stomach.

I murmured my congratulations while I prayed they would move on as quickly as possible.

Glancing at the empty seat across from me, Harvey asked, "Are you expecting someone?"

"Yes, I am," I said, "He should be here any minute."

"Is this someone special, Lydia?" Harvey asked. "Maybe you have some exciting news to share with us too."

The exciting news is that I'm not marrying you, I thought, but what I said was, "No, Harvey, nothing like that. But I'm fine. Everything is just fine, thank you." *It would be much finer if the two of you would move on and leave me alone*, I thought.

At last they seemed to get the message. "Oh well," Harvey said, "always the therapist, never the bride." He gave me a huge grin as he followed the waiter toward their table, his arm around his fiancée's teeny waist.

This was the ultimate humiliation. First, Rick Mann had stood me up and now Harvey Schwartzbaum had discovered I was still single—still alone, twelve years after my divorce. The waiter approached the table again and I felt my cheeks burn. I looked at my watch one last time: 8:45. I grabbed my coat and my purse, muttered an apology to the smug-looking manager—whose pity-filled eyes made me feel even more pathetic—and headed out the door.

When I got home, I threw my coat on the couch in the living room and headed straight for the phone. Once again, I checked my messages, but there was nothing from Rick Mann.

That son of a bitch, I thought. *Why didn't he call?* I found myself in the kitchen, in front of my old friend, the refrigerator. *You're always there for me*, I thought, patting its cold exterior. *I know I can count on you.*

And sure enough, as soon as I opened the door, I saw the leftover Chinese food from two nights ago. I opened the containers and dumped everything onto one large plate—moo goo gai pan and chicken egg foo yong, together with some yummy shrimp fried rice. I felt my eyes fill with tears as I realized how pathetic it was that I could even think about food at a time like this.

But I'm hungry, I told myself to justify my suddenly huge longing for food. *Is it really food I'm yearning for?* I wondered as I added some crunchy Chinese noodles to my already full plate. *Well, whatever it is, I'm not going to allow myself to analyze what's going on because I want to eat this pile of food*, I thought as I plopped down on the couch and hit the power button on the remote.

It was still early. I could eat the leftover Chinese, watch some TV, call a couple of friends if I felt like it. And say what? What would I tell them—I'd been stood up by a former client who wanted me to go into business with him? Well, I could kiss my social work license goodbye if that information ever got around.

I could say goodbye to my radio program too, I thought, *and my private practice, which was just starting to take off.* I had to face it. I was a fraud—a single, divorced, lonely, miserable fraud who'd messed up her own life along with everyone else's. This time, the tears really started to flow, cascading right down my face and into my egg foo whatever it was.

I was looking around for tissues when the phone rang. *It's not that late*, I thought. *I could still meet him somewhere for coffee and dessert. If he had a good excuse, that was, a really good excuse.*

"Hello," I said as brightly as I could, wiping my nose on my sleeve. I held my breath, hoping to hear Rick Mann's voice on the other end of the line.

"Lydia? Have you met someone new? I hope you've found someone better than that terrible musician—Richard or Ronald or whatever his name was, I don't even remember." Though *of course* she remembered. "The one who wrote that dreadful 'soup rap' or whatever it's called. You deserve the best, Lydia, and don't you forget it," my mother said.

"Mother, why are you asking if I'm dating someone?" *Oh God*, I thought, *I don't want to think about Robert right now. I can't handle any more pain at the moment.*

"Well, you were out late tonight and it's a weeknight," she said.

"I do go out sometimes, you know," I said, more to convince myself I had a life than to argue the point with her.

"Well, wherever you were, you didn't have your cell phone on and I couldn't reach you."

"I was meeting a friend for dinner and I forgot my cell phone. End of story. No new boyfriends in the picture, nothing interesting or exciting going on in my life." I paused for a moment. "Just a former client who's giving me a run for my money, that's all."

"Are you having a problem?" my mother asked. "I just read an article in the *Jewish Week* about a doctor whose patient was stalking her. It was terrifying."

"Nothing as exciting or dramatic as that. Just somebody who's basically a pain in the you know where. Nothing I can't handle. Right now, though, I'm exhausted and I have to go to bed."

"All right, but I think you're hiding something. I'm your mother and I can always tell, you know," she said, and it was true. She had a kind of radar for detecting any problems—particularly with men—in my life. "Get some rest and I'll call you in the morning."

Sure, Mother, I thought. *I'll be sleeping like a baby tonight.*

I hung up, went upstairs to my bedroom and threw myself onto the bed. I reached for the remote, turning on the TV, and praying I'd find something to watch that would distract me from thinking about how terribly this evening had turned out. It was now past ten and I knew Rick Mann wasn't going to call.

I thrashed around, thinking about what a rotten judge of character I was. Imagine, I had trusted Rick Mann—believed him when he said he wanted me to be his business partner. It was clear to me now that all he'd wanted was to humiliate me. What kind of therapist was I if I couldn't figure out what my clients were all about? *Maybe I need a break*, I thought. *Maybe I shouldn't be doing this anymore, intervening in people's lives, pretending I can help them.* I felt confused, so confused.

The more I thought about it, the more I liked the idea of getting away for a while. *That research project I started has changed everything*, I thought. *Nothing is the same anymore. Maybe I need to get away so I can take stock of who I am and what I've become.* I knew there was no point in trying to sleep, so I got up and went into the den. I plopped into my favorite chair, snuggling into the soft fabric and putting my feet on the ottoman. I turned on the TV and began to surf the channels, searching for a way to alleviate my misery. I found an *I Love Lucy* marathon and immersed myself in Lucy's wacky predicaments. It was all so innocent and lighthearted. Everyone seemed to be having so much fun. *Yes*, I thought, *that's what's missing from my life—fun.*

I was lost in thought for a while as I considered this. When I focused on the TV screen again, I saw Lucy sitting in a chaise, reading a book. She was wearing a floppy hat and sunglasses, and when I looked more closely, I saw she was on a ship. *Hey*, I thought, *Lucy's on a cruise*. I looked at her, sitting in a deck chair, carefree and relaxed. *That's what I need—a cruise*. It sounded so spontaneous, so exotic—in short, so unlike me, I decided to check it out right away.

I jumped up, turned off the TV, and sat down at my desk, turning on my laptop. *I wonder where I should go*, I thought. I began to surf the Internet for information about cruise lines. *You're heading into uncharted waters*, I said to myself. The truth of the matter was, I knew nothing about cruises. I'd never been on one and had never had a yearning to spend more than a few hours out on the water. But at the moment, the thought of sailing away across the ocean was very appealing indeed.

Maybe I should call Carol, I thought. She'd been on a cruise last year and had been urging me to join her on one ever since. I glanced at the clock. It was just after midnight, probably too late to call her. Better wait until tomorrow.

Rick Mann, I thought, *I'm going on vacation—far, far away from you.* Far away from any thoughts about Rusty Munson too, I suddenly realized. It had been weeks since I'd sent him that Friend Request on Facebook, and I knew there was no hope of ever seeing him again. *Things are muddled enough in the present*, I thought. *I definitely don't need to dredge up past relationship failures right now.*

I shut down the computer, turned off all the lights, and went to bed. *I ate too much*, I thought as I curled myself into a ball under the covers, *but I don't care. I needed that food to comfort me.* Then I pulled the soft, fluffy blanket over my head and prayed for sleep.

CHAPTER TWENTY THREE

I was up early the next morning. I lay in bed for a while, refusing to allow any thoughts about last night to seep into my mind. I couldn't wait to call Carol, but I knew she usually slept in on Friday mornings. I showered and dressed quickly and then—first removing my clothes that were hanging from the handlebars—I pedaled furiously for ten minutes, which felt like an hour, on the stationary bike in my bedroom. I kept myself busy until ten and then called Carol. She picked up on the first ring. "How about joining me on a cruise?" I asked. "I have this sudden, irrepressible yearning to get away."

Although Carol was surprised and somewhat suspicious at first, she recovered quickly when she realized I was serious. Her voice was buoyant as she reflected on the last cruise she'd taken and how many singles she'd found on board. She'd just broken up with another crazy boyfriend—one of the men she'd met during our night out at the Oasis—and was eager for an adventure. "We both need a getaway. I'll get right on it," she said and promised to call me back soon to discuss potential dates and destinations. As she said goodbye, I heard her fingers tapping on the keyboard. An hour later, she called me back. She'd contacted a travel agent who'd found a cruise leaving in just two weeks from Fort Lauderdale for the Panama Canal. Carol said she'd be happy to take care of all the arrangements.

"You and I know very well there won't be one decent man on board that damn ship. All I expect to meet are losers, losers, and more losers. Anyway, I'm not even thinking about meeting anyone right now." Even as I said it, I knew it wasn't true.

"Well, like I always say, 'you never know,'" Carol replied, sounding hurt. "I know I'm certainly going to keep my eyes open. I'm always looking and I don't try to hide it."

So I've noticed, I thought, as the word *desperate* flitted through my mind. "Oh, what's the difference?" I said. "The important thing is, we're going to leave the stress of our day-to-day lives behind us for a little while. We can be who we want to be—and escape from who we are. I need a break from being Lydia," I joked.

"You know," she said, "that doesn't sound like a bad idea. We could assume new identities while we're on the cruise and really escape from who we are. Doesn't that sound exciting?"

"Listen, Carol, I just meant we could let loose a little—forget about our problems and concentrate on having fun. I wasn't suggesting a complete identity change."

"Let's think up new names for ourselves. If we pick intriguing, exotic names, maybe we'll become more intriguing and exotic too. It's worth a try. You could be…Alexis Steele," she said, giggling.

"Sounds crazy to me," I said, feeling secretly pleased she'd remembered I'd always loved the name Alexis. "Even if I agreed to go along with your off-the-wall idea, we'd never be able to pull it off with all the security checks these days. Or are you suggesting that we get phony passports too? How about if we just try to pay off one of the guards when we go through the security checkpoint in the airport? Then we could have a really romantic vacation—in jail."

"Oh, stop taking yourself so seriously," Carol said. "We don't need fake passports or anything like that. We'll go as ourselves, but when we get to the ship, we'll slip into our other identities. I'll start calling you Alexis and you can call me…"

"Carol, can we talk about this tomorrow? My only chance to get in shape by the time we sail is to commit to a daily exercise routine, beginning right now, which means I have to get to the gym. I'll call you later and we can continue this crazy discussion."

"You're right about the gym. I'm adding aerial yoga and Pilates to my regimen for the next two weeks. And don't forget to schedule a bikini wax," she said before she hung up.

I sent a brief email to Steph and Nate to let them know I'd be going away for a couple of weeks—boy, would they be surprised—and then headed to my bedroom to find my sneakers. I was pulling them out from under my bed when I heard the phone ring. *I wonder if that's the electrician*, I thought, remembering I'd been trying to reach him for several days. I dashed for the phone, a sneaker dangling from my left hand.

"Hello," I said a little louder than I'd intended. What was wrong with me lately? So, the ceiling fan in my bedroom wasn't working. It wasn't a crime that the electrician hadn't returned my calls, was it?

"Lydia? It's Rick Mann. I know you must be angry, so I wanted to explain," he added, his voice quivering slightly. "I didn't mean to stand you up last night."

"Well, I didn't mean to sit there and wait for you for forty-five minutes but I did, and frankly, it wasn't much fun," I said. "Not by my standards, anyway. And what the hell did you mean when you said, 'You didn't mean to stand me up?' Is that like, 'I didn't mean to rob the bank, officer?' You ought to know better than to try that line on me, Rick. People pay me money to help them figure out why they do stuff like that, for God's sake." I heard the tremor in my voice and felt the trembling in my knees.

"You don't understand," he said, an urgent note in his voice. "I had every intention of meeting you."

"You had every intention of meeting me? Well, we won't be meeting anytime soon because I'm going away on vacation. Thanks to you, I had a chance to take a look at what's been happening in my life lately and how stressed I've been. So, I'm going on a cruise, and at last I'll have time to think about how I can do things differently from now on. I've made some rotten decisions lately, like taking you on as a phone therapy client and trusting you were being up front with me. I'll tell you one thing I do know for certain—you really need some help. Unfortunately, though, I don't know anyone else who would be willing to take you on." And I hung up without allowing him to utter another word.

Perfect, I thought. *Now I could go on my cruise in peace and forget all about him.* It occurred to me I'd sounded more like a jilted girlfriend than a disgruntled therapist but I decided not to take time to process that at the moment.

I sprinted to the bedroom to grab my other sneaker as the phone started to ring again. *Oh no, Rick Mann, you're not going to get to me today,* I thought as I pulled my gym bag out of the bottom of my closet and headed for the door. *I'm going to the Panama Canal and you can go straight to hell.* I felt juvenile but validated as I flew out the door.

JARED

He had his mouth open to reply when Lydia hung up. He sat there, stunned for a moment, and then tried to reach her again. He wasn't surprised when the answering machine picked up, and he hung up without leaving a message. She probably wouldn't listen to it anyway. He stared at the ceiling as he replayed their conversation in his head. Actually, he'd said very little. Most of the "conversation" had been hers.

So Lydia was going on a cruise. Now, that was useful information, if only he could find out the cruise line, departure date, and destination. He knew she wasn't going to tell him anything—hell, she wouldn't even pick up the phone when he called back—but maybe there was somebody who could help him find out what he needed to know.

He turned on his computer and scrolled through the list of contacts in his address book. As soon as he saw the name "Chuck Barnes," he knew he had the answer. Chuck was one of Lydia's greatest fans. He'd called her up after reading a newspaper article about Project Ex and had completed several months of therapy. He credited her for changing his commitment-phobic tendencies and told everyone who would listen that those therapy sessions had changed his life. It was all bull, of course, but Chuck believed it.

He sent an email to Chuck immediately and asked him to contact Lydia—taking care not to mention Jared's name, of course—for some recommendations on cruises for singles. *I bet she'll tell him about her upcoming cruise,* he thought, *and if I know him, he'll get all the details.*

Sure enough, later that evening, Chuck sent a return email. Although bemused that Jared would seek advice from Lydia Birnbaum, Chuck had called Lydia immediately. *And you'll never believe it,* he wrote. *Lydia's going on a cruise herself—to the*

Panama Canal! He then proceeded to provide all the information Jared needed. He sent Chuck a quick thank you note and immediately contacted the cruise line to book a cabin on the *SS Vandermeere*.

CHAPTER TWENTY FOUR

For the next ten days, I was in a frenzy of preparation for the cruise. Usually, when I went away, I was obsessed in the days and weeks before leaving about what to take. First, I would dig one of my suitcases out from the back of my closet and leave it open on the bed in one of the other bedrooms. Then the ritual would begin. I'd agonize for hours about whether I should pack that adorable pair of pink sandals I'd bought on sale—cheap—but somehow had never worn. *If you don't take them now,* I'd tell myself, *you may never wear them, and how wasteful is that?* After all the discussions inside my head, I'd throw the damn things in the suitcase, telling myself that "one more thing," or two more, in this case, couldn't possibly matter. And even though Carol had told me the cardinal rule of packing was, "When in doubt leave it out," my cardinal rule was, "If it makes you look thin, leave it in."

When it was time to close the suitcase, I had to climb on the bed and throw myself on top of it. Then it was usually so heavy that after I shoved it off the bed—and realized it felt like it was probably one hundred pounds over the weight limit allowed by the airlines—I'd open it up and start pulling stuff out, cursing at myself for my lack of discipline in the first place.

This time, however, I was feeling particularly organized. I already had a few things piled on the bed in the guest room. I'd spoken to my friend, Lisa, a fellow therapist, and asked her to cover my clients while I was away. I was crossing "cancel newspaper delivery" off my three-page list of things to do before we left when the phone rang.

"Hello," I said, as I tossed my light green sweater with the cute little sailboat appliqué onto the bed. *It'll be perfect for evening walks on the deck after dinner,* I thought, ignoring the pile of brightly colored sweaters right next to it.

"Hi, Mom," my daughter Stephanie said. "Are you getting excited about your cruise? It's so cool you're going to the Panama Canal."

"I am looking forward to it. It's been a long time since I've been away."

"We never took any vacations like that when Nate and I were growing up. The only place we ever went was Hershey Park."

"So," I said, deciding to change the subject, "How's Les?"

"My former boyfriend? He's okay, I guess."

"Your former boyfriend? Wait a minute—last I heard, you two were practically engaged."

"Well, everything's changed since then. We broke up a few days ago."

"What happened? Did he meet someone else?"

"No, of course not. You always imagine the worst. Basically, he's just boring—so boring. And he always wants to do everything his way. Now he's decided he wants to go to graduate school in some godforsaken place in the Midwest. Can you see me in Idaho or somewhere like that?"

Since I'm geographically challenged, I had no idea whether Idaho was or wasn't in the Midwest—although it sounded as if it ought to be—but I decided this was no time to discuss geography with my seemingly heartbroken daughter.

"Grad school is important for him, honey. It sounds like he's thinking about your future together. A couple of years in a new place could be fun and then…"

"It's just like you to take his side, Mom. You drive me crazy. First you tell me Les isn't good enough for me, and then you try to talk me into staying with him even though I don't love him anymore."

I was silent for a few moments. "You didn't say that. I didn't hear the part about not loving him anymore."

"You're right," Stephanie said, "I didn't say it, but it's true. I don't love him anymore and I don't want to talk about this right now."

"But you're the one who called me. All I asked was, 'How's Les?'" I reminded her.

"Well, you say that, but I know you're trying to get inside my head like you usually do. But that's not going to work. I don't want to talk about my relationship with Les today."

I paused again, struggling with my urge to hang up. "What *do* you want to talk about, Steph?"

"I just wanted to tell you that I hope you have fun on your cruise and let you know I'll be in Philly next Saturday."

"That's the day after Carol and I leave for Florida," I said.

"I know. I was wondering whether Les and I could stay at the house for a few days while you're away."

"Whether Les and you… Wait a minute—I'm confused. Didn't you just tell me a few minutes ago that you're not seeing each other anymore?"

"I never said that, Mom. I just said we're not together anymore—you know, as a couple. We're still friends. My friend, Mary Beth, who lives in Philly, is getting married next weekend, and you can be sure I'm not going to show up by myself."

My head was starting to pound, so I ended the conversation as quickly as I could after assuring Stephanie that she and Les were welcome to stay at my place.

As soon as I hung up, I called Carol. "Listen," I said, "I'm ready for a vacation. Are you sure we can't leave tomorrow?" Just then, I heard the call waiting beep. "Call you later," I said to Carol as I switched to the other call.

"Don't hang up, Lydia, please," Rick Mann said. "I need to talk to you."

"I'm busy, Rick," I said, "really busy. I can't talk to you right now."

"Well, when can we talk? It'll only take a few minutes, I promise."

"I told you—we have nothing more to talk about. And anyway, I'm going away soon and I have a lot to do."

"You're really going away?"

"Yes, I really am. Even therapists deserve a break, you know."

"Oh, I know you need a break. That's pretty clear."

"You can cut the sarcasm," I said, struggling to keep my voice even.

"I'm sorry," he said. "I wasn't trying to be sarcastic. I'm just glad you're getting away, that's all. You work so hard…"

I didn't work hard enough with you, I thought. *You're still a pain in the ass.* "I can't talk to you right now," I said, surprised at the firmness in my voice.

"I was hoping we could set up a time to get together—you know, to discuss our business venture."

"I thought I made it very clear last time you called—I'm not interested in your business proposition. Therapy and business deals just don't mix. So please, find another partner and forget about me." *Gee*, I thought, *this vacation is just what I needed. I haven't even left yet and I feel stronger already.*

"Forget about you? You really saved me, Lydia."

"The truth of the matter is, you never needed saving, and actually, that's a good thing. But now it's time for you to move on and for me to go on vacation. By the time I get back, you'll probably be on your way to becoming a millionaire," I said, trying to laugh but realizing I felt sad for some reason.

"So I'll never get to meet you in person, and I'll never be able to talk to you again? This is it?"

"When your business idea has taken off and the money's rolling in, you can give me a call to say, 'I told you so.'"

"And then?"

"I suppose I'll have a few moments of regret because I could have been rich too, but I'll feel validated because I didn't allow myself to cross any boundaries with you."

"Cross any boundaries?"

"The boundaries between therapist and client. They'll still be intact, and in the end, we'll both feel good about that. I know we will."

"If you say so. But frankly, I think it would be a good idea if you followed your own advice once in a while."

"What do you mean?"

"Well, when I told you how I couldn't get past my anger toward my dad—even after all these years—you told me something I'll never forget."

"And what was that?"

"'You have every right to judge him'—that's what you said—'but try to judge him with kindness in your heart.' I feel like you're judging me right now, but I don't feel any kindness coming through."

"I really have to hang up now," I said, sadness suddenly washing over me.

"Well, I hope you have a great vacation. Where are you going, anyway?"

"You're trying to cross over those boundaries again. I'm going away and that's all I'll say. Take care now, Rick."

"Yeah, you too. And don't lose any sleep thinking about me," he said before he hung up.

I sat there, tears stinging my eyes. He'd done it again. Rick Mann had had the last word.

PART III—LYDIA ADRIFT

CHAPTER TWENTY FIVE

It was a beautiful spring morning when Carol and I set out for the airport. There wasn't a cloud in the sky as we boarded the plane at Philadelphia International Airport. When we landed in Fort Lauderdale, we jumped in a cab and arrived at the dock in no time. An hour later, we were on board the *SS Vandermeere*, helping ourselves to a lavish buffet. There were people everywhere—passengers in all shapes and sizes, some more sizable than others. They looked relaxed and happy as they piled their plates with pasta, an array of salads, fruit, chicken, fish, and some gooey-looking desserts too. The staff members, dressed in their crisp uniforms, stood out in sharp contrast to the rest of us. I looked outside to the pool area and laughed when I noticed that a number of people were already in bathing suits, stretched out on chaises, drinks in hand.

Before long, we were on deck six, wandering down a long, winding hallway, searching for our cabin. When we found it, we looked at each other and grinned. As Carol slid the room card in the slot, she turned to me and said, "Are you ready for an adventure?"

"I'm not just ready. I'm raring to go."

Our luggage was waiting for us—astonishing, considering how many suitcases had been hoisted onto this huge vessel. I surveyed the neat, compact room and checked out the tiny bathroom. I looked out the window and felt a thrill when I realized soon we would be surrounded by nothing but ocean. We glanced at our bags but agreed we were too excited to unpack. Besides, we had a lifeboat drill in fifteen minutes. We each grabbed a flame-colored life jacket from the top shelf of the closet and dashed out the door to the hallway, where we joined a stream of passengers heading toward the stairs.

We followed the crowd to the third deck, where we found even more people milling around, most of them with their orange life jackets already in place.

"Do we have to put these on?" I asked. "I'm going to look like a blimp."

"Put on your life jackets and take your designated positions," a voice boomed overhead.

"There's your answer. Come on, you know you look great in orange. Maybe some guy will find you so irresistible, he'll want to rescue you—right here on deck," Carol said, unbuckling her jacket and pulling it over her head.

With a sigh, I hoisted mine over my head too. "It's a little tight," I said, wriggling into it.

Carol giggled. "It's kind of cute, really. Just think of it this way—you'll look ten pounds lighter when you take it off."

"Thanks a lot. We haven't even set sail yet and already I look big and round, not to mention orange."

JARED

Jared watched the two women from the other end of the deck. He wondered what was so funny about putting on life jackets. He peered at Lydia's friend through his dark sunglasses. She looked nice, pretty but tight, with every hair in place. Not his type at all. Lydia, on the other hand, looked relaxed and carefree.

Jared had only seen Lydia twice—once on that TV show, when her energy seemed to light up the screen. The other time had been at the Oasis, that terrible singles place. He had thought she was lovely then, as he'd watched her from his seat at the bar, her dark hair curling softly around her face, her curves accentuated by a sleek black dress that was just short enough to show off her legs. He remembered how much it had surprised him to see her looking so sexy, so stylish—sultry, even—and so unlike the other therapists he'd known, who had always seemed to wear long tops and longer skirts, everything flowing and decidedly—to him, at least—nonsexual. However, as alluring as Lydia had looked that night at the Oasis, somehow she seemed more beautiful to him right now, with that smile on her face and her eyes lit up that way.

He turned to look out over the rail. *Get a hold of yourself,* he thought. *You have a story to finish, remember?* Steiner was going to have his ass if he didn't get the column in by the end of the month. His job was to watch Lydia and find out whether she could apply that so-called wisdom everybody talked about to her own life. She was going to fall for some guy on this ship and make a fool of herself in some way. It was up to him to watch it all happen and then let her adoring public know how vulnerable she was.

Jared took a deep breath and turned around. He caught Lydia's eye and she gave him a shy smile. They gazed at each other for a moment and then he averted his eyes, bending down to tie his shoe.

CHAPTER TWENTY SIX

"Hey, Carol," I said when the lifeboat drill ended. "Did you notice that cute guy over by the railing? He looked kind of familiar."

"Oh, I saw him all right. He was adorable, but he didn't look familiar to me."

"Well, I tried to smile at him but he seems really shy."

"That's never stopped you before."

"It doesn't matter now," I said, glancing around again. "He's gone."

I suggested we go back to our cabin to rest for a while, but Carol insisted we go to the sail-away party on the top deck. "Everybody will be partying. We came on this cruise to have fun, didn't we? And hey, maybe that cute guy will be up there too. You never know…"

"Okay," I said, "Let's go find ourselves a couple of margaritas."

"And maybe a couple of guys to go with them," Carol said.

When the ship set sail half an hour later, Carol and I were standing at the rail, brightly colored drinks in hand. "I feel rejuvenated already," I said. I looked around the crowded deck, but there was no sign of the mystery man I'd seen earlier. *Oh well*, I thought, *he's probably married anyway.*

"I have a feeling this is going to be a cruise we'll never forget," she said.

We returned to the cabin several hours later and did some unpacking. I dressed carefully for dinner, checking myself one last time in the mirror before I stepped out into the hall. Carol looked happy and very sexy in her silky white shirt and tight black capris. Her amber skin was glowing and the golden highlights in her soft brown hair seemed to accentuate the sparkle in her almond-shaped green eyes. She squinted, scrutinizing me for several seconds before announcing I looked terrific in my new hot pink top and white pants. "You look ten years younger already," she said.

"Let's hurry up," I said. "I haven't eaten in at least an hour."

"Stop thinking about your stomach. I'm just hoping we get seated at a table with other singles."

Carol and I rushed to the dining room and got in line behind the other people who were waiting for the early dinner crowd to finish their meal. We looked around, our hearts sinking as we saw couple after couple get in line.

"We may as well accept it," I said. "There aren't any other singles around here. Somebody sold us down the river on this one."

"Stop being so negative. We haven't reached the dining room yet. Let's wait until we get to our table and see if they remember we asked to be seated with other singles."

At that moment, the line began to move. Before we knew it, we were in the large dining room, the gleam of crystal and silver sparkling in the iridescent glow of a huge chandelier that hung in the center of the room.

"Wow," Carol said.

"Double wow," I said. "This is some gorgeous room."

"Now all we need are some gorgeous men."

We started checking out the table numbers. I felt like I was at a huge wedding reception, without a date, as usual. Finally, Carol found our table, #122. "There it is. Over in the corner, near the window. There's only one couple sitting there. All the other seats are empty. Come on, let's sit down before anyone else gets here. If there are any single men, we'll give them the opportunity to sit right next to us," she said, dragging me along with her.

As we approached the table, the first thing I noticed was that the man and woman who were already there were seated side by side, rather than across from each other. Since the table was rectangular rather than round, this meant at least one other couple would also have to sit side by side too, directly across from them. The man was wearing a denim shirt with an American flag embroidered on each front pocket. He had a round, florid face and a friendly smile. The woman was blond and heavyset and had on lots of makeup and American flag earrings. She looked at least ten years older than the patriotic guy I assumed was her husband.

Carol and I tried to avoid them and headed for seats at the other end of the table. However, the woman motioned to the two chairs directly across from them and asked, "Why don't you sit here? Then we can get to know you. I'm Brenda and this is my husband, Stanley."

"I don't even want to talk to them, let alone get to know them," Carol whispered in my ear. But we were already past the point of being able to ignore them without being ruder than either of us was willing to be.

"I'm Mia and this is my friend, Alexis," Carol said.

What was she doing? I'd made it clear before we left that I had no intention of posing as someone else. I wanted to lean over and smack her, but it was too late.

"Our friends will be joining us soon," I said, trying to brush them off. "We thought we'd all sit together."

"We'd like to meet your friends too. You can save the seats next to you for them," Brenda said.

We were stuck. We sat down, glaring at Brenda and Stanley reposing like two baked potatoes on the other side of the table. I prayed they would get an emergency phone call: "Table 114 just called. They need someone to lead them in the Pledge of Allegiance. Can you get over there right away?"

No sooner had we plunked ourselves into our seats than two great-looking guys appeared. They were engrossed in conversation and didn't even look our way as they chose seats at the other end of the table, exactly where we had wanted to sit. After a few moments, they glanced in our direction and then returned to their conversation.

"Hello," Brenda, who seemed to have elected herself mayor of our table, said. "Did you notice these two beautiful women down at this end of the table? Why don't you move a little closer so we can all get to know one another?"

I felt my cheeks burn and kept my eyes down, pretending to be engrossed in checking out the items on the menu.

One of the men—he was very cute, I had to admit—turned to Brenda and said, "Thanks for the offer, but we're happy right where we are." Then he turned to look at us again, an amused gleam in his eyes.

"I'm Brenda and this is my husband, Stanley," she cut in. "And this here is Mia and that's Alexis."

"Hello, beautiful ladies," he said. "My name is Michael and this is my friend, Gabe." Gabe gave us a shy smile. "We don't want to be rude, but we still have some business to finish before we get down to having fun on this cruise, so you'll have to excuse us this evening. However, once we decide to let loose and enjoy ourselves, you two better watch out."

When he grinned, he looked like a mischievous little boy who was about to get into some serious trouble. I smiled back, noticing that he had olive skin and gorgeous pearl-gray eyes. The dark stubble on his cheeks and chin only added to his appeal. This guy was a heartbreaker and he knew it.

"Well, boys," Carol said, "we're on this cruise ship to escape from work, and we're definitely looking forward to having fun. So look us up when you're ready to party."

The guys beamed at us.

Gabe—who had sandy-colored hair and hazel eyes—murmured, "Oh, we will, Mia." He had a dimple that burrowed into one cheek when he smiled, and Carol's eyes were shining when she smiled back at him.

"Nice to meet you, Alexis—is it Alexis or Alex?" Michael asked, his gaze sweeping over me and resting a little too long on the swell of my breasts above my V-neck top.

Carol, I thought, *you're going to regret you ever got us into this identity switch situation. But we're stuck now, and if you want a new identity, I'll be happy to invent one for you.*

"Either—really—whichever," I said, "Mia and I have a lot to talk about too. She's an archaeologist. She just got back from her latest dig, and I can't wait to hear all about it."

"How exciting," the mayor said. "I've never met an archaeologist before. I want to hear every detail."

Carol gave me a devastating look. "Oh, I don't want to talk about it tonight. Alex and I are on this cruise so we can relax and get away from our work," she said, kicking my shin hard under the table.

I grimaced and leaned down to rub my ankle. At that moment, our waiter came over and introduced himself. Brenda immediately launched into what appeared to be her complete medical history, reciting the list of foods that made her nauseated, gaseous, tremulous, congested, or just plain grouchy. *Hell,* I thought, *even my doctor doesn't know that much about me.*

The rest of us sat in stunned silence as she recited the names of foods I always thought were innocuous and even therapeutic: black pepper, red pepper, onions, garlic, avocados, peanuts, zucchini... My head began to spin as I wondered if the poor woman could eat anything at all. Glancing at her across the table, however, I reminded myself that she clearly was not in any danger of wasting away.

Our waiter, Reuben, who bowed slightly when he told us his name, seemed nonplussed by the seemingly endless list of foods which—to hear Brenda tell it—posed a serious risk to her health. Just a quarter of a teaspoon of black pepper, she told him, could send her to bed for days. I found myself wondering how I could get my hands on some, and whether it would be possible to sprinkle it on her food while she was in the bathroom.

They'd better give this guy a huge tip, I thought. *I have a feeling he's going to earn it.*

I glanced at the two guys at the other end of the table who now seemed frozen in their seats. I guessed they were trying to figure out how quickly they could get a new table assignment so they wouldn't have to eat dinner with Brenda and bear witness to the rashes or, God forbid, worse symptoms she had just rattled off in such rapid succession.

Everything kind of went downhill from there. Michael and Gabe wolfed down their dinner and excused themselves, muttering they had some important emails to send. Brenda made it through the meal safely, thanks to Reuben's diligence. As a matter of fact, she made it through several meals—the chicken, the fish, and the beef, not to mention two different desserts. *Carol wasn't kidding when she said you can order every item on the menu when you're on a cruise,* I thought.

After Gabe and Michael left, I had to restrain myself from ordering two of every dessert. I could see that Carol was depressed too. "Let's go to the show," I said. "I wonder who's performing tonight."

Brenda was happy to fill us in on the program for the evening, as well as the menu and theme for the midnight buffet. I glared at her and said, "You know what? I'm not feeling very well. I think I'll just head back to the cabin and go to sleep."

"Uh-oh," she said as Carol and I got up and prepared to dash toward the door. "Sounds like you had an allergic reaction to something. Maybe it was the fish…"

Or maybe, I thought, as I sprinted through the dining room to freedom, *it was you.*

CHAPTER TWENTY SEVEN

Carol and I returned to our cabin right after dinner. As soon as the door closed behind us, I turned to her. "What were you thinking? I told you I wasn't going along with that stupid identity-switch scheme."

"Oh, come off it. An identity switch is just what you need right now. All you've been talking about for the last two weeks is how much you need to get away and clear your head. You may not realize it, Lydia, but you've been obsessed with that phone client of yours. Maybe it'll do you some good to put Lydia aside and get inside someone else's head for a while."

Although I was still furious, I realized what she'd said was true. My compulsion to go on vacation had been fueled by an irresistible urge to run away from my life and my problems—most particularly, my problems with Rick Mann. I was upset about my research project too—annoyed with myself because I still hadn't arrived at any major insights, even though everyone I knew seemed to believe I was going to write some kind of seminal article about relationships.

"I'm angry right now so I'm not going to say any more about this," I said. "All I want to do at the moment is sleep, and that's what I intend to do. We can talk about this again tomorrow and try to figure out a way we can get out of this mess you've created."

"Get out of it? No way. I like being Mia. She's much more sophisticated than I am, and I have a feeling she has a reckless streak. Chances are even if we do get to have some fun with Gabe and Michael while we're away, once we get home, we'll never see them again. So why shouldn't we enjoy ourselves while we can? It's just a game, Lydia. We're not going to hurt anybody."

I marched off to the bathroom without giving her an answer, washed up, brushed my teeth, and went straight to bed, turning my face to the wall so I wouldn't have to look at her or talk to her again. Even though I was fuming, when I remembered the way Michael had looked at me during dinner, I felt a little shiver of excitement.

The next morning, I awoke with a feeling of exhilaration. We were at sea. Nothing and no one from home could get to us. We were floating somewhere—*God knows where,* I thought, knowing I really didn't care—out in the middle of the ocean. Well, maybe it wasn't the middle, but it sure felt that way, our pasts and our histories far behind us.

"I still don't like the fact that you forced me into this new identity against my will," I told Carol as we got ready for breakfast. "But I'll give it a try for a little while—since I have no choice."

"You'll love being Alexis," Carol said, "You'll see. We'll have to sit down and flesh out the details of our new identities. It'll be fun to figure out what Alex and Mia are all about. And, by the way, I almost murdered you last night when you said I was an archaeologist. Where the hell did that come from?"

I started to giggle, remembering the look on Carol's face when Brenda asked about her "discoveries." "I was just trying to pay you back for catching me off guard that way. But it's true you've always loved archaeology. You took those courses in college, didn't you? And you have gone on a couple of expeditions."

"I wouldn't call them 'expeditions,'" Carol said. "I'd call them 'singles tours.' Yes, it's always been my 'thing.' But I'm hardly an expert. What if we meet someone who really knows archaeology? I'll be screwed."

"Isn't that the point of this whole vacation?" I asked, ducking as she flung her shoe at me. "Oh, lighten up, Carol. Who the hell is going to challenge you around here? Everyone's out to have a good time. Nobody wants to talk about work."

"Except those two adorable guys at our table last night. Do you think they really had work to do?"

"Well, they said they were trying to get their work out of the way so they could have fun. But maybe that was the only excuse they could think of at the moment to escape from Brenda's tentacles."

"Her what?"

"Her tentacles—with an *n*. She reminded me of an octopus, the way she tried to pull us all in. And you have a really filthy mind."

"Well, I wanted to strangle her."

"Ditto. Hey, let's get to breakfast and then we can discuss our schedule for the day."

"I don't know about you, but my schedule includes some time to look for Gabe. He had such a sweet smile."

"What if I'm interested in Gabe too? What if we're both after the same guy?" I asked as I headed to the bathroom for a quick shower. "Don't worry," I said when I saw her face, which had suddenly taken on a greenish undertone. "He's all yours. Michael's more my type, although I'll bet he's a handful."

"A handful?" Carol asked. "I guess I'm not the only one here with a filthy mind."

"We're wasting time," I said, feeling my face flush as I allowed myself to think about Michael's body, which, from all appearances, was solid and sexy. "Maybe Michael and Gabe are early risers. Let's get out there and find out."

"Early risers?" Carol asked. "Hmmm, now I wonder what Dr. Freud would have to say about that statement."

This time I was the one who threw the shoe—straight at her head.

The day was blissfully uneventful. We spent a lot of time sitting by the pool and reading, eating, and talking about which excursion to sign up for when we docked at our first port. We were on the lookout for Gabe and Michael, but they seemed to have vanished. When they didn't turn up at our table at dinner that night, we were disappointed.

"Don't worry," Carol said. "The cruise just started. We'll meet lots of other guys. You'll see."

Over the next couple of days, I felt myself begin to unwind. Carol and I loved to spend our afternoons at the pool, reveling in the shock of the hot water in the whirlpool followed by the crisp coolness of a dip in the swimming pool. When we felt the least bit hungry, we ate. When we were thirsty, there was always a waiter available to bring us an ice-cold drink. We rubbed sunscreen on our bodies until our combined UV protection was about 300. Then we allowed ourselves to bask in the sun until we felt like we were baking in an oven and we had to return once more for a refreshing plunge into the pool.

"This is the life," I said on our third day, groaning as I turned to face Carol, who was lying on the chaise next to mine. "I think you and I have a lot to learn from Mia and Alex."

"I'm not going to disagree on that one," Carol said. "I feel so light, so free. Of course, I always feel lighter when I'm on vacation, but part of it is this new identity. I really like being Mia. I feel so uncomplicated."

"Well, to be honest, Carol—and I am talking to Carol now—you always were pretty uncomplicated, in a good way. It seems as if your life always went smoothly—until Randy died, I mean."

"I guess you're right. Before I lost Randy, my life was pretty easy. I never struggled, never worried about money, or about whether he was fooling around or anything like that. I guess I was lucky; my parents loved each other and adored my sister and me. There wasn't much I really wanted that I couldn't have. Until Randy got sick, of course," she said, her eyes filling with tears.

"Oh God, I don't want to make you sad, not while we're away. I just wanted you to know that maybe, in some ways, Carol and Mia have more in common than you realize," I said, reaching out to squeeze her hand.

"Am I interrupting anything?" a deep, very male voice said. Carol and I looked up to see Michael standing over us, an impish grin on his face.

I pulled my hand away and sat up, knocking the book on my lap right onto my big toe. "Ow," I said.

"It looks like you two really are close friends," he said with a wink.

"Don't be ridiculous," I said, picking up my book and closing it with a thump. "Mia was just remembering something that made her sad." I sighed and took a moment to think. "It was the time she took me to Greece on one of her expeditions and our beloved guide risked his life to save us."

Michael turned to Carol, amusement dancing in his dark eyes. "He risked his life for both of you? I hope he's still around to tell the tale?"

"Oh yes," Carol said, lowering her eyes. "It was very close, though. I don't like to talk about it. It brings back such painful memories."

"I understand," Michael said. "You know, Gabe and I had a great guide when we were in Greece a couple of years ago. Maybe it's the same one. What was his name?"

Carol and I looked at each other as the blood drained from our faces.

"Zorba," I said. "His name was Zorba."

"Zorba?" Michael asked. "Zorba the Greek?"

"I know it sounds silly," I said. "But some people in Greece have to be named Zorba, don't they? Well, our guide was one of them. His name was Zorba, and he took plenty of ribbing about it. But he was very good-natured about it, remember, Mia?"

Carol seemed to have lost the ability to speak, but she nodded, giving me a pleading look that seemed to say, *Stop!*

But I couldn't. I simply couldn't stop. It was such a great story, really, and not so very far from the truth—at least, the truth that I was making up on the spot about Mia's adventurous life.

"You see, Mia was so fascinated by the caves that she didn't hear the avalanche," I said, avoiding Carol's eyes.

"An avalanche…in a cave?" Michael asked.

"Well, I don't know what you'd call it, but…"

"It was a rockslide," Carol burst in, giving me a look that said, *Shut up already!* "A rockslide. Avalanches happen in the mountains, where there's ice and snow."

"Of course, it was a rockslide. The worst rockslide in like, a hundred years, or something like that," I said, warming to the topic. *Maybe I was meant to be a screenwriter.* I thought. *Maybe I should be writing fiction instead of that stupid article about Project Ex.*

Thankfully, at that moment, Michael caught sight of Gabe and waved him over.

"We were just talking about one of Mia's archaeology expeditions," Michael explained. "You'd never believe the stuff she's been through."

Gabe smiled at Carol. "I'd love to hear about your work. I'm pretty interested in archaeology myself, but mostly I just read about it. It's great that you get to live it."

Carol gave me a withering look. "Most people's eyes glaze over when I talk about archaeology. I'm glad you're interested. I'd rather hear about you, though. What's this fascinating business you're in that keeps you busy even while you're on a cruise?"

"Well, it keeps me busy all right, but there's nothing fascinating about it."

"Maybe not to you," Carol said, her eyelashes fluttering. "What do you do?"

"Michael's a writer," he said, "and I'm a photographer. I don't do weddings or bar mitzvahs or stuff that like. I'm strictly into portraits—kids, families…"

"He's being modest," Michael said. "He's the photographer to the rich and famous—celebrities, sports figures, movie stars. You wouldn't believe the people he's photographed."

"And you said your job isn't fascinating? You've got to be kidding." Carol said. "Sounds like you get to meet some of the most glamorous people in the world."

"You'd think so, wouldn't you? But the truth is, when you get close to them, most of those so-called celebrities are just people like you and me, with a lot more money, of course. Their kids are no cuter than anyone else's, and they have problems too. Yeah, I guess some people would call it a glamorous job. I just don't see it that way," Gabe said, running one hand through his tousled hair.

I'm so glad we decided to get away on this cruise, I thought. *Here we are, lounging by the pool, flirting with two adorable men. We'll probably never see them again once we get home, so why shouldn't we have some fun with our little masquerade?* Carol was beaming and I was feeling pretty happy myself—happier than I'd been in a long, long time.

JARED

From across the pool behind his darker-than-black sunglasses, Jared Abrams watched the two men flirt with Lydia and her friend. He stared at them, trying to figure out if he could safely move any closer. He'd give anything to hear what they were saying. One thing was clear, even at this distance—they were having a really good time.

That fucking Michael Miller, he thought. It hadn't worried him too much when he'd noticed Michael at Lydia's table the other night. He'd assumed she was too smart to fall for a scumbag like Michael, but clearly he'd been wrong. Jared peered again around the newspaper he was holding in front of him and saw Lydia put her hand on Michael's arm. She was gazing intently into his eyes. *Hell*, he thought. *She'll be in bed with him by tonight at the rate she's going.*

Wait a minute. What difference did it make? He wasn't responsible for Lydia, and God knows, she was supposed to be the guru on relationships, wasn't she? If she fell for Michael Miller, it was her problem, wasn't it? And anyway, wasn't he following her on this cruise so he could prove she was just as vulnerable and clueless about relationships as everybody else?

But he hated that goddamn Michael Miller—hated everything about him. They'd been rivals for years, and once Michael had even borderline-plagiarized something Jared had written. He should have pressed the matter, but Michael apologized, said it was all a misunderstanding, begged Jared to leave it alone, so he did. But man, right now, he wished he'd ruined the guy—sent him in disgrace to live on some desert island or something.

Jared had to admit he knew very little about Michael's personal life. He'd never cared if he was married or had kids or anything like that. He had a feeling he'd heard something about Michael that was downright slimy, but he couldn't remember what it was.

He made a silent promise to check that out with the guys in the newsroom when he got back to Philly.

Pulling his baseball cap farther down over his eyes, Jared got up and moved quickly to a chaise at the end of the pool. From here, he had a better vantage point. He had to be careful, though. Michael knew who he was, and that was dangerous. The man could blow his cover, and then he'd never get to finish his story. If Lydia found out who he was, it would ruin everything—everything. No, Jared—and Rick Mann, for sure—had to stay in the background so he could put his story to bed and find some peace at last. Lydia was in his head too much of the time already—and now she was right in front of his eyes as well. Though, whose fault was that?

He kept his face hidden behind his newspaper and drifted a couple of chairs closer to Lydia and her friend. They were still deep in conversation with the two men and never glanced his way.

"Are you following me?" he heard someone ask. He lowered the newspaper slightly and looked over at the next chaise. A woman in a bright pink bathing suit that revealed altogether too much as far as he was concerned was smiling at him.

"Hi there," she said in a thick New York accent. "I don't mind if you follow me. It's actually kind of cute." She fluttered her eyelashes and leaned over, her mountainous breasts hovering over him like birds of prey.

"So sorry," Jared said. "I was just trying to find a shady spot over here." He saw the disappointment on her face and said, "You look great in that bathing suit. If I weren't engaged…"

"You're engaged?" she asked, leaning back again on her chaise. Her eyes narrowed. "So, where's your fiancée?"

Jared squirmed. "She's in the cabin," he said, "taking a nap. She's not feeling too well." *Why did I just tell her I'm engaged?* he asked himself.

"Well, I'm sure you're lonely out here all by yourself, but I really can't spend time chatting with you. Sorry, but I'm looking for guys who are unattached. I could have sworn you were flirting with me."

"I would never cheat on Gail. We've been together for seven years," he said, doing his best to end the conversation.

"Seven years? No wonder she's not feeling well. That's not for me," she said, shaking her head. "If a man can't commit, it's over. Maybe," she said after a moment, "that's why I'm still alone."

"Hmmm…maybe," Jared said. She glared at him. "Well, everyone knows we guys are all commitment-phobes at heart anyway," he added quickly.

"You can say that again," she said, returning to her book. "I'm not going to disagree with you there."

Jared said a silent prayer of thanks as she bent her head over the book. He didn't feel like talking to anyone. He wanted to move closer so he could hear what Lydia and her friend were saying, but he was afraid Michael would notice him. It might be worth the risk, though. Those four were so into one another, they probably wouldn't have noticed if he took off his bathing suit and draped it over his head.

Just as he was about to make his move, Lydia stood up and stretched. "I'm going to relax for a while in the whirlpool. Anyone care to join me?" she asked, looking right at Michael.

"I'm game," he said, getting up so quickly he almost knocked over his chair.

"Mia, would you like to see the three o'clock movie? It's something with Tom Hanks. I forgot the name, but it sounded good. Hopefully, it's not the one about being shipwrecked," Gabe said. "I've had enough sun for today."

"Me too," Carol said. "Give me ten minutes to change and I'll meet you. Where is it?"

"Deck eight," Gabe said. "See you in a few…"

Jared was having trouble controlling his building rage. These guys really knew how to move. How could Lydia be so stupid? Couldn't she see what a phony Miller was? Was it possible she could be falling for him? Boy, was he glad she wasn't his therapist anymore—or Rick's therapist, anyway. He'd never even be able to pretend to take her advice again, now that he knew she was so undiscriminating about the men in her own life.

He waited until Lydia and Michael climbed into the whirlpool, then he folded up his newspaper, tucking it under his arm. Keeping his gaze on the deck, he slipped out the door. He hated to leave Lydia alone with Michael, but what could he do? He pictured them, side by side in that churning whirlpool, their bodies rubbing against each other. He shook his head to clear the disturbing images from his mind and started to jog toward the elevator. *What he needed,* he told himself, *was a shower—a nice, cold shower to calm his nerves. Or maybe a warm shower and a cold drink would be better.*

CHAPTER TWENTY EIGHT

By five o'clock, I was exhausted so I returned to the cabin for a refreshing nap before dinner. Carol had just stepped out of the shower when I arrived. She emerged from the bathroom in her robe with a towel around her hair, face flushed and eyes bright with excitement.

"Well," she said, "I don't know about you, but I'm having the time of my life."

"You're not going to hear any complaints from me. Michael Miller is the best thing that's happened to me in a long time, or at least I think he is."

"Go ahead and say it. He's perfect—smart, funny, sexy—and he's definitely after you. He's just the kind of man you've been looking for, and you know it."

I felt my face redden as I peeled back the bedspread and threw myself on my bed. "You're probably right, Carol, but you know me. I'm a pessimist when it comes to men. I'm allowing myself to feel happy at the moment, but I'm also waiting for something to happen—something that will ruin everything."

"Well, I'm no therapist," Carol said, plopping herself on her bed and fluffing up the pillows, "but frankly, I think you should lighten up a little and enjoy it while it lasts. That's what I'm planning to do."

"I know you're going to kill me if I mention anything about our lives back home, but to tell you the truth, I really miss my radio show. I was so burned out before we left that even my show didn't excite me anymore. But now that I'm away from it, I realize how it's become a part of me. I hope my listeners don't forget about me while I'm away. With my luck, the therapist who's filling in for me has already become ten times more popular than I'll ever be."

"Lydia, you're being ridiculous. Your fans love you and you know it. We'll only be away for ten days—not ten years. Relax and get a grip."

"You're right. I'm being totally neurotic about this. And, by the way, I don't like to think of them as fans. They're my listeners."

"In your world, they're listeners. In mine, they're fans. Either way, they adore you, along with your neuroses. You don't have anything to worry about. I'm sure they're all waiting for you to return so they can dump their problems on you again."

"I swear I won't even mention my radio show again. What was I thinking? Once I get home, I'll be in over my head just like before, swamped by all my commitments. I have to finish up the interviews for my research project, and then I have to write that stupid article, not to mention that my clients will be calling as soon as I walk in the door. You're right—my radio show and everything else will be right there, waiting for me as soon as I get back."

"So, now that we nipped that problem in the bud, I have a question for you," Carol said.

I gave her a suspicious glance. "What kind of question?"

"It's a simple one, really. What do you think of Gabe, now that we've had a chance to get to know him a little?"

"I think he's terrific. You two were made for each other—especially with your passion for archaeology."

"Don't you dare bring that up again," Carol said, leaning back and grabbing *People* magazine from the stack on her nightstand. "Forget the archaeology crap. I told Gabe it's just a hobby. I also told him you get carried away sometimes and exaggerate just a little."

"You told him I'm a liar? Thanks a lot. Now Michael will never believe anything I say. Not that he would anyway once he, you know, sees my driver's license or any other form of identification without the name 'Alexis' on it."

"Lydia, stop being so damn literal. We're not hurting anybody with our new identities and we're having fun. And if we're toying a little with these guys, what the hell. We don't owe them anything and they're here for the same reason we are—to escape from their lives for a while. We're just helping them escape a little more than they realized."

"Okay, if you say so," I said, suddenly feeling exhausted and settling down for a catnap.

"While you're taking a nap, I'll catch up on my reading," Carol said. "And, by the way, Gabe suggested that we all meet for a drink before dinner around seven."

"Well, then, Mia dear," I said, "I'd better get some beauty rest. It may be a late night tonight."

When the four of us arrived in the dining room at 8:15, I could feel Brenda's beady eyes following us as we made our way to Table 122.

"Well, looks like you've all hit it off. I was wondering where you were. I thought you were going to miss the appetizers. I ordered the lobster quesadillas. Reuben assured me they wouldn't have a speck of black pepper or red pepper in them," she said.

What a shame, I thought, as Brenda patted the seat beside her, urging me to sit there. I sat down with a sigh and glanced at the menu as Michael rushed to sit across from me. Poor Carol and Gabe were forced to sit side by side, directly across from Brenda and Stanley. They looked just as miserable as I felt. The rest of the seats at the table were empty and it wasn't hard to figure out why. The other people assigned to this table from hell had probably rushed to the office and demanded new seating assignments. *We're the only schmucks stupid enough to hang in there with these lunatics*, I thought, *but not for much longer. This is the last night I'm going to put up with this torture.*

Dinner turned out to be uneventful, and I was feeling guilty that I'd had such traitorous thoughts when the time came to order dessert. "Oh, look," Brenda exclaimed. "Rice pudding—my favorite." Even though she was ecstatic at the prospect of having rice pudding, she proceeded to order three other desserts too, including a hot fudge sundae. The more she ordered, the more full I felt.

"I'm going to skip dessert," I said. "I'm stuffed."

She stared at me, her flinty eyes reflecting shock and disbelief.

"No dessert? You have to get something. Try the raspberry tart—it sounds delicious. Don't worry, I'll eat it if you don't," she said, leaning over and patting my hand.

"You know," I said, suddenly remembering Brenda's peanut allergy. "I think I'll try the peanut butter pie. I love peanut butter."

Brenda shuddered. "I won't be tasting that," she said. *Exactly*, I thought.

Michael and I were engrossed in conversation when Brenda's rice pudding arrived. It looked delicious and I was just thinking that I if I weren't such a mean, vindictive person, I would have ordered it myself when I noticed her husband Stanley's face had turned whiter than the pudding.

He stared at the bowl with a look on his face that could only be described as horror. Pointing to the brown sprinkling on top, he asked, "Is that nutmeg?"

All of us stared at the pudding, which frankly looked scrumptious to me—smooth and creamy and everything rice pudding ought to be. I couldn't understand why Stanley and Brenda were now staring at it as if they knew a terrorist had infiltrated the ship, crept into the kitchen, and dusted it with anthrax.

"I think it is," Brenda cried. "It's a good thing you noticed."

Michael gave her a puzzled glance. "What's wrong with nutmeg?" he asked.

Both Brenda and Stanley turned, wide-eyed, toward Michael. "Brenda has a psychedelic response to nutmeg," Stanley said. "You have no idea what just a little can do to her."

The four of us sat there, our eyes riveted on Brenda. "A psychedelic response to nutmeg?" I asked, struggling to repress an uncontrollable urge to laugh. "What do you mean? If you eat it, will you put on dark glasses and start quoting Timothy Leary?" *Shit*, I thought. *I really dated myself just now. Why the hell did I mention Timothy Leary?*

Stanley had a serious look on his round face. "This isn't something to joke about," he said. "Some people, like Brenda, have out-of-body experiences when they have just the tiniest taste of nutmeg. Believe me, I checked into it after she flipped out the first time. It's rare, but once it happens—trust me—you'll do everything in your power to make sure you never eat it again."

I could feel the tension welling up inside me as I stared at the now sinister-looking bowl of pudding in front of Brenda. Michael gave me a nervous look and I shrugged, shaking my head. I figured he was probably wondering—like I was—whether just sitting near the damn pudding was enough to make Brenda flip out. Whatever she was going to do, I was sure neither of us wanted to be there to watch it happen.

I was about to reach over and shove the bowl away from her when Brenda picked up her spoon and began skimming the nutmeg from the top, dribbling it into the saucer of her coffee cup.

She then dipped the spoon into the remaining pudding and, as I watched with a mixture of horror and fascination, she ate every bite, a beatific expression on her pudgy face.

"Brenda," I cried, "are you sure you should be eating that?"

"Oh, don't worry," she said. "I took off all the nutmeg."

Gabe and Carol gave each other a furtive glance. Stanley smiled in relief. "Smart move," he said, putting his arm around Brenda's ample shoulders.

Right, I thought. *And we get to watch you go completely bonkers, because we all know damn well there's a speck of nutmeg in there somewhere.*

I have to admit that Brenda seemed fine and very happy, so I allowed myself to relax a little, although I devoured my dessert as quickly as possible. I noticed that Michael, Gabe, and Carol were shoveling in their desserts too, barely taking time to swallow.

Brenda yawned and began to rub her eyes. "I'm so sleepy," she said. "I just can't keep my eyes open."

"Well, it's a good thing your bed is only a couple of floors away," I said, watching her carefully out of the corner of my eye.

She reached for the hot fudge sundae she had ordered, pushing away the empty bowl that had once contained the questionable pudding. As she polished off the now-melting ice cream, her eyelids began to droop. The spoon was perched midair, halfway toward her mouth, when her head lolled to the side, plopping onto my shoulder. A moment later, she was snoring, her head nuzzling my neck, a fine line of drool dribbling from the side of her mouth.

I kept my gaze on the last crumbs of peanut butter pie on my plate and held my breath, willing myself not to look at Michael, Carol, or Gabe and praying I wouldn't laugh. After a few minutes, I turned to glance at Stanley, who was taking an odd-looking contraption out of his pocket. I watched, transfixed, as he pulled some kind of thread out of his other pocket and proceeded to wind it through the contraption. Satisfied, he gave me a grin and began to floss his teeth.

At that moment, Brenda's head jerked up and she lurched to the left. Before anyone could move to stop her, she slid off her chair and onto the floor. There was a clunk as her forehead grazed Stanley's chair.

I heard myself scream, saw people rushing over, watched as Stanley kneeled down beside her. Reuben, our waiter, came too, hovering over Brenda, his face pale. *Poor man*, I thought. *There goes his tip. Was it possible the stupid nutmeg had killed her? I hadn't objected when she ordered the pudding, so clearly I was an accomplice as well. But how was I supposed to know the damn stuff could kill her?*

We sat there—Michael, Carol, Gabe, and I—unable to move or speak. I said a silent prayer: *please God, don't let her die and please don't make us sit at this table again.*

I looked down and felt a sigh of relief when I saw Brenda heave herself into a sitting position, with the help of several hefty men who looked like linebackers. However, within moments, she slid back to the floor, turned onto her side, tucked her hands under her head, and fell fast asleep. As Stanley leaned over to check her pulse, she began to snore again.

Stanley looked up at us, the dental floss contraption hanging out of his shirt pocket. "Oh well," he said, "we wanted to get to sleep early tonight anyway."

"Sounds like a good idea," Michael said, grabbing my hand. Carol and Gabe jumped to their feet too, and the four of us raced toward the door.

"Do you want to go to the show?" Michael asked when we were outside the dining room. We stood in the hallway, bunched together, laughing until our sides hurt, gasping for breath. The tears streamed down my cheeks as wave after wave of laughter swept over me.

"I think we've had our entertainment for the night, thank you very much," Carol said as she started giggling again. "I mean, a psychedelic response to nutmeg—did you ever hear anything like that before?"

"No," Gabe said, smiling at Carol and pulling her closer to him. "And I hope I never will." I looked at Carol and the two of us burst into laughter once more.

"Let's get out of here," Michael said. "They may wheel Brenda out of the dining room at any second. How about if we head upstairs to the lounge for a little dancing?"

"Dancing?" Carol and I said at the same time. "You guys like to dance?" I asked.

Gabe looked down at his feet. "Well," he said, "I'm not the greatest dancer. However," he added, glancing at Carol, "I'll give it a try, although I'd feel better if you were wearing hiking boots. I'd sure hate to step all over your toes while you're wearing those," he said, pointing at Carol's strappy sandals.

"I think I'll take my chances," Carol said, gazing up at him with a look I hadn't seen in her eyes for a long, long time.

Embarrassed, I turned to Michael. "What about you? Are you in the mood for some serious dancing? Because I'm ready to dance the night away."

"Well," he said, as that boyish grin I liked so much took control of his face, "I can think of some other things I'd like to do all night long, but we can start with dancing."

My mind became a movie screen and I watched Michael making love to me, felt his hot kisses as his mouth moved from my lips to my breasts. What I'd already seen of his body at the pool—the dark hair curling on his chest, the powerful muscles of his chest and arms and the spectacularly tight butt beneath his bathing suit—made me feel quite certain that it would be a pretty damn wonderful way to end the evening. Of course, I wasn't going to let him know I felt that way, not yet, anyhow. And besides, I wasn't that superficial, was I—yearning for someone just because he had great abs and an adorable ass?

Gabe gave Michael a shove. "You're a pig, do you know that? These two have class—not like the women you usually hang around with. So shut up and let's get to that dance floor." He pulled Carol tighter, gave her a squeeze, and headed for the elevator.

"Okay," Michael said, bringing my hand to his lips. "I promise I'll behave myself if you really want me to."

It's a good thing he put his arm around me, because my knees felt weak. I was an easy target and I knew it. Would he know as soon as he put his arms around me on the dance floor that my son was the only man who'd even touched me in almost a year? "Oh," I said, "I definitely want you." I paused, feeling my face turn bright red. "Want to, I mean."

The rest of the night passed by in a dreamy haze. The four of us went up to the gorgeous, starlit lounge on the top deck. We drank piña coladas and strawberry daiquiris—or at least Carol and I did—and we allowed the magical spell of the night to envelop us. At around 2:00 a.m., I told Michael I wanted to get back to my cabin. Carol and Gabe were cuddled up next to each other on a banquette, chatting quietly.

We said goodnight to them and Michael walked me to my cabin. Hesitating for a moment at the door, he wrapped his arms around me. He kissed me and then we kissed again, his lips hot and urgent against mine. I felt myself melting into his body. I was shocked by the intensity of my feelings, the heat that was surging through me. I wanted him and yet I was afraid. *Who is this guy?* I asked myself. *What do I really know about him?*

"Michael, I have to go," I said, wriggling out of his arms. "Thanks for a wonderful evening."

"The evening doesn't have to end yet, you know," he said, giving me a quizzical look.

"For me it does. Everything was perfect, but now I'm tired and ready for bed."

"Isn't that the point?" he asked, leaning down to kiss me again.

I laughed and turned quickly to unlock the door. "Goodnight," I said over my shoulder as I scooted inside. I caught a glimpse of the shocked expression in his eyes before the door closed behind me.

I rushed through my nightly routine and got into bed. I knew sleep was out of the question. Tossing and turning, I relived every moment of the evening and heard again what he'd whispered in my ear while we were dancing, his body pressed against mine. "I can take you to sexual heights you've never experienced before." And while I believed him, at least as far as recent history was concerned—I mean, let's face it, I hadn't been climbing any sexual peaks lately—for some reason, I just couldn't go to bed with him yet. *It's too soon*, I thought. *I just met him a few days ago.*

"Sex isn't as important to me anymore," I heard Rick Mann's voice say in my head. "Not without feeling. Not without love. Damn you. You taught me that, Lydia."

I sat up, shaking my head to clear my thoughts. Why the hell was I hearing Rick Mann's voice now, when just a few moments ago I was reliving every second of my romantic evening with Michael Miller?

Damn you, Rick Mann. You don't expect me to follow my own advice, do you? I thought as I shoved the pillow over my head to block out his voice.

CHAPTER TWENTY NINE

Even though I spent very little time sleeping, I was up early the following morning. Carol was awake too, looking bright and very cheerful. *I wonder when she got in last night*, I thought. We decided to take a brisk, half-hour walk on the top deck before breakfast. Carol couldn't stop raving about Gabe, and thankfully she didn't seem to notice she was doing most of the talking. My brain felt fuzzy and I wasn't in the mood to do any soul-searching so early in the day.

I was standing in line at the breakfast buffet when the young man next to me turned to stare. "Excuse me," he said, "are you Lydia Birnbaum?"

I had tongs in my hand and was in the process of deciding whether to choose a yummy-looking banana nut muffin or a lusciously appealing chocolate croissant, but the question stopped me dead in my tracks. "Do I know you?" I asked, tongs poised in midair.

He laughed as he spooned scrambled eggs onto his plate. "I live in Jersey and I listen to your show all the time. I'm not stalking you or anything. I've seen your picture in the paper and I recognized you right away. I just wanted you to know I think you're terrific."

I tried to smile and thanked him for the compliment. Then I grabbed the muffin and looked around frantically for Carol. I saw her seated at a small table in the corner and rushed over to her. She eyed my almost-empty breakfast tray and gave me a puzzled look. "What's up, Lyd?" she asked. "Breakfast is usually your favorite meal. Didn't you see the strawberry pancakes and that huge tray of exotic-looking pastries?" She eyed me suspiciously. "You're not getting sick, are you?"

"No, I'm not sick," I said, sitting down and glancing around to make sure the man from the breakfast line hadn't followed me. "I lost my appetite, and you'll understand why when I tell you what just happened."

After I told Carol about the man who had recognized me in the buffet line, she said, "I know he took you by surprise, but, after all, somebody was bound to recognize you sooner or later. I mean, you are semifamous. But it's no big deal. Forget about it. Most people here have no idea who you are."

"You're right," I said, trying to push down my feeling of uneasiness along with a large piece of muffin. "He just caught me off guard."

After breakfast, we headed for the spa and luxuriated side by side while two incredibly young and beautiful women gave each of us a facial and then a full massage. I felt stress oozing from my pores and realized again how much I needed this getaway.

Carol turned to me, her eyes shining. "Aren't you glad we did this? Isn't this just the best?"

"How did you know what I was thinking? I know we're best friends, but this is too much. Now we even have the same thoughts."

Later, when we were back in our cabin, relaxed and glowing, each of us sprawled on our beds, Carol asked, "Lydia, have you spent any time thinking about that crazy phone client of yours and why he had such a strong impact on you? I've never known you to get so worked up over a client before."

"That's not true," I said, immediately defensive. "I've lost sleep over plenty of clients…"

"Lost sleep, yes," Carol said, shrugging. "Left town to get away from them—I don't think so."

"That's ridiculous," I said, but I knew she was right. Why else would I have gone away just when my radio show was taking off and my research project still needed so much work? What had Rick Mann triggered in me that had made me feel so desperate to run away?

"Listen," I said, shaking my head to clear away the negative thoughts, "I don't want to think about him right now. I just want to concentrate on having fun. You don't mind, do you?"

Carol grinned. "Those words are music to my ears."

By four o'clock, we were feeling sleepy, so we settled in for what had become our daily routine—a nap before dinner. I had just snuggled up to my pillow when the phone rang. Carol picked it up, gave me a quizzical look, and said, "No problem, Captain Jorgensen. She's right here."

"The captain?" I mouthed as she handed me the phone. "Hello," I said, wondering if I'd broken some rule and was going to be thrown in the brig. *The brig*? I asked myself. *Where the hell did that word even come from? I hadn't read a book about pirates since I was about ten years old.*

"Ms. Birnbaum," the captain said, his voice smooth as silk, "it's an honor to speak to you."

It is? I thought, but what I said was, "Well, it's nice to talk to you too, Captain." I glanced over at Carol, who was sitting on the bed, frozen to the spot. "What can I do for you?"

"Actually," he said, "I called to ask for a favor."

"A favor?" I asked. What could the captain possibly want from me?

"I believe you ran into my son, Kyle, at breakfast this morning."

"Your son?"

"He said you were standing next to him in the buffet line."

"That was your son?" Just my luck. Thousands of people on this cruise, and the one person who had recognized me was the captain's son. Maybe I'd offended him when I brushed him off and now the captain was angry with me too.

"I've been trying to be incognito," I said. "I never expected anyone to recognize me."

"Oh, he's become quite a fan," the captain said. "And he's seen you on YouTube too. I listened to your show when I was visiting Kyle and his family last month, and frankly, I'm impressed too."

"Thank you, Captain," I said, feeling my cheeks begin to flush.

"Could you possibly come and meet with me this afternoon? Actually, both Henry, the cruise director, and I would like to chat with you. We have an interesting proposition for you."

"Sure," I said, wondering what kind of proposition they had in mind. There was no way I could refuse. How could I say no to the captain? I certainly didn't want to upset the man. The way I saw it, my life was in his hands.

"What time did you have in mind?"

"How about 4:30? I'll send the steward to come and get you."

I looked at my watch. It was 4:04 now. "No problem," I said, giving my pillow one last squeeze. "I'll be waiting for him."

Sure enough, the steward was at our door twenty minutes later; he escorted me to a large room at the front of the ship where Captain Jorgensen and Henry were waiting. "Please sit down," the captain said, pulling out one of the armchairs surrounding a small round table that held a pitcher of lemonade and a tray of cookies. "Would you like a glass of lemonade?"

I shook my head and declined the cookies too.

"Ms. Birnbaum," the captain began.

"Please call me Lydia," I said.

"Lydia," he said as he leaned forward and looked directly into my eyes. He was a tall man with close-cropped, wispy blond hair. He looked striking in his crisp white uniform, and when he smiled, his clear blue eyes sparkled like sapphires

"We're in a bit of a bind," Henry chimed in. "And we're hoping you can help us out." Henry wasn't too bad on the eyes either. He had smooth, brown skin and deep brown eyes that crinkled when he smiled.

"What kind of bind?" I asked, as I calculated how old Henry might be and wondered whether he was single.

"Did you read about the show we're having on Thursday night?" Henry asked.

"You have so many events," I said. "And, by the way, they've been terrific—very well organized. My friend Carol and I are definitely impressed."

"Well, this show is right up your alley. It's kind of a competition…for couples."

"A competition?"

"You're too young to remember *The Newlywed Game* that was on TV back in the 70s," the captain said, "but our show is loosely patterned on that, except we're not out to humiliate anyone, of course."

"I've seen it a few times," I said, feeling flattered he thought I was too young to have seen the show that was a precursor to the current-day reality shows I detested. I remembered David and I were addicted to the show for a while and used to love feeling superior to the imbeciles who bared their souls every week. "But I don't think I'm the kind of participant you're looking for. I'm single, you know. Maybe you thought I was married because of my radio show…"

"We don't want you to be a contestant," Henry said. "We want you to be the moderator. We call the show, 'So You Think You Know Your Spouse.' You'll love it. It's right up your alley. You'll pick the winning couple too, with a little help from the audience."

"You want me to be a game show host?"

"We're hoping you can help us out because the person we were counting on had an unfortunate mishap," Henry said.

I gave him a look that said, *What kind of mishap?* "Sorry," he said, "I can't go into the details. Listen, you'll be compensated. We can't pay you anything, but we can offer you a $500 credit toward your next cruise."

The captain put his hand on my arm. "Lydia," he said, "please say yes. It would mean so much to me."

They really weren't asking for much, and who knows, maybe I'd enjoy moderating their stupid couples show. It sounded harmless, really. I thought for another minute, took a deep breath, and said, "I'm flattered you asked me to host the show, and I'd be delighted to do it." Then I asked them to excuse me so I could go back to my cabin and get ready for dinner.

Carol pounced on me as soon as I opened the door to our cabin. "Tell me what's going on. You can't imagine the things I've been thinking. Did they find out about our identity switch? Will we be prosecuted?"

"Carol, you've been watching too many *CSI* episodes. There's nothing wrong. On the contrary, we're in demand, or at least I am."

"In demand? What the hell are you talking about? Have you been drinking?"

"It's really very simple. The captain and Henry—you know him, that adorable cruise director—have a problem and they asked me to help them out."

"Help them out? What do they need?"

"No big deal. They asked me to host a game show on Thursday night—a take-off on *The Newlywed Game*. Can you believe they thought I was too young to remember that ridiculous show?"

"*The Newlywed Game?* How the hell are you going to do that?"

"As if you don't remind me every day that I'm the expert on relationships? If I can do a weekly radio call-in show, I can handle this. It'll be a piece of cake," I said with more confidence than I felt.

"Oh yeah? And what are you going to do when Gabe and Michael turn up at this little competition and find out who Alexis Steele really is?"

I hadn't thought about that. It hadn't even occurred to me that Michael and Gabe might come to the show. "They're single," I said. "Why would they go a stupid couples show?"

"You never know. I'm sure there'll be lots of laughs."

"Well, I'm giving you an assignment. Make sure they don't show up."

"And how am I supposed to do that—slip a mickey in their drinks?"

"You have to get a life, Carol, and get away from those TV shows you watch. All I'm asking is, keep those two away. I don't care how you do it."

"Well, I'll try. A *ménage a trois*—this could be fun."

"You can't fool me. I know you only have eyes for Gabe."

"You're going to owe me big time if I can pull this off," she said as she scooted into the bathroom.

JARED

Jared was trying hard to relax and get into the spirit of the cruise. He forced himself to spend at least a few minutes a day on his balcony, staring at the ocean. But no matter what he did, he couldn't seem to calm down. He wasn't sleeping too well either, and he walked around feeling tired all the time. No matter how much he tried to get himself into other activities, the truth was, shadowing Lydia had become an obsession.

It annoyed him that he couldn't remember the secret he'd heard about Michael Miller. The guy had gotten away with plenty of stuff over the years—stories with questionable sources, allegedly objective interviews that reflected his definitely biased point of view—but he also had a reputation for being a real asshole with women. Jared couldn't remember the specifics about Michael's past, but he knew one thing for sure—the man was cruising the waters in more ways than one. The schmuck had been flirting with several women. When he wasn't with Lydia, he seemed to be spending a lot of time with a glamorous-looking blonde who wore her tops cut high at the midriff and low at the neckline. Somehow or other, Michael seemed to be able to string along the two women at the same time, although Jared couldn't figure out how he got away with it.

On Thursday, Jared decided he needed a break and forced himself to go to the gym, hoping it would give his energy level and his spirits a lift. When he got there, he opened the door slowly, watchful for Michael Miller. Some people were gathered on the floor at the other end of the room. It looked like some kind of yoga class. He couldn't make out their faces, but he didn't think Michael would be the yoga type anyway. As he headed for the treadmill, a pretty young woman in a yellow and white tank top touched him on the arm.

"Hi," she said. "I'm Maryanne, one of the fitness instructors here. We're having a great class today. How about joining us? We could really use another person."

"No, thanks," Jared said. "I just came in to relax for a while. I thought I'd put in some time on the treadmill, lift a few weights…"

"Well, if you need to relax, this is the class for you," she said, pointing toward the other end of the room. "Come on, you're going to love it."

Hell, Jared thought, *if this is some kind of special relaxation class, I could definitely use it.*

"What's your name?" Maryanne asked.

"Chad…Chad Stevens," he said, not sure why he didn't want to use his real name.

"Well, Chad," she said, drawing him over to the group. "I'd like you to meet Alexis."

Jared looked down—directly into Lydia's luminous hazel eyes.

Jared stared at Lydia, waiting for her to tell Maryanne she'd called her by the wrong name, but Lydia just smiled—God, she had an amazing smile—and said, "Hello. Glad you can join us."

"Hi," he said, feeling more uncomfortable by the minute. What kind of damn class was this, anyway? And why was Lydia using somebody else's name? What the hell was going on? Did she have a reason to go incognito, just as he did? What could she possibly have to hide? He panicked for a moment, wondering whether she'd recognize his voice. *Don't worry*, he reminded himself, *Rick Mann has a New England accent.* All he had to do was be himself and she'd never make the connection.

"Chad, why don't you sit down on the mat behind Alex? You don't mind if I call you Alex, do you?" Marianne asked, smiling at Lydia. "Stretch out your legs and lean back just a little," she said, giving Lydia a gentle backward push in Jared's direction.

Maryanne arranged herself in the middle of the group. "Let's get started. Couples Massage 101 is about to begin."

Jared glanced around the group and noticed with a jolt there were couples only—eight in all. No one else seemed to be seated with someone they'd never met before.

"Now," Maryanne said, "everyone take a deep breath and blow the air out slowly through your mouth. Relax your shoulders, breathe deeply and quietly for a few minutes, and feel yourself begin to let go of any tension you may be feeling."

That's a joke, Jared thought. Just being this close to Lydia made him feel like there was a hundred-pound weight sitting on his chest.

"Let's start out with a simple back rub," Maryanne said. "And don't worry, you folks in the back. You'll have a chance to get a massage too. First, you'll give your partner an exhilarating back rub to get their juices flowing, and then you'll get a relaxing neck and shoulder massage to calm you down after all your hard work."

Just the thought of touching Lydia anywhere made Jared feel warm all over, the way he always felt when he was getting aroused. Jesus, if just the idea of touching Lydia made him feel this way, what would happen when he began to give her a massage? He glanced down at his clingy exercise shorts and wished he hadn't changed out of the bulky khaki shorts he'd been wearing earlier.

Rubbing his hands together briskly, he placed them on Lydia's shoulders and began a gentle massage, following Maryanne's instructions as closely as possible. He was just beginning to get into the whole experience when he looked up for a second. There, in the doorway on the other side of the room, was Michael Miller. Even at that distance, Jared recognized him immediately. He was chatting with a sexy-looking woman in a bright green top and hadn't glanced yet in the direction of the group on the floor.

Jared clenched his fingers and felt his heart lurch in his chest. He didn't realize how hard he was pressing down on Lydia's shoulders until she said softly, "Hey, Chad, take it easy, will you?" He apologized and lightened up a bit as he sorted through what to do. It wouldn't take Michael long to spot him, and then what would he do? He'd have a whole lot of explaining to do, not that he believed Lydia would ever listen to him. No, once his cover was blown, his ass would be grass and he knew it.

He looked around, searching for a way out. He noticed that the door to the men's locker room was only about ten feet away. If he made a dash for the locker room right now, he might escape before Michael looked this way. He jumped up quickly. Lydia slumped backward onto the floor. He heard her yelp in surprise or possibly in pain, but he couldn't risk turning around. "Sorry, something's come up," he said over his shoulder as he bolted for the locker room door.

Jared was almost at the doorway to the locker room when he collided with a woman who seemed to have appeared from nowhere. They both went down hard, sprawling onto the floor. Jared lay there for a moment, the breath knocked out of him. Then he opened his eyes and saw the voluptuous woman he'd met at the pool leaning over him, her overflowing breasts practically touching his nose.

"Oh, it's you," she said. "Are you okay?" Without waiting for an answer, she continued, "I was on my way to massage class. Even though it's supposed to be a class for couples, I figured, what the hell? Hey, were you there with your fiancée? I'd love to meet her. What was her name again?" She hesitated for a second before triumphantly calling the name to memory. "Gail," she said. "I remember now. Her name is Gail. Where is she? And where were you going in such a hurry, anyway?"

Jared lay there, speechless, grateful that her buxom figure was shielding him from the people in the massage class, but also aware that she couldn't stand there forever.

CHAPTER THIRTY

Maryanne and I and several other people from the massage class saw the collision and rushed over to see if everyone was okay.

"Are you all right?" I asked, rushing over to Chad.

"You must be Gail," the blond woman said, smiling up at me.

"Who's Gail?" I asked.

"His fiancée," the woman replied, pointing to Chad and giving me a funny look.

"I didn't know Jared Abrams was engaged," Michael Miller said, strolling up beside me and putting his arm around me.

"What?" I asked, recoiling in shock and horror at the name.

"Jared Abrams, the columnist from the *Philadelphia Globe*," Michael said, a condescending smile on his face.

"That's not Jared Abrams," I said. "I just met him a few minutes ago. His name is Chad Stevens. He was my massage partner."

"Well, maybe he was your massage partner, but make no mistake about it—this is Jared Abrams. And, by the way," Michael said, bending down to shake Jared's hand, "let me be the first to say, congratulations on your engagement."

"Lydia, I can explain," Jared said as he struggled to get to his feet.

I stared at him.

"Who's Lydia?" the blond woman asked. "I'm getting so confused."

"So am I," I said.

"You don't have to pretend with me. You see, I know who you are," Jared said, finally getting to his feet.

"Obviously you've confused me with someone else. My name is Alexis."

"You don't have to play this game anymore. I know who you are, but I can't figure out why you're masquerading as somebody else. Were you afraid people would recognize you and ask for your advice all the time? I don't get it."

"I told you, my name is Alexis Steele. I'm not who you think I am. And, by the way, you're hardly the one to accuse anybody of deception since it's pretty clear you were trying to fool me. Isn't that so, Chad?" I asked as I turned to walk away.

"It was wrong," Jared said. "Wrong to deceive you. But I had my reasons…"

"None of which she cares to hear," Michael Miller interjected, moving in between Jared and me.

"Lydia, please—don't listen to him. He's a fraud," Jared pleaded.

"Oh, he's a fraud?" I asked. "You mean, he's not who he says he is either?"

"No," Jared said. "He's really Michael Miller. But he's not the nice guy he's pretending to be. He's a liar and…"

"And you're exactly who you said you were, just a few minutes ago, in massage class?"

"No, of course not, but I can explain all that. I mean, I wasn't going to tell you who I really am—not yet anyway, but…"

"But now that you were caught, you have no choice," Michael Miller said. "Is that what you were going to say?" He was grinning now.

Just as I turned to leave, Jared blurted out, "When you judge people, keep kindness in your heart."

I spun around so quickly I could feel my thoughts sloshing around in my head. "What did you say?" I asked.

Jared's eyes were riveted on mine.

"Sounds like that song, 'Killing Him Softly with Kindness,'" the woman—who had since identified herself as Shana—said. "Very poetic. By the way," she said, smiling at Jared, "Are you engaged or aren't you?"

No one spoke or moved. All I could hear, over and over inside my head, were Jared's words—my words, really—the very words Rick Mann had repeated to me just days before I went on vacation.

My face turned white and my knees began to tremble. I felt weak all over, like I was going to faint. Staring at the man I now knew was that dreadful newspaper columnist Jared Abrams and wondering what connection he had with Rick Mann, I asked, "Who in God's name are you, anyway?" And then I fled.

CHAPTER THIRTY ONE

When I reached the cabin, I locked the door and sat down on my bed. I stared out the window and marveled at how calm everything looked outside, where the sky was blue and cloudless. Outside, everything looked so serene. The words that Chad, who had turned out to be none other than Jared Abrams, who had turned out to be—was it really possible?—none other than my former client, Rick Mann, had spoken right before I rushed out of the room swirled incessantly in my brain: "When you judge people, keep kindness in your heart." How could he have the nerve to quote my advice when clearly it meant nothing to him—nothing at all?

Just then, there was a knock on the door. "Lydia, it's me, Carol. Are you in there?"

I was silent, hoping Carol would go away. As close as we were, I didn't feel like talking. Not yet. Right now, I needed to be alone.

"Lydia, I know you're there. I have my keycard and I'm coming in. I'm worried about you."

"Please don't come in," I pleaded. "I really need to think things through for a little while."

"I saw your face before you ran out of the gym. I know you're upset, but I don't know why. Please, please, can't I come in for just a few minutes? I want to make sure you're all right. You know if I were in there and you were out here, I wouldn't stand a chance at sending you away before you knew I was okay."

I knew I couldn't continue to carry on an entire conversation with Carol through a closed door. Besides, she had a point. The poor woman didn't have a clue about what was going on. I couldn't blame her. I hardly knew what was going on myself.

I sighed, wriggled off the bed, and opened the door. We stared at each other for a moment before she came rushing in. As soon as she put her arms around me, I began to sob again.

"Lydia, what is it? What happened? I can't imagine what could make you unravel like this."

"No," I said, wiping my eyes. "You could never imagine what happened a little while ago. Trust me, 'never' doesn't even begin to cover it."

"Tell me already. I can't take it anymore."

"Look, I'll tell you everything—or at least, everything I know," I said, pushing her away and giving her a gentle nudge back out the door. "But not now. I really, really need to be alone."

"Well, I guess I don't have any choice. You obviously aren't going to tell me anything at the moment. I'll leave, but I'm only going to be able to tolerate the suspense for so long—half an hour, maybe."

"Make it an hour, and I promise I'll fill you in on everything," I said, giving her a tentative smile. "Come back in an hour and then we'll talk."

Carol gave my hand a final squeeze and then headed out the door. I sighed in relief, plopping down on the bed just as the tears began to flow once more.

The incident in the gym popped into my head again. I saw Jared's face turned toward me, remembered the look in his eyes. I thought again about my last phone conversation with Rick Mann, remembered how hurt he'd been, how he'd accused me of running away from my problems, how he'd asked me to hear him out, and begged me to judge him with kindness. I couldn't believe I'd been conducting therapy sessions all along with Jared Abrams, the man whose columns had caused me so much humiliation. What kind of therapist was I if a client could get away with a hoax like this?

I leaned over and picked up the phone. When the operator answered, I said, "Please connect me to Captain Jorgensen." She put me through to his extension and I left a message, asking him to call me as soon as possible.

When the phone rang about ten minutes later, I picked it up on the first ring. "You can see me now?" I said. "Thank you, thank you so much."

I glanced again at my watch. I wasn't sure how long it had been since Carol left, but I figured at least half an hour had gone by. I rushed into the bathroom and splashed cool water on my face. Then I stood and stared at my reflection for what seemed like a long time. "You can do this. It's the only way."

Grabbing my keycard from the night table, I scribbled a note to Carol, "I'm okay—talk to you later," took a deep breath, and headed out the door.

JARED

After Lydia raced out of the gym, Jared stood there, struggling to collect his thoughts. Everything had happened so fast. One minute he was in the massage class with her and the next minute he was on the floor, the breath knocked out of him. And of course Michael Miller had showed up in time to ruin everything.

It wouldn't take Lydia long to figure out he'd created Rick Mann for only one purpose—to deceive her and unveil her as a fraud. But so what? Wasn't that the purpose of the article he'd been working on for so long—too long?

Something had been shifting inside him for a long time now, but he hadn't wanted to acknowledge it and hadn't even attempted to understand it. The truth was, he didn't feel vindictive toward Lydia anymore. He actually felt a kind of connection to her and no longer had a burning desire to expose her vulnerabilities to his readers, or anyone else. As a matter of fact, that was the last thing he wanted to do. As he'd watched Michael Miller make his moves on her, he'd begun to realize how much he wanted to protect her from him. He had no idea why he was feeling this way, or what had caused the shift in his feelings toward her. He just knew he had very little desire to finish the exposé he'd been so gung ho about writing a few months ago. But he knew Steiner, his editor, would have a lot to say about that. He'd really sold this column—told Steiner he would get the dirt on Lydia Birnbaum and expose her to her adoring public as a fraud. How could he shift gears now and tell Steiner he'd been wrong?

Suddenly, nothing seemed more important to him than to apologize to Lydia for the humiliation he'd caused her and to ask for her forgiveness. He knew it made no sense that just a few months ago, he'd felt no compunction about his one-man campaign to destroy her reputation and her radio career. But now that he was up close and personal this way, he had to admit there was definitely something charismatic about her, something shimmering and special. It was easy to understand why people warmed up to her as easily as they did. Of course, that didn't necessarily mean she was a great therapist. But he certainly hadn't uncovered anything to prove she wasn't, had he?

CHAPTER THIRTY TWO

It took me only half an hour to convince the captain that my plan made sense. I had to bend the truth just a little, murmuring that my beloved Aunt Bessie was soon to take her last breath, but it had worked. He was disappointed, of course, but relieved when I said I'd still host the couples show that night. I was just grateful he didn't try to talk me out of going home.

Rushing back to the cabin, I peered in all directions, dreading another confrontation with Jared Abrams. I didn't want to see anyone except Carol. When I returned to our cabin, I was surprised she hadn't returned yet. *Maybe I'll have time to pack before she gets back*, I thought, as I began opening drawers and piling sweaters, pajamas, underwear, and socks on my bed. I was pulling one of my suitcases out from under the bed when she came in.

"What are you doing?" she asked.

"Carol," I said, taking a deep breath, "I'm leaving."

"Leaving? You can't leave. We're out in the middle of the ocean."

"Tomorrow, when we dock in Costa Rica, I'm taking an excursion of my own—right back home."

"Home? You can't go home. We're on vacation."

"My vacation is over, but you can still enjoy yours. You won't even miss me with Gabe around."

"Gabe has nothing to do with this," Carol said, starting to cry. "Why do you have to leave? This doesn't make any sense."

"Actually, it makes more sense than anything else that's happened today. I'm going home, and that's all there is to it. If you want to know why, I'll tell you, but then I'm not going to talk about it anymore. And I'm not going to leave this cabin until the ship docks in Costa Rica, except to do that stupid couples show tonight."

Carol looked me up and down and then sat down on the bed. "All right, so you'll go home. I don't understand why you feel like you have to leave, but maybe after you explain, I'll have some idea whether you've finally developed some mental illness yourself after all those years of counseling other people or whether this crazy idea about leaving tomorrow makes sense. Either way, I'll support you. It's just that—well, I'm used to relying on your decision-making abilities. I'm not sure about this one."

"I understand how you feel," I said, tears springing to my eyes again. "And I'll be honest with you—I'm not sure whether this is a rational decision or not. I just know I have to get off this ship as soon as possible."

And then I told Carol what had happened—how, right in front of my eyes, Chad had turned into Jared Abrams and then into Rick Mann. "Gabe already told me the part about Jared Abrams," she said. "I know he's written some nasty things about you, but I can't believe he was vindictive enough to go undercover as Rick Mann just to get a story. And I understand why you're hurt and angry. But why do you have to run away again?"

"You know my history—when things get rough, the first thing I want to do is run. I've been working on that issue my whole life. I'm not saying I'm proud of it. But it's how I'm constructed, and in my heart I know it's the only thing I can do right now."

There was a knock on the door, startling both of us. "Who is it?" Carol asked as I headed for the bathroom and called over my shoulder, "I don't want to talk to anyone."

"It's the steward," a voice on the other side of the door said. "I have a delivery for Ms. Birnbaum."

I scooted into the bathroom as Carol went to open the door. "Are you sure these flowers are for Ms. Birnbaum?" she asked.

"Oh, yes," the steward said. "Quite sure. The captain feels just terrible about her aunt."

"Her aunt?" Carol asked as I poked my head out of the bathroom.

"Yes, poor Aunt Bessie," I said. "We're not sure she's going to make it through the night."

"Oh, Ms. Birnbaum, I have something else for you. This is from Mr. Abrams," the steward said. He turned and picked up a huge flower pot. In the center was the biggest cactus I'd ever seen, except in cowboy movies, surrounded by an assortment of smaller ones in brilliant colors.

Carol pointed to a spot on the floor and asked the steward to place the pot there. He put it down carefully and then scurried out the door. Carol leaned over to pick up the card that was tucked into the soil and handed it to me.

"I've been a prick," it said. "Jared Abrams" was scrawled underneath.

"Well," Carol said, "at least the guy has a sense of humor. That's some phallic symbol."

"He's a prick all right. He asked me to judge him with kindness, but who wants to be kind to a cactus? If you try to touch it, you'll bleed."

I threw down the card and turned again to my packing. "I'm through with Jared Abrams or Rick Mann or whoever the hell he is." I shoved my dirty laundry into a duffel bag.

"I can see you're not going to change your mind. Let me remind you, though, that whenever I'm about to do something totally irrational, you always say, 'There might be another way to handle this.' I can see you're not willing to consider any other option at the moment. So, I guess you'll have to leave. I'm not saying I agree with you, and I'm certainly going to miss you—considering we're on this vacation together—but I understand."

"That's why you're my best friend," I said, giving her a hug.

CHAPTER THIRTY THREE

I picked at the early dinner I ate alone in our cabin and tried to take a nap before the couples show but I couldn't sleep. Negative thoughts clicked like a ticker tape in my brain: *you're a loser, you always screw up, you let everyone down, you're a fraud*...on and on and on. Feeling exhausted and wired from lack of sleep, I forced myself to get out of bed at 7:00. Henry had asked me to meet him at 7:30 so he could prep me before the show. It took all my energy to get dressed and brush some blush on my cheeks.

I rushed to the second deck and followed the signs to the "So You Think You Know Your Spouse" show. I was surprised to see that many of the seats in the large room were already filled. People were laughing and talking, drinks in hand. I put one hand on the wall to steady myself, trying to decide whether to stay or run when Henry caught my eye and waved. He hurried to my side and put his arm around my shoulder.

"So sorry to hear about your aunt, Lydia. You don't know how grateful we are that you're here tonight. And, by the way, we were able to schedule a flight to Philadelphia for you—first thing in the morning, about an hour and a half after we dock in Costa Rica. You'll be home soon."

"Thanks so much, and thanks for the flowers," I murmured, lowering my eyelids. "They're beautiful."

Henry had already told me there were three couples who'd made it to the final competition. "Let me introduce you to everyone," he said as two of the three couples filed onto the stage.

I met Terri May and George from Mississippi, who'd been married for forty-two years and assured me they had no secrets from each other, and Tanya and Frank from Toronto, who acknowledged they'd been married for "only" thirty-five years but had known each other since grade school.

I felt the professional Lydia taking over. She was the one who was needed tonight. There was no place here for the insecure Lydia, who'd been beating herself up emotionally ever since that dreadful incident in the gym. Taking a deep breath, I smiled at the couples and shook everyone's hand, doing my best to put them at ease. Everyone was counting on me to pull this off, and I was damn well going to do it.

Henry glanced at his watch and looked around the crowded room. "Where's our last couple?" he asked. "They should be here by now. I hope they didn't get cold feet."

Just then, I saw Brenda and Stanley—the "mayor" and her husband, my former dinner companions—approach the stage.

"Brenda! Stanley!" Henry said, greeting them like long-lost friends.

Their mouths fell open when they saw me. "What's she doing here?" Brenda asked in her squeaky voice. "You told us a therapist named Lydia Birnbaum would be the moderator tonight."

Henry laughed. "This is Lydia Birnbaum."

"I hate to break it to you, Henry," Brenda said, "but she's not Lydia Birnbaum. I ought to know—we had dinner with her several times, and her name's Alexis something or other. By the way, where have you been?" she asked me. "I could be dead for all you know or care."

I remembered the last time I'd seen Brenda, she was lying on the floor next to my feet. I felt myself turn scarlet as I did my best to explain about the new identity I'd adopted just for the cruise. "But now I'm back to being Lydia again," I said.

Henry looked at me with questioning eyes. "Nothing for you to worry about," I said. "Just a harmless charade." *Not like the rotten one Jared Abrams pulled on me*, I thought. "I hope you've been feeling all right," I told Brenda. "I really was worried about you that night, but I knew you were in good hands."

She seemed somewhat mollified by my apology. "So, it's true you have your own radio show?" she asked.

Thankfully, at that moment, Henry motioned the couples to their seats and escorted me to the podium.

"All the questions are ready," he said, pointing to the cue cards at the side of the room. "So let's get started."

The first round began with questions for the wives; their husbands dutifully left the room. "Terri," I said, "what will your husband say is on his nightstand at home right now? Please be specific."

"Oh, that's easy," she said. "Nothing. The man don't read a thing and he hates clutter. There's nothing on his nightstand—except the photo of his dear, departed mother, of course."

There was a roar of laughter from the audience. I thought it was pretty funny myself, but I tried to keep a straight face. I couldn't resist the next question, which I ad-libbed: "Isn't it kind of hard to make love with that picture of his mother right next to the bed?"

I could hear murmurs of support, along with snickering, from the audience, but Terri looked at me, her eyes wide in surprise. "Lord, no," she said in her lilting southern accent. "My mama's on the other nightstand. When George is in the mood, he gives me a cue and we turn both those pictures right to the wall. Works every time."

The questions got raunchier and raunchier, and the people in the audience—who were drinking fast and furiously—were loving every minute of it. *This is all in fun,* I reminded myself. *Nobody's out to hurt anyone. You may be feeling humiliated, but most of these folks are drinking so much, they won't remember anything in the morning except that they had a great time.*

Things were moving along and I was doing my best to maintain my dignity. After that first question, I made up my mind I wasn't going to do any more ad-libbing. After an agonizing hour and a half, it was time for the final round. The husbands had just returned for their last question. I turned to Stanley and, reading from the cue card, asked, "Who will your wife say is your favorite coworker?"

George looked at me with a puzzled expression. "My favorite coworker?" he asked. "Gee, I don't know. I'm not too friendly with the people at work."

Maybe if you didn't floss your teeth at dinner, I thought, *you'd find it easier to make friends.* "Well, think about it for a minute, George. There must be someone you talk to during coffee breaks or at lunch."

"I guess it would have to be John, the new IT guy. He's only been there for a few months, but we hit it off right away."

The other husbands gave their answers and then the wives returned to the stage. Everyone knew the show was almost over, and there was a quiver of excitement in the air.

"Who is your husband's favorite coworker?" I asked, turning first to Brenda for her response. Terri had a smug look on her face and Tanya looked pretty self-assured too.

However, Brenda's pallid skin had turned a shade lighter. She swallowed several times before she answered. "Oh, I know who his favorite coworker is. Everybody in Parsons Springs knows too."

"Brenda," I hurried to reply, "I think you're reading too much into this question. All we want to know is, who is George's favorite person to hang with at work?"

"I know who he hangs with," she said, lingering over the word *hang*, "but I can't believe he'd have the nerve to talk about it here." She pulled herself out of the chair and stood, looking down at her husband, whose face had also turned chalk white. "You bastard!" she shouted. "Did you think I didn't know about your torrid little affair with that hussy, Joanne?" She reached over to grab the pitcher of ice water that was on top of the podium and strode over to George.

"It was John," he said, looking up at her with pleading eyes. "I told them John was my favorite coworker."

"Then you're not only a cheating son of a bitch, you're a liar too," she said as she poured the water over his head. Flinging the pitcher across the stage, she ran down the steps and out of the room.

Henry rushed onto the stage and grabbed the microphone. "Well, everybody, thanks for joining us tonight. You never know how things will turn out when you have a live show, and I guess I'd have to say this one had a real surprise ending. Don't worry—everything will be okay. I'm sure Lydia will be glad to advise Brenda and Stanley how to find a marriage counselor when they get back home."

I just hope they both get home, I thought. *If their cabin has a balcony, one of them is a goner for sure.*

"And," Henry continued, "We're going to consider this a tie. It gives me great pleasure to present both of our other couples with a bottle of champagne."

"Thanks for being such a trouper," he said, moving away from the microphone. "Who knew that Brenda was a nut case?" I gave him a weary smile.

There was sporadic clapping and then some people in the audience got up and began to file out. It was over and there was only one thing on my mind. Now I could go home.

PART IV—LYDIA IN RETREAT

CHAPTER THIRTY FOUR

When I left the ship the following morning, I stood on shore for a moment, squinting in the bright sunlight. Costa Rica. I'd always wanted to come here, and now, before I'd had even one glimpse of the rain forest, I was leaving. *So what*, I told myself. *You can come back someday.* I straightened my shoulders and picked up my suitcases. Then I glanced around and hailed a taxi to take me to the airport.

The trip home was uneventful. I was too on edge to sleep, but I closed my eyes for most of the flight, praying no one would talk to me. As soon as the plane touched down in Philly, I felt tears spring into my eyes. *Home*, I thought. *I'm home. You're being ridiculous*, I told myself as I waited for my luggage. *Just a week ago you couldn't wait to escape and now you're acting like Dorothy in the* Wizard of Oz. *There's nothing waiting for you back here—just the same problems you couldn't deal with before you left.*

I'd thought about calling one of my friends to ask for a ride home from the airport but had decided it wasn't a good idea. I really didn't feel like facing any questions about my early return.

I was hoping the taxi driver would be the silent type because I wasn't in the mood for small talk either.

When I got home, I left my suitcases right inside the front door then went upstairs, kicked off my shoes, and changed into my pajamas. I closed the blinds and climbed into bed, letting the soft darkness in my bedroom envelop me. All I wanted was sleep. I felt fragmented, as if there was a jagged hole inside me. Sleep was the answer—it would make me whole again. I laid my head on the pillow and thankfully, I slept.

When I woke up, I knew I didn't want to get out of bed, so I turned my face to the wall and tried to sink back into slumber. But my stomach felt empty so I sat up in bed, trying to decide what to do. I went downstairs to the kitchen and opened the refrigerator, hoping there was something in there I'd forgotten to throw out before I went away.

But no, it was pretty barren inside, except for a container of orange juice that was almost empty and a few slices of cheese with hardened edges that definitely looked unappetizing. With a sudden surge of hope, I opened the freezer, expecting to find at least a half-gallon of frozen yogurt, but all I saw were those old tuna steaks I'd meant to throw out ages ago, along with a couple of veggie burgers and a package of frozen string beans.

Feeling hungry and still exhausted, I sat down at the kitchen table and thought about my options. I could call and order takeout. That was easy enough, and yet, at the moment, it seemed to require more energy than I could muster. I could call my mother and ask if she had some chicken soup she could bring over. I knew I'd regret it later if I chose that option, but the thought of the warm, soothing liquid that had been my panacea since childhood—"Jewish penicillin" as one local deli called it—was very appealing. Or, I could go upstairs, sleep some more and try to figure all this out when I woke up.

I turned off the light and headed back upstairs to my bedroom, ignoring the sounds my stomach was making. I tried to remember what I'd had for dinner last night, but I couldn't. I just knew my stomach felt as empty as my heart, and frankly, I didn't care.

As I trudged upstairs, I began again to review all the stupid things I'd done over the past ten months, all the things I should have done differently. I never should have started that stupid research project. It was a mistake from the beginning. What made me believe I was an expert on matters of the heart? The truth was, I didn't feel like an expert at the moment since, in spite of all the research—all the interviews with my former boyfriends and the men they'd referred to me, not to mention all the people who'd called in to my radio show—I still hadn't reached any earth-shattering conclusions. Or any non-earth-shattering ones either.

A cold fear crept over me. What if in the end I discovered I had nothing new to say about relationships—no words of wisdom to offer that hadn't been written before? What would my clients, ex-boyfriends, and radio listeners have to say about that? I could say goodbye to my radio career and my private practice if word got around that I was nothing but a charlatan.

And then there was the matter of my own love life—or lack of one—to consider. I had expected this project to be some sort of cathartic experience. Somehow I'd thought the insights it provided would propel me toward the ever-elusive goal of finding a truly intimate and loving relationship. Now I realized that was bullshit—pure bullshit.

I thought back to my terrible marriage. It hadn't seemed so bad on the outside, to other people. But David was a difficult, demanding guy, and we really didn't have much in common. He was charming, though—charismatic, people said—bright and very ambitious. We were married only a few months when I realized how lonely I still felt. He was a great guy to have around in a crisis—taking over, making phone calls, getting things done. But the day-to-day routine of married life—the little intimacies and intricacies that draw a couple closer together—were irritating and much too mundane for him. His intense way of dealing with just about everything had alienated almost every friend we had.

I'd been looking for intimacy—for a truly loving relationship—for a long time, and it was now clear I was never going to find it. And what right did I have to call myself a relationship expert when I was such a failure in that area myself? Despair seeped through my veins and made its way straight to my heart. What would I do now? I'd lost faith in myself and my ability to help people transform their lives. I couldn't even return to the life I used to have because everything—everything—had changed. How could I help other people when I no longer believed in myself?

I climbed back into bed and pulled the covers up to my chin, closed my eyes, and prayed for sleep. *At least I'm not thinking about food*, I thought as I felt myself drifting off.

JARED

Jared paced in his room. It had been a long trip home. The captain had not been pleased when Jared went to see him and insisted he needed to leave. "Something urgent has come up. I must go home immediately," he'd told the poor captain, who'd seemed to take it personally. Having two passengers "jump ship" during the cruise seemed to have unnerved the poor man. But nothing could convince Jared to change his mind or his course of action. And now that he was home, he was focused on one thing and one thing only—getting Lydia Birnbaum to accept his apology.

He had not had one night of peaceful sleep since the incident on the ship three days ago. He couldn't write either and had no patience for his colleagues, his family, or even his closest friends. As soon as he got home, he'd called a few of his buddies from the newsroom and asked what they knew about Michael Miller. Sure enough, it turned out the guy was a real lowlife. He'd been married at least three times, but the marriages never lasted more than a year or two. His latest girlfriend—a twenty-something alleged actress who'd made a name for herself on the porn circuit—had dumped him just a couple of months ago, and ever since, he'd been making the rounds of every singles haunt in town.

He'd thought about sending Lydia an email, warning her to stay away from Miller, but had rejected the idea. She would never open it. It was a waste of time for him to write emails that would only end up in some cyberspace graveyard. *So*, he asked himself as he paced around his lonely bedroom, *what should I do?*

The phone rang; he checked the caller ID screen and saw that it was his daughter, Emily. She was one of the bright spots in his life, but today he didn't feel like talking to anyone. However, he forced himself to answer. "Hi," he said. "What's up?"

"What's up with you? How was the cruise? I thought you weren't coming home until Thursday. I was just going to leave you a message now, in case I forgot at the end of the week."

"Uh, I left a little early."

"You left the cruise? I've never heard of anyone doing that. No, wait a minute, wasn't Grandma flown home when she and Grandpa were on that cruise to Hawaii? Remember, she fell and broke her shoulder and… Dad, are you okay? Did you get hurt or something?"

"No, honey, I'm fine. I just had a deadline to meet and…"

"I don't believe you. I talked to you before you left, and you told me you cleared your calendar so you could have a real vacation. I was suspicious, because you never go away, especially by yourself, and besides, I couldn't imagine you on a cruise with a bunch of old people."

"Excuse me, but they weren't all old. And even the ones who were looked pretty damn good to me."

"Don't change the subject, Dad. I want to know why you came home so suddenly. You're hiding something from me, and I don't like it." Emily's voice had risen now, and it had a slightly whining edge.

"Calm down, sweetheart. I just had to get home, that's all." Suddenly his voice broke. "Actually, there's more to it than that, but I can't talk about it right now."

"Dad, what's wrong? Now, I really am worried. When can I see you? I need to know you're okay."

"I'm okay, Em—honest. I'm just hurting, that's all. Emotionally, I mean. I did something I'm not very proud of, and now I'm paying the price—big-time," Jared said.

"Dad," Emily said, "you just don't sound like yourself. I'm coming over." And she hung up.

Twenty minutes later, she was at his door, and before long they were sitting at his kitchen table, a pot of coffee in front of them.

Emily looked beautiful in a soft green sweater that brought out the green flecks in her golden eyes. He couldn't believe his little girl was twenty-seven and an accomplished writer herself with one of Philly's top ad agencies. He'd told her the whole story: his attempts to discredit Lydia and her project in his columns, which Emily had read, of course; his decision to go undercover as Rick Mann in order to expose her as a fraud; how, in the end, he was the one who'd been exposed, and how he now felt driven to apologize to Lydia for everything. Emily sat there staring at him without saying a word.

"Dad," she said at last, "why did you come home early? Why did you leave the cruise?"

Jared tried to say something, but his lips felt frozen.

"I was shocked when I called and you said you were in emotional pain. I never heard you say your emotions got in the way when you were working on a story. As a matter of fact, I've never heard you talk much about emotions at all."

"I'm not myself right now," Jared said. "Ever since those damn therapy sessions with Lydia, I don't seem to know who I am anymore." He got up and began to pace around the room.

"Well, I think Lydia's affected more than your psyche. Don't be angry when I say this, but I think you've fallen in love with her, Dad."

Jared knew his feelings about Lydia had been shifting for some time. When he'd begun playing the role of Rick Mann, it had been a game and he'd enjoyed the deception. But over time, he realized it was his own heart and soul he'd opened up to Lydia in those therapy sessions—the sessions that had expanded him and softened his edges in ways he still couldn't understand. And, as the months of therapy had unfolded, he'd begun to look forward to his sessions with her. Although he'd called himself Rick Mann, it was he—Jared Abrams—who had grown to rely on her support. But had he fallen in love with her along the way? It seemed more than a little farfetched and yet...

He sat down and put his head in his hands. "I just want to apologize to her. Then I'll be able to get back to myself again."

Emily gave him one of her sweet smiles. "You'll find a way. I know you will." She came over and gave him a hug, but then glanced at her watch and groaned. "Gotta go, Dad." She gave him a peck on the cheek and rushed out the door.

After Emily left, Jared sat at the kitchen table, his untouched coffee long forgotten. He was racking his brain, trying to figure out how to get through to Lydia. She wouldn't talk to him on the phone or in person or answer his emails.

He thought again about his column. The deadline was the next day and he hadn't written a single word. Thank God he'd called Steiner and told him the column wasn't going to turn out the way he'd expected.

His mind was blank, but he forced himself to go into his study and sit at his desk. He turned on the computer, looking around for Millie, but he couldn't find her. Sighing, he began to write and was surprised when the words began to flow immediately. His fingers barely touched the keyboard, and when he was done, he felt lighter. He read it over twice, made a few changes, and then sent it off to Steiner.

When he stood up to stretch, he realized his stomach felt empty but he was too tired to even think about making himself a snack. He went to his bedroom and found Millie, curled into a ball on his pillow, her gray and white face nuzzled between her paws. Smiling, he lay down next to her, leaning over to scratch the downy soft fur under her chin. Within minutes, he was fast asleep.

Early the next morning, Steiner called and woke him up. "Hello," Jared said, his voice scratchy.

"Are you still in bed, you bastard?" Steiner roared.

Jared felt his stomach clench.

"Abrams? Are you there? I read your damn column this morning. I hope you know what you're doing. I'll run the frigging thing as long as you can assure me that you're not turning into goddam Dear Abby."

"Thanks," he managed to stammer. "Will it be in this weekend?"

"Yeah, may as well get it over with," Steiner said before he hung up.

CHAPTER THIRTY FIVE

So far, every day since my return home had been pretty much the same—I dragged myself out of bed by 10:00, showered, and then settled onto the couch in the living room, where I ate breakfast, lunch, and dinner in front of the TV. Then I was back in bed by 9:30. I was grateful that, since my friends and family thought I was still away, very few people had tried to reach me. Several days passed this way, and then, suddenly, the phone started ringing again. I tried to ignore the calls by snuggling deeper into the soft pillows on the couch and adjusting the volume on the TV to drown out the persistent ringing.

I can't hibernate forever, I told myself one night when the ringing just didn't seem to stop and my curiosity was boiling over. *I'll check my messages to see who called. I don't have to call anyone back if I don't feel like it.* I checked my personal line first. There were two messages from Steph—nothing from Nate, of course. He'd probably forgotten I was out of town. Then there was a frantic-sounding message from Carol: "I'm back. Where are you? I'm worried about you," and a message from Michael Miller: "Lydia? Are you there? I'd love to see you again. Can't we pick up where we left off on the ship? Call me."

There were two messages on my business line, one from Sam Sloane, asking me to call him right away, and one from a woman named Emily Andrews: "Hi, Ms. Birnbaum. I heard about you some time ago but just got up the nerve to call you. I really need to talk to someone about a very sensitive issue, and I was hoping I could make an appointment to see you soon." She had left her cell phone number and asked me to contact her right away.

I played the message several times. Emily's voice sounded strained. I wondered if she was in some kind of serious trouble. She'd said she needed to talk about a "sensitive issue." Could she be pregnant? Or maybe she was having issues about her sexual identity? I sighed. I wasn't sure I was ready yet to return to my role as psychotherapist. Psycho maybe, but therapist—what did I have to offer anymore in the way of advice?

I sat there, lost in thought, while the TV droned on. My mind wandered again to a phone session with Rick Mann, aka Jared Abrams. It had been a particularly intense session and he'd sounded close to tears at the end. "Lydia," he'd said, "I don't know what I'd do without you."

Why does he want to destroy me? I asked myself for the hundredth time as I got up and went to the kitchen, where I began a frantic search for chocolate. I wanted to grab a bag of peanut M&Ms but stuck a piece of gum into my mouth instead. Self-pity seeped through me; I allowed myself to wallow in it for a while as I chomped on the gum, thinking about whether I should give in to my cravings for M&Ms after all, when the doorbell rang. *Now, who the hell is that?* I wondered as I lifted myself off the couch and headed to the front hall.

It was Carol. I knew it even before I peered through the peephole. I thought about pretending I wasn't home, but she had a key and, knowing her, she'd let herself in if I didn't open the door.

Maybe, I thought, *she's here to rescue me and restore me to the Lydia I used to be.*

I opened the door. Carol's green eyes registered shock for just a second, and then she threw her arms around me.

"Am I glad to see you," she said, pulling back and looking me up and down.

"I'm glad to see you too," I said, surprised to discover I meant it.

"You look so thin," Carol said. "You're pale and you look like you haven't slept for days, and I bet you've lost at least five pounds. I don't know what you're doing but maybe I should try it too…"

I shot her a baleful look. "Trust me, Carol," I said. "This is not the way to lose weight. I feel like shit."

Carol put her arms around me again and patted me gently on the back. "I'm sorry, Lyd. I know this isn't the time for joking around. I was just trying to make you smile."

"I haven't been doing that lately, that's for sure. I think I forgot how."

"Come on, let's sit down and talk."

Once I started talking, I couldn't stop. I couldn't stop the tears either. As soon as I'd peered through the peephole and seen Carol, I'd felt them welling up in my eyes. She'd brought a box of tissues with her—"I know you always forget to buy them"—and a bag of lentil chips. *With a name like that, how could they possibly be bad for you?* I asked myself as I wrapped my arms around her and hugged her with all my might.

CHAPTER THIRTY SIX

After Carol left, I sat there and thought things over for a long time. She had just about convinced me to call Sam Sloane. Everything she'd said made sense. After all, I'd been away from my show for only a couple of weeks and—for my listeners, at least— nothing had changed. They were waiting for me to come back, looking to me for advice. My show had expanded to twice a week not long before I'd left for vacation. I was making really good money, doing something I loved—something most people only dream of doing. All I had to do was pick up the phone and call Sam to let him know I was back.

If I gave up on my radio career, I'd be sabotaging myself. Now, that was a behavior that was all too familiar. It seemed that whenever I came close to success or happiness, something always got in the way and prevented me from reaching my goal. I winced as I popped another piece of sugarless gum in my mouth and asked myself if that was really true, but I knew it was.

Over and over again, I'd set myself up to fail, in my career and my personal life too. It had started out as an unconscious process, but I'd been doing it long enough now to know there was a self-destructive pattern. Maybe I recognized it, but I sure hadn't changed it. Changing the pattern would take work, commitment to change—and something else that I didn't seem to have—the willingness to put myself first. The more I thought about all the ways I sabotaged myself, particularly in romantic relationships, the louder I chewed on the gum and the harder my head throbbed. *A nice dose of sugar would calm me down*, I thought, but then I remembered that I sabotaged myself with food too.

Totally disgusted, I spat the gum into the trash can and went to get a glass of water. I was filling the tallest glass I owned with ice cubes when the phone rang. *Who's calling now?* I asked myself as I grabbed the phone, pushed the "talk" button, and cradled it next to my ear.

"Lydia? It's Sam Sloane. I'm so glad I reached you."

"I've been meaning to call you, Sam."

"Well, I was beginning to get a little nervous since you haven't returned my calls. But I know how trustworthy you are, so I was pretty sure you'd keep the promise you made before you left."

"Promise?"

"You promised you'd be back on the air no later than the 23rd, this Thursday night."

"This Thursday night?" I asked, feeling like a two-year-old, repeating everything he said. I'd forgotten all about that conversation with Sam Sloane.

"I hope you've seen the ads." He chuckled. "Your face is on almost every bus that drives by. That new photo we took looks great. We're getting quite a response."

"Ads?" *Stop it already*, I told myself.

"They're in the newspapers too. Don't tell me you haven't seen them—unless you've been hibernating," he said, laughing again.

You have no idea, I thought.

"How was the cruise?"

"It was…unbelievable."

"Did you meet anybody? If you did, I'm sure your listeners would love to hear all about him."

"Don't get excited, Sam. It wasn't like that. I went with my friend Carol. It was supposed to be a girlfriends' getaway, and that's what it was."

"Girlfriends' getaway—sounds pretty sexy to me, and I'm sure our callers would be interested in hearing about it."

"I'm not planning to say anything about my trip, Sam," I said a little too sharply. "Sorry, I didn't mean to snap at you. I'm still adjusting to being back, that's all."

"Well, get some rest and enjoy your last couple of days of freedom. I'm looking forward to seeing you."

"Me too," I said, swallowing hard. "Can't wait."

The next morning, I sat at my desk, looking at the phone. Emily Andrews' phone number, scribbled on a crumpled pink Post-it, was sitting in front of me. After hours of persuading, Carol had talked me into giving Emily a call.

"It sounds like she really needs some help," she said. "And it'll be good for you to focus on someone besides that horrible Jared Abrams. You've blown this thing with him way out of proportion."

I sat for a moment longer and then picked up the phone and dialed Emily's number. She answered on the first ring. We scheduled an appointment for the following day at ten o'clock. I was surprised to feel the stirrings of curiosity inside me. I used to get excited when I began with a new client. It was uncharted territory, a new horizon about to be explored. I'd thought those feelings were gone forever but maybe I was wrong.

After I hung up, I took a deep breath and tried to meditate for a few minutes. I felt more nervous than usual, but, as I told myself, that was natural, considering I'd been feeling fragile and inadequate since the dreadful encounter with Abrams on the ship just two weeks ago.

The phone rang and I picked it up immediately, wondering if Emily had changed her mind. But it was Michael Miller.

"Lydia, I'm so glad I reached you," he said. "I've been worried about you."

"Sorry. I got your messages but… Well, I've been kind of tied up since I got home. How did you find me, anyway?"

"There aren't too many Lydia Birnbaums in Philly who have become overnight sensations."

"Fly-by-night is more like it. Here today, gone tomorrow."

"What's that supposed to mean? I hear you're a terrific therapist and a great radio talk show host. I'm planning to tune in to your show myself from now on."

"Well, you'd better tune in soon. I don't know how much longer I'll be on the air. Why would anyone want to take advice from me when I let myself get duped by Jared Abrams?"

"Lydia, you've had a shock. You just need time to recover, that's all. You're not going to let that schmuck Abrams ruin your career, I hope."

"He played me for a fool, and I played right along with him. Now he's planning to write a column about me and everyone will know what happened. My life, my career, will be destroyed overnight."

"You need to forget about Abrams for a while. How about if we get together? I'm sure we can find something fun to do."

"I know you're trying to help, and I appreciate that, but I just want to be alone. I'm not up to being sociable at the moment. Thanks for the offer, though. It's flattering to know you tracked me down."

"We were just getting to know each other when Abrams came along and ruined everything. Promise me you'll think about meeting me soon, even if it's just for a drink. It would be good for you to get out and forget about all this for a while. I'd really love to see you again."

Tears started running down my cheeks. I didn't even attempt to wipe them away. "I'm not sure I'm ready to go out with you or anyone else right now."

"Why don't you think it over and give me a call tomorrow? Let me give you my cell number—it's the best way to reach me. Maybe I should get your cell number too."

"Okay," I said, reciting the number. *I don't know why you want to go out with a loser like me*, I thought as I hung up.

CHAPTER THIRTY SEVEN

When the phone rang early the next morning, I just knew it was Emily. *She probably has cold feet*, I thought.

I was right—it was Emily, but she wasn't backing out—she just wanted to change the time for our session. "Is it possible I can see you this afternoon instead of this morning?" she asked. "Are you free at four?" The truth was, I was free all day, except for my session with her. But of course I didn't tell her that. Instead, I said I'd had a last-minute cancellation and would be happy to see her later in the day.

I might as well sit down and try to revise that outline, I thought as I pulled myself out of bed, got dressed, ate a quick breakfast, and headed to my office to review my notes. I sat at my desk, reading over my outline, trying to force myself to focus on the article. I turned on my computer and wrote the first paragraph, hitting the delete button as soon as I put the period at the end of the last sentence. I began over and over again but hated every word. Finally, I decided to forage in the kitchen for a midafternoon snack and then watch some reruns until Emily arrived.

At 3:55, the doorbell rang. Sighing, I turned off the TV and headed to the front door. I peered through the peephole and saw a slender young woman standing on my doorstep. As I opened the door, I smiled and extended my hand. "Hello, Emily," I said. "It's nice to meet you."

In just a few moments, she was sitting on the green couch in my office, her hands clasped in her lap. She looked so vulnerable and so young. She was really quite beautiful, with her pale skin and thick, dark hair that fell to her shoulders. She was tiny—no more than five feet tall—with fine, chiseled features and dimples that blossomed when she smiled.

"It's nice to meet you, Emily. Why don't you tell me a little about yourself and what brought you here."

"First of all, thanks for making time for me this afternoon. I know how busy you must be, and I really appreciate it."

Oh, if you only knew, I thought. *You may be my last client—ever. I've never felt more like a fraud.* But what I said was, "You look nervous. Have you ever seen a therapist before?"

Emily blushed. "To be honest, I would never dream of going to a therapist. It was my dad who suggested I see you. Uh, he's been in therapy, and he said it really helped him a lot."

"Your dad?" I asked. "Well, it's great he's been a role model for you in that way. Are you close?"

Emily hesitated and sighed. "Yes, now we are. But after he and my mom split up, we barely spoke to each other for close to three years."

"When did they split up?" I asked, feeling a wave of empathy wash over me.

"It was exactly fifteen years ago. I remember I'd just turned twelve when my parents separated, and my sister, Sarah, had just graduated from high school."

"You have an older sister?"

"Yes, I love her to death, but we're very different."

"What do you mean?" I asked.

"Well, she's such a homebody. She went to college then came back home and married her high school sweetheart. Now she has a baby and she's perfectly happy to stay home and be a mom. She's just so…normal," Emily said as tears welled up in the corners of her eyes.

Suddenly the phone began to ring. *Damn*, I thought. *I forgot to turn off the ringer again.* I heard the answering machine pick up and made a dive for the "stop" button when I froze. Not only had I forgotten to turn off the ringer on the phone, I'd forgotten to turn down the volume on the answering machine too. Jared Abrams' voice filled the room.

"Lydia, if you're there, please pick up. I need to talk to you right away. I'm truly sorry for everything, and I need you to forgive me."

I turned to Emily, whose face was devoid of color. She looked like she was going to faint. She stood up, her hands covering her pale face. Grabbing her coat from the rack near the door, she said, "I have to go. I'm sorry—I had no right to come here like this."

And before I could stop her, she rushed out of my office. I ran to the front door and called after her. "Emily? Emily? What's wrong?" But she had already jumped into her white sports car and started the engine. Before I could get to the car, she had backed down the driveway and was on her way down the street.

I stood in the doorway, dumbfounded. What the hell was going on? Everything had been going so well until the phone rang and then…

The phone call from Jared Abrams had seemed to unnerve her. But why? It was jarring, yes, and certainly unprofessional of me to have let it happen. But why had Emily rushed out like that?

Furious, I picked up the phone and hit the "redial" button. Jared picked up on the first ring. "Lydia?" he said. "I was hoping you'd call."

Before he had time to say another word, I exploded. "You listen to me, Jared Abrams. I know you think I'm the worst therapist in the world, and maybe I am. But I'll be damned if I'm going to let you ruin my career, do you hear me? You can write anything you want about me, but I'm not going to let you destroy everything I've worked so hard to build. Do you hear me? Do you hear me?" I was sobbing and I hated the choking sounds I was making into the phone. "Why can't you just leave me alone?" I asked, slamming down the phone.

Grabbing my purse from the table in the foyer, I flew out the door just as the phone began to ring again. I jumped into my car and started the engine. Then I put my head down on the steering wheel and let the tears flow as desperation welled up inside me. I had no idea why Emily had run off, and I just couldn't put any energy into thinking about it at the moment. I sat there, weeping and staring into space, until I remembered I had nowhere to go.

My cell phone rang and without thinking, I answered it. "Lydia, I'm worried about you. You just didn't sound like yourself yesterday."

"Oh Michael, it's you," I said, taking a deep breath. "I thought you were Jared Abrams."

"Jared Abrams called you?"

"He keeps calling me. He just won't stop. Why can't he understand I never want to see or hear from him again?"

"How could he have the nerve to call you after what he did?"

"My sentiments exactly. Why can't he just get on with his life and stay out of mine? Let him write his damn column—I don't care. Then maybe he'll find someone else to persecute for a change."

"Do you want me to call him? I'll tell him you're prepared to sue for libel if he prints that damn thing."

"Please don't call him. I don't want to sue him. I just want him to back off. Now he's saying he wants me to forgive him—that he's apologetic for everything he's done. Like I'd ever believe a word he said."

Michael was quiet for a moment. Then he said, "I won't call him if you don't want me to, but I think somebody ought to set him straight. But hey, how about if we meet for a drink tomorrow night? I'd love to see you."

"Sorry, Michael, but I can't see you tomorrow. I'm doing my radio show and then I'm going away for a few days."

"Going away? Where are you going?"

"To the place where I always go when I need to think," I said, deciding on the spot. "The Shore. I'm leaving first thing Friday morning."

The minute I said it, I knew it was true. I needed to get to the Shore. I had a desperate yearning to escape to someplace safe, someplace where I could think. I smiled sadly to myself, remembering I'd felt the same way when I left the cruise ship. Now, even though I was home, I was still yearning for safety somewhere else. Could I really blame this desperation to get away again on Jared Abrams or was he just the catalyst—bringing up unresolved feelings and insecurities from the past?

"I promise I'll call you as soon as I get home," I said. "And then we can make plans to get together. Okay?"

"Listen," he said, "I have an assignment at the Shore on Friday myself. I'll be in Atlantic City. Maybe we can meet up…"

"Maybe," I said, but what I thought was, *I don't want to run into you or anybody else I know.*

"Well, so long, Michael, and thanks for offering to help. I'll talk to you soon."

I hung up and then dialed Carol's work number. I listened to her familiar voice mail greeting and said, "Hi, it's Lydia. I wanted you to know I'm going away for a few days. I'm going down the Shore first thing Friday morning. I have a lot of thinking to do, mostly about me. I need to get my life back on track. Oh, and I'm not going to return any calls, so don't bother trying me on my cell. I need some time alone. Don't worry, I'm fine."

I hung up, found a tissue in my bag, blew my nose, turned off the engine and got out of the car. Then I went back inside to begin to make plans for my trip to the Shore. I sorted through the magazines I had piled on the nightstand in my bedroom until I found the "Best Places at the Shore" issue of *Philly Now*. I remembered reading a review of a brand-new bed-and-breakfast in the Atlantic City area. I started leafing through the magazine, searching for the review, but dammit—I couldn't find it.

I loved the small towns that stretched beyond Atlantic City—Margate, Longport, Ventnor. When I was a child—before people began building multimillion-dollar homes along the shoreline—I spent many happy summers on the beach in Ventnor, a small, charming, and once predominantly Jewish town just minutes from Atlantic City. However, they were residential towns, and I'd never heard of a bed-and-breakfast or a hotel opening up anywhere nearby. The new B&B I'd read about had somehow managed to open up right outside of Ventnor and I couldn't wait to see it.

I was getting frustrated and was about to give up when I turned the page and saw the article, along with a photo of the proprietors, Chris and Rachel Sandler. The phone number and address were listed in a box at the top of the page. I pulled out my cell phone and dialed the number, praying they'd have a room available immediately.

JARED

That evening, Jared was sitting at his desk in his home office, thinking about his column, which was supposed to run in just a few days. He wondered whether Lydia would ever read it.

Suddenly the phone rang. It was Emily.

"Dad?" she said. "I've decided to go to the Shore for a couple of days."

"The Shore? You're going to the Shore?"

"I'm leaving tonight. Something's come up and I need a break. I'm so disappointed in myself."

"Disappointed in yourself? What do you mean?"

She was crying—he could hear the gasps between her words. "I thought I could help you work things out with Lydia, but I was wrong, so wrong."

Emily—his usually composed daughter—sounded close to hysteria. "Calm down, honey. What didn't work out? What are you talking about? You don't even know Lydia."

"I'll explain when I see you. Right now, I need to clear my head. I called my office and said I wasn't feeling well. I want to spend some time by myself for a little while, but I'd love to have dinner together Friday night, if that's okay."

"Whatever you need. Will you stay in Margate, at Grandma and Grandpa's place? You know where they leave the key."

After he hung up, he headed for his bedroom and threw a few things into an overnight bag. *I'd better be ready, just in case she wants me to come tomorrow*, he thought. He was concerned about her, but he knew he had to honor her request for privacy for a little while. He'd leave for the Shore on Friday afternoon and get there in plenty of time for dinner. What the hell was going on?

He decided to go for a run and changed into his running shorts. As he was on his way out the door, his cell phone rang again. He checked the caller ID: Michael Miller. *Why is that bastard calling me?* Jared wondered, turning off his cell phone.

CHAPTER THIRTY EIGHT

I was touched by the warm welcome I received when I arrived at the radio station the following evening. Sam Sloane came out of his office and threw his arms around me. "Lydia," he said, "we're so glad you're back. Your listeners have been waiting for you."

I felt like crying. Here, at least, I was still Lydia Birnbaum, accomplished therapist, soon-to-be author, and talk show host. No one knew about the fiasco on the ship. I was in a cocoon—safe and protected.

I went to the booth and began to prepare for the show. The phone lines lit up as soon as I finished my short intro. The callers wasted no time letting me know they'd been anxiously awaiting my return.

"Lydia," a woman named Joan said when I picked up the first call, "I've been dying to talk to you about my new boyfriend."

"Tell me about him," I said.

"He's terrific—dependable, funny, kind, loves my kids…"

"So what's the problem? Is he unemployed?"

"No, he has a great job."

"An alcoholic?" I asked. "A drug addict?"

Joan laughed. "Lydia, what's wrong with you? I told you he's dependable and he has a steady job. It's nothing like that…"

"What is it then? Because frankly, there are lots of people waiting to get some air time with me, and it sounds like you have it all together at the moment."

"He's short," she said.

"Short?" I asked. "How short?"

"About five one, I guess. Much shorter than I am."

"And how tall are you?"

"Five eleven. Over six feet in heels."

"I'd forget about the heels. Didn't you know how tall he was before you agreed to go out with him?"

"Not really. We found each other on the Internet. There was only a headshot next to his profile. He described his height as 'average' so I figured he was 5'9" or 5'10"."

"So I guess you were kind of surprised when you met him."

"I let him pick me up at home. Kind of stupid, I know, but he sounded so nice. He rang the bell, but when I looked through the peephole, I thought there was nobody there."

"Was it some kind of prank?"

"No, nothing like that. He was so short, I couldn't see him. But I found him as soon as I opened the door."

"You honestly couldn't see him when you looked through the peephole?"

"Nope. I opened the door, looked down, and there he was."

The crew in the sound booth was going crazy. They were doubled over with laughter, wiping their eyes.

I'm in trouble now, I thought. *My sponsors will probably drop my show once they start receiving hate mail from "Short but Equal" support groups around the tri-state area.* I did my best to turn my interchange with Joan into a discussion of how prejudices constrict our lives. I reminded her of the positive things she'd said about her boyfriend and suggested she try to live with the situation if she could. I knew I was a hypocrite since I'd ended more than one relationship because the guy didn't meet my "stature standards." It was stupid, I knew, but I'd always had a "thing" about tall men and knew I'd never get past it. However, there was no reason Joan needed to know that.

"When we go out I always walk on the outside," she said. "That way, if someone I know drives by, they don't even know he's there."

"Whatever works for you," I said as I ended the call before I burst into uncontrollable laughter.

There were a couple of serious calls after that, one from a guy whose wife had just run off with his best friend. Several listeners who'd been abandoned by their spouses or lovers called in to give him encouragement and support. I felt proud to be the host of this amazing show that brought people together and helped them resolve their problems.

Everything was going smoothly and my spirits were soaring. At 9:45, I glanced at the clock. *Only fifteen more minutes,* I thought, *and then I can go home.* Several phone lines were blinking. I picked up the next call and said, "This is Lydia. How can I help you tonight?"

"Lydia," Jared Abrams said. "Please don't hang up on me. There's something important I need to tell you."

"Don't do this," I said, feeling the hairs on the back of my neck start to quiver. "Not on my radio show—please."

"I have no other way to reach you. You won't talk to me, and I know you won't read my emails. I wanted to warn you about someone you met on the ship. I know for sure he can't be trusted."

I tried to take a deep breath, but I couldn't. My chest felt tight and I was afraid I was going to faint.

Sam Sloane poked his head into my booth and slid a note onto my console. "Take line two now. The caller says it's urgent." He gave me a quizzical look and shrugged his shoulders.

I shrugged back, rolling my eyes as I put Jared on hold and picked up the other call. I glanced at the clock: 9:55. Five minutes and I was out of here.

I hit the talk button and then heard another familiar voice. "Don't listen to him," Michael Miller said. "He's lying through his teeth. The man's looking for a lawsuit, and he's going to find himself in court very soon."

I sat there, gripping the sides of my chair, taking in gulps of air. I looked again at the clock. Only two minutes to go.

"I think it's time for a word from our sponsor," I squeaked, ending the call. Then I grabbed my purse and rushed out the door.

Sam was standing outside his office, waiting for me. "I'm not feeling very well. Please ask Joanne to sign off for me tonight. I'm going to the Shore for a few days, but I'll call you," I breathed as I whizzed by. "I'll explain everything when I get back."

Then I ran to the parking lot and jumped into my car.

CHAPTER THIRTY NINE

I didn't check my messages when I got in. I knew Michael had probably called, and possibly Jared too. I didn't want to talk to them or anyone else. I was furious they'd used my radio show for their propaganda—furious they'd violated the place where I still felt safe, confident, and secure.

No, I reminded myself. *You still have one more refuge—the Shore.*

I was so worn out, I could barely keep my eyes open. I climbed the stairs one step at a time, like a spent old woman, and went straight to bed.

The next morning, I got up early and finished packing. I was so glad I'd already made the reservation at the B&B. I didn't have the energy to focus on anything today except getting to the Jersey Shore.

There was very little traffic, and before I knew it, I was at the Atlantic City tolls. I followed the directions Rachel and Chris Sandler had given me, and about fifteen minutes later, I saw the hand-painted sign: "Sandler's Seaside Spot—5 miles ahead on the right." My heart gave a little flip-flop when I pulled into the narrow drive and saw the charming front porch, with geraniums planted in old-fashioned wicker planters along the railing. I opened the trunk, grabbed my suitcase, and took a deep breath, feeling the ocean air fill my lungs.

Rachel Sandler greeted me at the door with a smile, a tall glass of iced tea and a ceramic plate piled high with still-warm, home-baked chocolate chip cookies. I nibbled on a cookie as she led me to my room. "I think you'll love this room," she said. "It's my favorite. Whenever I need a break, I come here and hide out for a while. There's something so comforting about it—I planned it that way."

I gasped when she opened the door. The little room was decorated in shades of pink—my favorite color—with fresh flowers on the windowsill and pillows in a profusion of colors on the bed. Light streamed in through the windows and a ceiling fan over the bed lazily circulated the air. There was a fluffy chair with an ottoman in the corner. An adorable little calico cat was curled in the center of a crocheted pillow that sat on the chair.

"Muffin," Rachel said, "I've been looking for you." She turned to me. "I hope you're not allergic. I can put you in another room if you are. She's not supposed to be in the guest rooms, but I guess this is her favorite room too."

I laughed in delight. "Believe me, Muffin is just the kind of company I need right now," I said as Rachel smiled and then slipped out the door.

I laid down on the bed and closed my eyes. Muffin jumped up beside me and started to purr. *I'll just rest for a little while*, I thought as I drifted off.

At one o'clock, Rachel knocked on the door and asked if everything was all right. I told her I was catching up on some lost sleep. She was very sweet and offered to make me a sandwich, which she brought to my room a few minutes later. I gobbled it down—I'd forgotten to eat breakfast, I suddenly remembered—and then curled up again with Muffin at my feet.

When I looked at my watch again, it was 4:00. I couldn't believe I'd been sleeping all day. I jumped up and grabbed my jacket then headed straight out the door. If I hurried, I could still get some time on the boardwalk before dark. Fifteen minutes later, I was walking on the boards in Atlantic City, the salty sea breeze blowing through my curls. *I could walk on these boards forever,* I thought. After a brisk half-hour walk, I stood by the railing for a while and looked out over the ocean. Dark storm clouds were gathering overhead, but I ignored them. *Who cares if it rains?* I thought. *I'm here and that's all that matters.*

JARED

Jared parked his car in the driveway of his parents' summer home in Margate and sighed. He glanced at his watch and wondered why Emily's car wasn't there. *Maybe she's out on an errand*, he told himself, but he felt uneasy. However, as soon as he opened the front door, he felt some of the tension slip away. He'd forgotten how much he loved this place, with the gleaming white wicker furniture and brightly painted walls. He smiled when he saw the glass flamingo salt-and-pepper shakers his mother loved still sitting on the tabletop. Even though his parents hadn't been here since last summer, it looked like they'd left just last week. He'd made the right decision; at the moment, this was where he needed to be.

He plopped on the sofa, turned on the TV, and tried to relax. He was yearning for the ocean but felt too lazy to get back in the car again. He kept clicking the remote until he found *Judge Judy*. Just then, his cell phone rang.

"Emily?" he said, checking the caller ID.

"Dad," Emily said, her voice sounding strained. "I'm on the boardwalk in Atlantic City, right outside Harrah's. Can you meet me here?"

"Are you okay?"

"I think so. I just want to talk to you, that's all."

"I'll be right there," he said, searching through his pockets for his car keys as he hung up.

He was out the door in an instant, Judge Judy's gravelly voice still ringing in his ears.

CHAPTER FORTY

I was staring at the ocean when the first raindrops hit my arm. I looked up and saw a bolt of lightning streak across the sky. Startled, I glanced around and calculated whether I should make a run for the nearest casino—Harrah's—or head for my car. I wasn't in the mood for a casino and decided even if I got soaked, I'd rather dash for the car.

The downpour came just as I turned on the ignition. Torrents of rain streamed down my windshield. I leaned forward, driving cautiously along the small residential street. Suddenly, I saw a large sign on a lawn to my left: "Bingo Tonight." I peered through the rain and saw some people entering what looked like a church. I glanced across the street and saw more people approaching, bending forward against the pelting rain.

I turned into the driveway, maneuvered into a small parking space—one of the few left—and then dashed inside. If my mother ever found out about this, I'd never hear the end of it. She played bingo religiously every other Monday evening with her best friends, Ethel and Sylvia. *I'm here already*, I thought. *It's pouring outside and*

I have nothing else to do. I may as well play a few games in her honor—what the hell. Come to think of it, I was feeling kind of lucky, for a change...

No one seemed to care that I was a newcomer and didn't have a clue how to play the game. The nice lady who collected my money at the door and gave me the multicolored bingo cards assured me I would have no trouble figuring out what to do. I walked to the front of the room and took a seat at one of the long tables. A board with flashing numbers was right in front of me. *I have done this before*, I thought, remembering a disastrous bingo night Carol and I planned years ago for our Hadassah group. I giggled, recalling how the two of us had volunteered to run the event, even though neither of us knew the first thing about bingo. From the beginning, everything had gone wrong.

Then, Carol's boyfriend, Kurt Klein—who was supposed to call the numbers—showed up drunk, and Carol broke up with him on the spot. He was so angry he threw the bowl with all the bingo numbers out the window. Everyone wanted their money back and then we had to return all the gifts to the sponsors who'd donated the prizes.

I just had to call Carol—she would crack up when she heard I was planning to play bingo. I took out my cell phone and dialed her number. She picked up on the first ring.

"Lydia, I'm so glad to hear from you. Are you all right?"

"I feel a lot better now that I'm down the Shore. But you'll never guess where I am right now."

"Give me a hint."

"Well, I'm in a church."

"I know you've been feeling confused lately, but is this really the time to consider converting?"

"I'm not here to convert. I'm here to play bingo."

"Bingo? You haven't played bingo since that disaster with Kurt Klein God knows how many years ago."

"You're right. As soon as I got here, the memories came flooding back and I had to call you."

"Exactly how did you find this bingo game?"

"I was on the boardwalk, right near Harrah's, and then it started raining. So I decided to go back to the B&B—it's really nice, by the way—and I jumped in my car, drove a few blocks down the street, and saw a sign that said, 'Bingo Tonight.'"

"I guess it was meant to be. Hopefully, it'll be a lot calmer this time than that crazy night when Kurt Klein went berserk."

"I certainly hope so. I came to the Shore to unwind. One thing I don't need at the moment is chaos—or any more drama, for that matter."

Carol laughed. "I agree with you. Gabe and I feel like we need a getaway this weekend too. He's picking me up later and we're driving down to Ventnor. His parents have a place there. They just use it in the summer, so we'll have it all to ourselves."

"You're sure you're not planning this impromptu trip to the Shore so you can check up on me?" I asked.

"Get over yourself. I'm planning to spend a romantic weekend at the Shore with my boyfriend. Is that okay with you?"

"Just remember—I came here to escape. No surprise visits, please."

"Do you really believe I'll be thinking about you when Gabe and I have a chance to be alone together in a beach house in Ventnor?"

"Coincidences do happen, I guess," I said, sighing. "But it does seem like a bit much. I'm here, you and Gabe are coming tonight, and Michael Miller's on assignment down the Shore this weekend too. You can't blame me for feeling a little paranoid when Jared Abrams has been stalking me for weeks now."

"Well, he's not going to find you there, so just relax. I assure you that Gabe and I will be very busy with indoor activities. And Michael will probably be busy working. Forget about it and have a good time. You never know—maybe you'll be a winner tonight."

"Maybe I will be," I said before I hung up. *Maybe, I thought, I really will be a big-time winner tonight. It's about time for my life to turn around.*

JARED

It was raining heavily when Jared pulled into the parking lot at Harrah's. He found a parking space, jumped out of his car, and raced for the elevator. As he emerged onto the crowded first floor, he looked around quickly and then headed for the front door. He tried to stay calm, but he couldn't stop thinking about how tense Emily had sounded.

He ran through the casino to the front door and almost barreled right into her. "Dad," she said as he hugged her, "I made a terrible mistake."

"Come on," he said. "Let's find a place where we can talk." He put his arm around her and hugged her again as they headed back down to the parking garage. "I'm taking you to Grandma and Grandpa's house. No one will bother us there. We can pick up your car later."

"Could you pull over for a minute?" Emily asked after they were in the car, had turned the corner, and were heading down a small residential street. "I need to talk to you—now. I did something stupid, and I'm afraid I might have made things worse for you and Lydia."

Jared stared at her for a moment and then pulled the car into a small parking lot that was packed with cars. He squeezed into a space behind a small red car and then he asked, "What's wrong? What's bothering you?"

She began to cry, the tears spilling down her cheeks. "I went to see her on Saturday," she said.

"You went to see Lydia?" His face was white.

"I didn't just go to see her. I made an appointment with her—for therapy. I didn't use my real name, of course," she added, her voice low. She turned to him, her eyes pleading. "I know it was wrong, Dad. I was just trying to help."

Suddenly her eyes widened.

"What is it, honey?" he asked.

She was staring at something outside. She pointed. "Dad, that's Lydia's car. Look at the license plate."

Sure enough, it was her car. He saw the license plate, *Lydia B.*

Looking around, she asked, "Where are we, anyway?" but Jared had already flung open the door and was on his way to the entrance. Emily jumped out and sprinted behind him through the rain.

CHAPTER FORTY ONE

A silver-haired, distinguished-looking man began calling the numbers. I kept my eyes riveted on my bingo card. I was feeling lucky tonight. Something exciting was going to happen; I could feel it in my bones. I turned around once to survey the room and noticed there was still a long line of people waiting to get in. There were plenty of seats left, although most of them were in the back of the room. Because I'd arrived early—quite by chance, of course, since I had no idea I'd end up playing bingo tonight—I'd been able to grab a seat near the front of the room where I could keep a close eye on the numbers as they lit up on the screen.

I sat there for twenty or thirty minutes, my head bent low over my bingo card. It was already starting to get stuffy in the overcrowded room. I wiped the perspiration off my forehead as I stared at the numbers on the screen. I was disappointed I hadn't won anything yet and was starting to get a little bored with the whole thing. *This is just a waste of time,* I thought. *Maybe I should go back to the B&B and curl up with that new mystery I bought.*

I barely glanced up when a woman in the back yelled, "Bingo!" What difference did it make who won if it wasn't me? The winner started shouting, "I won! I won!" *Get a grip, lady*, I felt like shouting back. How could people go bananas over a stupid bingo game? After a couple of minutes, though, I started to get impatient. Pushing the floppy hat I was wearing away from my eyes, I turned around—and saw Jared Abrams standing in the doorway. A wave of shock swept through me.

I jumped up, leaving my bingo card on the table, my straw hat falling to the floor. My mind raced, the rhythm of my heart quickening along with it. How did Jared Abrams turn up here? Could it be just one more coincidence? Of course not. He must have followed me to the Jersey Shore, but why? This had to be a dream. No, it was a nightmare.

I looked around frantically, searching for another exit. Jared caught sight of me and began moving toward me. Although I wanted to run, my feet wouldn't budge. I was frozen to the spot, my mind still racing, anger boiling inside me.

Before I knew it, he was there beside me, reaching out to touch my arm. I tried to pull away, but his fingers had closed over my arm. "Lydia," he said, "We have to talk. Please…"

"How did you find me?" I asked. "Have you been following me? Why are you doing this?"

"I wrote an apology to you. It's in my column. I wanted to let you know," he began, his voice trailing off as he stared at me.

"Don't you have anything better to do than write about me? Why can't you just leave me alone?"

People were murmuring now, gesturing toward us. The silver-haired number caller moved toward us, waving his hands. Then Emily Andrews—the client who had rushed out of my office so suddenly on Saturday afternoon— was there too, standing next to Jared. What was she doing here?

"Please listen to him, Lydia," Emily said. "My dad never meant to hurt you. Please—just hear him out."

She spoke softly, but the word "dad" seemed to reverberate, filling the space around me. I turned to her, grabbing on to the edge of the table for support, my chest—or was it my heart?—constricting.

"Did you just call him 'dad'?" I asked. "You called Jared Abrams 'dad'?"

Emily nodded as she hung her head, tears spilling out of her eyes. "Please—let me explain."

I tried to run away, but Jared had a firm grip on my arm. I looked around and watched as the silver-haired man from the front of the room came closer. Everyone was looking at us.

"Haven't you humiliated—and deceived—me enough? *Both* of you?"

"I'm the one who should feel humiliated," Jared said. "I just shared my feelings about what I did to you in a column thousands of people are going to read tomorrow."

Looking around, I did the only thing I could think of doing at the moment. I kicked him—hard—in the shins.

Jared released his grip for a moment as he leaped backward, leaning down to rub his ankle. "What the hell?" he said.

Bending over to grab my purse, I ran toward the exit, praying that Jared and Emily wouldn't follow me. "Enough is enough," I called over my shoulder as I flew toward the door. "If you don't stop stalking me, I'm going to call the police."

When I reached the doorway, I paused for an instant and tried to catch my breath. Then I raced down the stairs. As I flung open the door, panting, I almost collided with a tall man in a dark parka who was about to cross the threshold. His eyes met mine. It was Michael Miller. I stood there, my mouth wide open. *This must be a nightmare*, I thought. *It can't be real. Why is everyone following me? Why does everybody want to find me when all I want to do is disappear?* I felt my heart, beating wildly inside my chest. I stood there, taking in huge gulps of air. Suddenly, I felt myself falling. *I'm passing out*, I thought, and then—blackness.

CHAPTER FORTY TWO

When I opened my eyes, I saw Michael Miller leaning over me.

"Are you okay?" he asked.

"I think so," I said, sitting up gingerly and looking around. "I think I fainted—probably because I was hyperventilating. I do that sometimes when I'm really stressed. How long was I out?"

"Just a few seconds, I guess, but you scared the hell out of me."

Just then, Jared and Emily appeared. When they saw me, their faces turned white too. Jared rushed to my side, bending over to offer his hand.

"Lydia," he said, "What are you doing on the ground?"

"It's none of your business, Abrams," Michael said. "Leave her alone."

"What are you doing here?" Jared asked.

"That's none of your business either," Michael growled. "Just stay away from her."

"I've had about enough of you," Jared said.

"And since when do I listen to anything you tell me?" Michael asked, moving closer to Jared and glaring at him.

At that instant, I pulled myself to my feet and started running feebly toward my car. My knees were wobbly and I felt exhausted, as if I'd just finished running a marathon. I made a beeline for my car, praying neither of them could catch me. All I wanted was to get back to the cozy room at the B&B and cuddle up with Muffin, that adorable little cat. Once I got there, I'd have plenty of time to try to figure out what had happened tonight. Or maybe I didn't want to think at all—about Jared or Michael or the research project that had led me straight to hell.

I heard their voices rising in anger behind me and tried to pick up speed. Then people were shouting, "Stop it. We're going to call the police," and I heard a thud. I glanced back over my shoulder and saw Jared, sitting on the ground, struggling to his feet.

"Dad, are you all right?" I heard Emily yell before I turned and fumbled in my bag for my car keys.

Michael ran up beside me, breathing hard. "Lydia," he said, "don't worry—I'll take care of you."

I stared at him. I felt as if my head was stuffed with cotton and all I wanted to do was lie down.

"Take care of me?" I asked. "I just need some rest. I can take care of myself."

"Trust me," he said, putting his hand over my trembling fingers as I tried to insert the key in the lock and open the door. "You want to get away from Abrams, don't you? I can take you to a place where he won't find you."

I nodded through the tears that had started falling again. "Yes," I said. "Please, take me away from that man."

He grabbed my hand and we flew to his car. He flung open the door and practically shoved me inside then jumped in on the driver's side. He backed out of the narrow parking space and then floored it.

I turned around and caught a glimpse of Jared, picking himself up from the pavement. He was calling after us, but I couldn't hear his words over the roar of the engine and the sound of the rain.

"What about my car?" I asked Michael after we'd reached the end of the street. "I have to get it out of the parking lot. I don't want it to be towed. I can't handle anything else."

"Is there an extra key anywhere?"

"Why, yes," I said. "As a matter of fact, there is. I keep an extra set of car keys in my desk at home, and Carol has a key to my house. She and Gabe are driving to Ventnor tonight—I guess you already know that. I'll call and ask her to stop there on the way here."

I pulled my cell phone from my pocketbook and dialed Carol's cell number for the second time tonight. As soon as she answered, I said, "I need a favor—and no questions, please. You just have to trust me, and I'll fill you in on everything later."

"So you lost all your money in the bingo game, huh? Bingo just isn't for you, my friend."

"Carol, this is no time for joking around. I'm with Michael Miller, and Jared Abrams is hot on my trail."

"Jared Abrams followed you to the Shore? I know he seems to be obsessed with you, but isn't that going a little too far?"

"Michael followed me too," I said, glancing over at him as he drove down the street.

Carol was silent for a moment. Then she said, "Michael didn't follow you, Lyd. It's my fault he found you."

"Let me guess," I said. "You told Gabe and..."

"I begged him not to tell Michael. But then Michael called Gabe and he sounded really worried about you. It was right after you called to tell me about the bingo game..." Carol's voice trailed off.

"Well, at least that makes sense. I was beginning to get paranoid, wondering how both of them knew where I was. Now the only mystery is how that bum Jared Abrams tracked me down. But you know what? Right now, I don't care. I called you to ask for a favor. Can you move my car so it doesn't get towed? It's in the parking lot at the Church of Our Savior, right in the heart of Atlantic City. Can you and Gabe move it to the B&B where I'm staying? Sandler's Seaside Spot—the new place I told you about. You can get the address on the web."

"I don't have your car key," she said.

"But you have my house key. And I keep an extra set of car keys in my desk, remember? Could you possibly stop by my house and pick it up before you come tonight? I know it's an inconvenience but…"

"Of course we'll do it," she said. "Gabe's on his way now. We'll pick up the key and take care of moving the car. But where are you going? I'm concerned—you sound so stressed. Are you all right?"

"I'm just worn out, that's all. Michael promised he'd take me someplace safe for the night. Don't worry about me. I promise I'll call you tomorrow, and then I'll fill you in on everything I know… which isn't much, believe me." As soon as I hung up, I put my head in my hands and started to cry.

"Abrams won't find you again," Michael said, reaching over to touch my arm. "I promise you that."

I turned to him with a grateful smile. "Thanks."

"I wish I could have reached you before he did."

"I don't know what's going on," I said, the tears still streaming down my face, "I don't really understand why you showed up tonight or how Jared found me. But I do know one thing—I'm thankful you got me away from him. I owe you one for that."

I sniffled and wiped my eyes. My eyelids were heavy and I felt myself drifting off to sleep as Michael turned the car onto the highway, his steel-gray eyes focused on the road ahead.

CHAPTER FORTY THREE

The next morning, I woke up in the big feather bed at an inn in Cape May and rubbed my eyes. Michael Miller was amazing; he'd taken care of everything. It was as if he had a plan, the way he'd arranged things so quickly. When we'd arrived in Cape May last night, a beautiful suite was waiting for us, with two separate rooms—thank God—and a cozy sitting room in between. It was perfect, and I'd felt some of my tension ease as Michael kissed me on the cheek and nudged me toward my bedroom. "Go to sleep. We'll get your clothes and other stuff in the morning."

One thing had been odd. Actually, everything was more than odd—it was surreal. Before I went to bed, Michael had asked me to give him my cell phone. "I don't want anyone to bother you," he'd said. "Just give me your cell phone, and I'll hold it for you for the next day or two. Carol knows you're safe. And you'll be seeing her tomorrow anyway."

I was exhausted and I didn't want to argue. Besides, maybe Michael was right. It might be a blessing if nobody could reach me, just for a little while. So I gave him my cell phone and went straight to bed. I nestled under the covers and tried to push all thoughts of Jared Abrams out of my mind, but it was impossible to keep him out of my dreams. All night, his words echoed in my head: "I wrote a column about you. It's an apology. I humiliated myself in front of thousands of people…" I'd tossed and turned, and finally, when the early morning light was beginning to peek through the curtains, I'd fallen into a state that felt more like a trance than sleep.

There was a knock on my door. "Are you up yet?" Michael called. "It's almost ten o'clock."

"Ten o'clock?" I asked, jumping out of bed. "I don't believe it."

"How about if I meet you in the coffee shop downstairs in half an hour? I'm going to take a walk."

"Sounds perfect," I said, heading for the bathroom. "I'll see you there."

Thirty minutes later, I slid into a booth in the coffee shop and sat facing Michael. "You look happy," I said.

"Well, I guess I am," he said. "I mean, I'm not happy about what Abrams pulled last night, but I'm glad you and I are here together. By the way, I'm sorry I called in to your radio show like that. I know I caught you off guard. When I heard his voice on the air, I went kind of berserk. I didn't mean to upset you. That's the last thing I want to do. I've been thinking about you a lot lately. I guess I should say, I've been thinking about us."

"You have?" I asked. "I thought we were just a fling. I loved our time together on the cruise, but then, after I got home…"

"You thought it was over? I have to admit, that is my usual M.O. But somehow, with you, it was different."

"Maybe because I wasn't really me," I said. "Maybe it was the exotic Alexis Steele who intrigued you. It's possible, you know, that boring old Lydia Birnbaum may not interest you at all."

He threw his head back and laughed. "Lydia Birnbaum—boring?" Again, he laughed out loud. "Alexis was fun, but she was no match for the real thing. It's Lydia who's been on my mind," he said, his eyes boring into mine. I looked down at the menu, trying to think of something to say, but my mind was blank. He seemed to sense my discomfort and changed the subject. "How about if we have some breakfast and then take a nice long walk on the beach? It looks like a beautiful day."

"The truth is," I said, "I'm still so confused. I just don't understand how Jared found me at the bingo game last night."

"I'm a bit confused myself, but I'll tell you everything I know—after breakfast. Let's eat first. I don't know about you, but I'm starved."

I sighed. "I have to get to the B&B at some point. Was it only yesterday I checked in there? I feel like it's been a thousand years." I blinked back tears. "I have to find a way to put the pieces of my life back together. I can't hide out here forever."

He smiled. "Not forever, no. Just for a day or two. Don't worry, we'll get all your things. I think it would do you good to relax for a little while—forget about everything. Let me take care of you right now. I promise you're in good hands," he said, putting his hand over mine.

The gesture brought the tears out from behind my eyelids. "Okay, it's a deal. For today, I'm all yours." And I squeezed his hand.

Just then, his cell phone rang. He glanced at the number on the screen and said, "Can you excuse me for a minute? It's my editor. I need to talk to him. I'll be right back."

"No problem. I was going to the ladies' room anyway."

I stood up, glancing around for the bathroom. "It's in the back," the waitress said as I passed her. "Last door on the right, near the back door."

CHAPTER FORTY FOUR

I took my time in the bathroom, inhaling deeply in front of the mirror to calm down my racing heart. So much had happened in the last twenty-four hours. I splashed some cold water on my face and freshened my lipstick before I headed back to the booth. The coffee shop was crowded, and I could hear snatches of conversation as I passed by each table. I noticed a man with thinning white hair in a plaid shirt that bulged over his middle sitting by himself, reading the newspaper. The paper was spread out on the table in front of him, and as I passed by, I glanced down and saw…my face. The man turned to me, recognition in his eyes.

"You're Lydia Birnbaum," he said. "You must be feeling pretty good right now."

I was mesmerized by my picture and completely bewildered by his words. "Feeling good? Why?"

"Well, you must be some therapist. It's clear that Jared Abrams thinks so, anyway. He's really changed his tune. Your phone's going to be ringing off the hook. I was thinking of calling you myself.

You sound like a miracle worker. Do you happen to have a business card with you?"

I stood there, my eyes still riveted on my picture. "Haven't you read this yet?" he asked. "Here." And he handed me the paper. "If you don't have a business card, could you just write down your number for me? I'd really like to schedule an appointment. Hey, do you think I could get a discount? I mean, you might never have seen Abrams' column if not for me." He chuckled, folding the newspaper neatly and handing it to me.

Hands trembling, I took the newspaper from him and then scanned the column. "To put it simply, Lydia Birnbaum changed my life. Actually, she saved my life," it began. I plopped into the seat across from him and kept reading, tears filling my eyes.

After I read the last paragraph, my knees felt weak. "Even though I posed as someone else, Lydia got through to the real me and touched my heart in a way that no one—no one—has been able to before."

I clutched the edge of the table, praying I wouldn't pass out. I had touched Jared Abrams' heart? Hell, I didn't think he had one!

"Could I borrow your cell phone?" I asked the man. "I'll trade you one free therapy session for the use of your phone—just for a few minutes."

"Sure," he said, handing it to me. He was still beaming.

"I'll be right back," I said, glancing toward the booth in the front of the restaurant. Michael was still outside. I made a beeline for the back door, dialing Carol's cell phone number as I ran.

She picked up on the first ring. "Who is this?"

"It's me," I said.

"Have you seen the column? Did you read it?"

"Yes. Yes." It seemed to be all I could manage to say at the moment.

"Where are you? Are you okay? And whose phone number is this, anyway?"

"It's a long story. But there's no time to explain."

"We ran into Jared when we picked up the car last night. He was planning to watch over your car and make sure no one towed it away. He told us about the column. He's not so bad, after all," Carol said.

"Did he happen to tell you he sent his daughter to me for a fake therapy session?"

"You've got it all wrong. He didn't know his daughter set up that fake session with you. He doesn't want to hurt you."

"And since when are you having intimate conversations with Jared Abrams?" I asked as the world spun around me.

"Since all of us went to his parents' house in Margate last night and talked until 3:00 a.m.—that's since when."

"All of you, meaning…" My voice trailed off as I tried to process what she'd said.

"Yup, all of us, meaning Jared, Gabe, and me, and that adorable Emily too. We've had quite a night and we've learned a lot."

"I don't have time to listen to all this right now," I said, feeling the panic well up inside me. "Just bring my car to me as fast as you can. I'm at the Purple Rose Inn in Cape May. Remember, that pretty place right across from the beach? I'll tell you everything when you get here."

"Don't worry—I know Cape May like the back of my hand. My parents always took us there when we were kids, remember?" She hesitated. "Jared is worried sick about you, Lydia. And he's sick about what he did to you too. Do you think you'll ever be able to forgive him?"

"I can't believe you'd even consider taking his side. But I don't want to think about all that right now. Just bring me my car. And please, hurry." I hung up and rushed inside to return the phone and the newspaper to my newfound friend. Scrawling my phone number at the top of the newspaper, I told him to give me a call to schedule a session. "Remember, the first one's free. Thanks so much for letting me use your phone. You'll never know what you did for me."

As I hurried back to the booth, I saw Michael walk in the front door. He sat down just before I joined him. Scooting into my seat, I said, "Hi."

"Hi, beautiful," he said. "You're starting to look like a woman who's taken a load off her mind."

"You can say that again," I said, turning to the waitress who had arrived to take our order.

It was then I noticed a cute but very tense-looking young man who was standing just inside the front door, a black gym bag at his feet. His eyes seemed to be scanning everyone in the room. I watched as he directed his gaze at a beautiful young woman who was sitting near the window, her head cocked to the side as she listened to the older-looking but quite handsome man who was seated across from her.

Suddenly the young man pulled a gun out of the bag and shouted, "I told you I'd never let you go, Lori. Why didn't you believe me?"

It seemed as if everyone in the restaurant froze for an instant, except for a man who was coming out of the men's room. I watched as he slipped quietly out the rear exit—the one I had used when I made the call to Carol.

Then, the woman at the table next to us started to scream. "He's got a gun! He's going to shoot us!"

The taut-faced young man wheeled around, aiming the gun at the hysterical woman. "Shut up, you stupid bitch!" He looked around the coffee shop, his eyes hard. "Get down on the floor. All of you." He noticed a man at the next table eyeing his cell phone, which was right beside him. "I'll shoot anybody who tries to call for help, so don't even think about it."

"Brian," the woman he'd called Lori said, "please…"

"Don't talk to me," he spat out, his eyes boring into her. "You know what you did. Don't you think you deserve to die?"

People began scrambling to get down on the floor. Someone started to cry. Michael and I hesitated, looking at each other. I nodded to him as I slid to the end of the seat. We both slumped down to the floor, huddling next to each other.

I was watching the young man carefully. I saw the slight tremor in the hand that held the gun, noticed the way he kept blinking, as if the sun was shining in his eyes. This guy was fragile and he was scared—scared and angry. We were in danger and somebody had to do something to calm him down. Otherwise... I shuddered as I thought about what could happen if he went on a rampage in this crowded coffee shop.

"Brian," I said as he spun around, aiming the gun right at my head, "it sounds like something's happened that's made you feel very angry and very hurt." I held my breath as he glared at me, the gun barrel focused at the spot between my eyes.

"Who the hell are you?" he shouted. "And how do you know anything about me?"

"Oh, I don't," I said. "I don't know you at all. But I can feel that you're hurting. And I'm sorry—really sorry—you're in so much pain."

His eyes narrowed as he moved toward me, looking me up and down. "I know who you are," he said. "I recognize your voice, and I've seen you on TV too. You're that crazy shrink who tries to fix people on the radio."

I tried to smile, but my face felt tight, as if it was going to shatter at any moment. "Yes," I said, "that's me. I wish I could 'fix' people, Brian. I can't do that, but I do listen to them. And I'd be happy to listen to you too."

"You hear that, Lori?" he shouted, swinging around suddenly and pointing his gun at her again. "She wants to listen to what I have to say, which is more than you've done lately."

"Well, I think she'll listen now," I said as he turned to face me again. "Why don't you tell her why you're so upset? And, by the way, would you mind if I sat back up on the seat again? I'd love to talk to both of you."

And that's what I did. I scrambled to my seat and then I sat there with my hands folded on the table in front of me, talking quietly while my heart raced, counseling another couple—very aware that all our lives were on the line. I listened and I talked and I prayed as I waited for the police to arrive.

Although it seemed like forever, I found out later it had taken only half an hour for the SWAT team to show up. And later too I learned that police helicopters were circling overhead. I saw the news crews outside the window, behind the barricade the police had set up. And when I heard the phone ring, I urged Brian to pick it up, to hear what the police had to say, to work with their negotiator. Through it all, I remained calm and composed, although my chest felt like it was going to explode. Not until he threw his gun outside and agreed to surrender to the police did I allow myself to breathe—really breathe.

From that point on, I watched everything happen through a mist that had settled over the whole scene. As the police entered the coffee shop and people scrambled to their feet, I made my way over to Lori, who sat, sobbing, her head in her hands. I sat down beside her and wrapped my arms around her. We held each other for a few moments without speaking. Then I sat back and asked, "Are you okay? This has been quite an ordeal. I'm so sorry you had to go through this."

Lori looked at me, astonished. "Are you kidding? I'm so sorry everyone here" —her hand gestured to the other people in the coffee shop— "had to suffer because of me and my problems. I'm just so sorry." Again, she put her head down and cried.

People nearby came over to comfort her. "It's not your fault, dear," a tall woman in a multicolored pantsuit said, coming up to us. "Don't blame yourself. We all have our issues. Thank God for her," she said, pointing to me. "She saved all of us."

And then everyone began to clap and cheer, and people—including the man with the newspaper—rushed over to thank me. I rose and hugged them, one by one. At that moment, I loved them—each and every one of them—with all my heart. Michael Miller came over too and planted a kiss on my cheek. "Jeez, Lydia," he said. "You blew me away."

"Well," I said, my eyes brimming with tears. "Let's just thank God that Brian didn't." I looked him right in the eyes. "I was scared, Michael."

"You could have fooled me. You were so damn calm. I don't know how you pulled it off."

"Neither do I. It was all like a dream."

"You know, I wasn't kidding earlier when I said you've been on my mind a lot. Maybe you and I…"

Just then, I saw a flash of red at the window and heard the beep of my horn. "Sorry, Michael, but something's just come up." I gave him a quick kiss on the cheek, grabbed my purse, and then turned back for an instant. "By the way, can I have my phone now?" He pulled it out of his pocket reluctantly and handed it to me and then I flew out the door. The police were waiting for me. "We'll need to talk to you," an adorable young man in uniform said.

"No problem," I said, pulling out a business card. "Just call me. Believe me, I have plenty to say, and I'll help in any way I can. Brian needs treatment, you know. I'm going to work hard to see that he gets what he needs."

"I have no doubt you will, ma'am. No doubt at all." *Shit*, I thought, running my fingers through my hair, *did he just call me "ma'am"?*

CHAPTER FORTY FIVE

Sprinting to my car, I turned and saw Michael, staring at me from the other side of the plate glass window. Opening the car door, I jumped in. "Did you hear?" I asked, turning to give Carol a hug.

But it wasn't Carol. It was Jared Abrams. Jared Abrams was driving my car. What the hell was going on? Furious, I reached for the door handle, but he pushed the automatic lock button, shifted into drive, and headed out of the parking lot.

Fury like hot lava was bubbling inside me. Once again, I was trapped, and once again, all I wanted to do was escape. *Wait a minute*, I thought. *This is my car. The person who should be in charge here is me.*

"Listen," I said, "I don't know what you think you're doing, but it won't work. You can't hold me against my will. That's called kidnapping, and believe me, I will press charges." I glared at him, my arms crossed over my chest, my fingers pressed against my furiously pulsating heart.

"Lydia, I know you have no reason to trust me, but please—just give me a chance to explain. I don't want to hurt you. I've done everything wrong, and I have no right to expect you to forgive me. I just want you to listen to what I have to say. And what the hell is going on here? The police are all over the place."

I turned my head and glanced out the window as we passed the pastel-colored Victorian inns that lined the streets of Cape May. "There was a situation and it's over. Really, it's none of your business. And you can go ahead and talk, but I can't guarantee I'll hear a word you say. It's kind of hard to pay attention when someone's forcing you to do something."

I saw him flinch and then he pulled over, turned off the car, and handed me the keys. "If you want me to leave, I will. I'll call my friend who lives in Margate and ask him to pick me up. You and I have a lot to talk about and I thought we could drive back to Philly together, after you pick up your things, of course. I was going to leave my car at my parents' house. But I don't want you to feel I'm forcing you to do anything."

I sat there, collecting my thoughts. I was still angry, but I felt a whole lot better now that I had my car keys in my hand.

"Maybe you'd better call your friend, because I'm not going to take you back to Philly, that's for sure. However, I will give you a chance to tell me your side of things. Let's find some place where we can talk. I'll give you thirty minutes—no more."

"Whatever you say. I'm turning everything over to you. You're in control."

It felt good to hear him say it, but I wasn't sure yet that it was true.

We changed seats and I drove to the corner and turned right. The beach was on our left now, and people were walking along the promenade beside the sand. I drove to the end of the street, parked the car, and pointed to the restaurant across the street. "Let's go in there for a few minutes."

I'd eaten there many times over the years. It was a real dive, but I loved the place because you could eat outside on a screened-in porch that overlooked the beach. Although every single item on the menu was fried—except the coleslaw—and the waitresses rarely smiled, I had lots of fond memories of sitting on that porch with Steph and Nate, all of us munching on fried fish sandwiches while we stared at the ocean.

I turned off the engine and we climbed out of the car and walked across the street. I felt the sun on my back and realized how much I'd missed being near the ocean. As soon as we entered the restaurant, a waitress nodded at us and led us to a small table right in the center of the restaurant. No one else was inside. I was grateful it was early November and too chilly to eat outside. There was no way I was going to share that beautiful view with Jared Abrams.

We barely glanced at the menus the waitress handed to us as we sat down at the little table, face-to-face at last.

"I wonder what would have happened," I said, "if you hadn't stood me up when we were supposed to meet in person. And, by the way, did you have any intention of showing up for our 'business meeting' that night or were you just trying to humiliate me?"

Jared closed his eyes for a moment and then looked at me. "I'm not going to lie to you. The meeting was a setup. I wanted you to agree to go into business with me so I could prove to my readers that you were a fraud."

"Why? Why did you want to destroy me?" I had an overpowering urge to jump up and run out the door, but I willed myself to remain in my seat.

"Shrinks just piss me off. It was nothing personal, really. I've had my issues with them over the years, and I guess you kind of took it on the chin for all of them."

"Oh, I see. That really makes a lot of sense. You thought that by ruining my life, you'd be getting back at all the shrinks who've done you wrong. Very sensible and extremely mature."

He couldn't look me in the eye. "I'm not proud of what I did. It wasn't professional or even rational. But I couldn't see that at the time. Also, I've dated my share of therapists and more than a few of them have turned out to be nut cases. That didn't help either. I didn't understand how much all this stuff bothered me or how angry I really was until I started therapy with you, or until Rick Mann did."

"How can you even mention Rick Mann to me? Do you know how humiliating it is for a therapist to spend hour after hour in session with someone who turns out to be someone else—someone who hates her so much he goes to great lengths to ensure no one will ever be able to trust her again? It's true you changed your mind and never published that exposé, but your deception made me question whether I could ever trust myself to help anyone again. And what hurts the most is, it made me question my ability to manage my own life." The tears were rolling down my cheeks. Damn, I hated to cry in front of him.

"Lydia, I swear I never meant for it to go that far. I got carried away. It got out of hand."

"Oh, really?" I said, furiously rubbing away the tears with my fingers. "I guess that explains why—even after you sent me your stupid apology cactus on the ship—once you got home, you still couldn't let it go. And to think that you got your daughter involved—I just can't believe you'd sink that low."

"I didn't! I wouldn't!" Jared shouted. "Sorry," he said, lowering his voice. "I didn't mean to shout at you. But it isn't true—I didn't ask Emily to contact you. She came up with that idea on her own, after I told her about everything that happened."

"No surprise, really," I said. "You two are quite a team. Your phone call in the middle of her session with me was nothing short of brilliant. And the way she ran off—it was amazing, really. She should be in theatre. She's quite the actress. Although I can't figure out how you could possibly have known I'd forgotten to turn off the volume on my answering machine..." I added, hearing the tremor in my voice.

"I swear I didn't know Emily was there when I called you that day. Don't ask me where she came up with that wacky idea." I shot him a look and he said, "Sorry—I know what you're thinking—like father, like daughter. But honestly, it was all a coincidence. After we left the bingo game the other night, she told me everything. She wasn't trying to hurt you. She thought she might be able to change things between us."

"Change things between us? What does that mean? She couldn't change what you did, how you deceived me..."

"No, of course not. She felt there was something else going on..."

"Something else going on? Like what?"

He took a deep breath and said, "I know this is going to sound ridiculous. The truth is, she had the crazy notion I was falling in love with you, and maybe you were falling in love with me too."

"Falling in love?" I asked, feeling something lurch in my chest. "That's ridiculous, all right. I'm not sure exactly how I feel about you at this point, but I definitely wouldn't call it love."

"I understand. You've made your feelings about me very clear. I'm not saying you were falling in love with me. It was Emily who came up with everything. She's been seeing too many of those chick flicks, I guess," he said, smiling. Even though his mouth was turned up at the corners, his eyes still looked sad.

At that moment, I glanced at the flat screen TV on the wall in the corner and saw my face on the screen. Underneath were the words, "Breaking News Story." I froze.

Jared turned around and saw it too. The waitress, strolling over to take our orders, turned to look at the screen, glanced back at me and then at the TV again. "Hey," she said, "you're that therapist I heard about on the radio—the one who saved all those hostages."

I felt myself blushing. "Well, it wasn't quite as heroic as they probably made it sound. I just happened to be in the right place at the right time."

"Hostages?" Jared asked. "That's why the police were all over the place...."

The waitress was beaming at us. "Didn't she tell you? The guy had a gun." She turned to me. "I heard you calmed everything down, had that guy eating right out of your hand. Pretty damn impressive, if you ask me."

Jared couldn't take his eyes off the TV. "It could have been a disaster," he said.

"Can I have your autograph?" the waitress asked. "My friends are never going to believe I ran into you in this joint." She shoved a napkin across the table; I signed it quickly and handed it back to her.

Desperate to change the subject, I glanced down at the menu and said, "Can I have a bowl of soup? I don't care what kind it is—I'll take whatever you're serving today."

"It's fish chowder and it ain't half bad," she said, tucking the napkin with my signature carefully into her pocket. "And what about you?" she asked, turning to Jared.

"Soup sounds good to me. I'll have the same," he said, handing her his menu.

Jared's eyes were still on the TV. "You know," he said, "you're a real celebrity now. Your phone is going to be ringing off the hook. Everyone will want to interview you and find out what really happened in that coffee shop."

"There's no way I'm going to capitalize on this hostage thing. I wouldn't do that."

"I admire you for saying that and I believe you. But this is news and reporters will be hounding you."

"Hounding is certainly something you would understand."

"Lydia, I'm trying to make amends. I really want to help you. I'll even be a guest on your radio show if you want me to, just so I can tell everybody what a fool I was and how I've learned that relationships should be based on honesty, not duplicity."

"You on my radio show? I don't think so…"

"I know you're still angry with me, but think about it. My being there would put a whole new spin on things. I bet I could help with the article about your project too."

"The article? Frankly, it's one of the things I've been running away from. But I'm tired of running and, you know what—I finally realized I don't have to run anymore. I lost faith in myself for a while—lost faith in my ability to help others since it seemed as if my own life was falling apart. But I've really learned a lot from Project Ex—not just about relationships, but about myself too. It's true that I've barely started writing that damn article, but I'll get it done. I know I will."

"Well, I'm here if you need me. After all, I am a writer."

"Why are you suddenly so desperate to help me? You wrote your apology. It's done. Don't you think it's time to move on?"

"You helped me," he said softly. "I wasn't kidding when I wrote that you changed my life. I thought I was playing a role, but I couldn't pull it off. It was Rick Mann who called you but I was the one who took your advice to heart. You seemed to know me better than I know myself. And I'm different somehow—changed in some ways—ways I'm still coming to understand. I feel like I owe you."

We sat there staring at each other for what seemed like a long time. "Look," I said, "All I know is, I have a radio show to do soon and a life I can't wait to get back to."

He grinned—a wonderful, lopsided grin that made him seem vulnerable somehow. In spite of myself, I felt myself smiling back at him. Just then, my cell phone rang. I grabbed it from my bag and pressed it to my ear.

"Lydia?" Sam Sloane said. "Are you okay?"

"Yes, Sam, I'm fine," I said. "You don't have to worry—I'm still at the Shore, but I'll be back for my next radio show."

"You'd better be here. The calls and emails are pouring in. Your listeners are worried about you, and of course they want to hear about what happened today at that restaurant in Cape May."

"I understand. But the focus of my show is on them, not me. I'm not going to make a big deal out of this, Sam."

"You can explain that to Terri Gross from NPR when you talk to her."

"Terri Gross? Why would she want to talk to me?"

"She wants to interview you. I just spoke with her a few minutes ago. She wants you to call her ASAP."

"Terri Gross wants to interview me?" *Why not?* I asked myself. *Why shouldn't she want to talk to the therapist and talk show host who just defused a scary hostage situation in scenic Cape May?*

"Do you want to call her back or should I?"

"Oh, I'll call her," I said. "I'll call her in just a few minutes. You can be sure of that."

"I thought you'd say that. This could be a real breakthrough for you, Lydia. I'm texting her phone number to you right now."

"A breakthrough," I repeated. First my own radio show and now a "breakthrough."

"So Terri Gross wants to interview you," Jared said when I hung up. "I'm not surprised. You have a real gift for helping people, and you deserve all the success that's going to come your way."

The strangest thing was, I believed him. For the first time, I believed he really, truly didn't want to hurt me. As a matter of fact, he seemed proud of me, but that wasn't the important thing. What was important was how I was feeling about myself.

"Look, Jared, I know our soup hasn't arrived yet, but I need to go now. I've got a lot to do and an important phone call to make. And I might—just might—consider taking you up on that offer to join me on my radio show at some point. But I'm not making any promises yet."

"That's good enough for me. I have no reason to expect any more than that."

"You certainly don't," I said, pushing back my chair and throwing a twenty on the table.

Then, without a backward glance, I turned and walked out the door and into the shimmering sunlight of Cape May.

ACKNOWLEDGMENTS

It's a privilege and a joy to thank the wonderful people whose love, support and guidance have been the wind beneath my wings:

- My devoted, ever-patient and slightly-*meshugah* husband Steve who never wavered in his belief that I could and would finish this novel.
- My extraordinary children – Avi and Anne, Jon and Kristin. Without your support, love and multifold talents, this novel would never have come to fruition. And my precious grandson Ezra, for reminding me that every day should be lived with a sense of wonder.
- My blended family, including my wonderful grandchildren, Daniel and Brooklynne.
- My dear friend and fellow writer, Anna Lefler, who unfailingly and lovingly propelled me forward with her wisdom, humor and amazing guidance.
- My brilliant editor, Hop Wechsler, who believed in Lydia Birnbaum right from the start.
- My life coach and best-ever cheerleader, Ruth Jenkin.
- My family, friends and fan club – Diann and Mark Saltman, Joyce Saltman and Sol Hitzig, Iris and Julian Tishkoff, Missy

Grotz, Kathy Snead, Penny and Ernie Bernabei, Leslie and Allan Slan, Bonnie Kaye, Judi Ahram, Ellen Kalkstein, Tina and Bill McDonnell, Elaine and Dick Roy, Lesley and Bob Haushalter, and the incredible volunteers and staff at the Philadelphia Ronald McDonald House, my professional "home away from home" for the past seventeen years!
- Illustrious author and scholar, Richard Lederer, for his words of wisdom and encouragement.
- Avi Doar, how I miss you. You taught me everything is possible!

ABOUT THE AUTHOR

Project Ex is Helen Reese's first novel. She is also a contributor to Listen to Your Mother, a recently released collection of essays highlighting motherhood's joys and challenges. In addition to her day job as social worker, Helen has worked as a freelance writer and publicist. Learn more at HelenVReese.com.

Made in the USA
Middletown, DE
01 November 2019